JAKE'S FORTUNE

A NOVEL BY
RAY COMFORT

WITH ANNA JACKSON

BRIDGE
LOGOS
FOUNDATION

Alachua, Florida 32615

Bridge-Logos
Alachua, FL 32615 USA

Jake's Fortune
by Ray Comfort
with Anna Jackson

Edited by Hollee J. Chadwick

Printed in the United States of America.

Library of Congress Catalog Card Number: 2009939896
International Standard Book Number 978-0-88270-004-5

Unless otherwise indicated, Scripture quotations in this book are from the *King James Version* of the Bible.

G218.316.N.m912.35250

DEDICATION

To Julia, Summer, Luke, Robby, Danny, Jonathan, Kylie, Janie, Calvary, and Benjamin.

ACKNOWLEDGEMENTS

I created the skeletal bones of this novel.
Anna Jackson brilliantly gave the story
flesh and blood realism.

May God breathe life into it, raise it up,
and use it to speak to many.

shot

Jake was in the barn when he heard his mother scream. The sound of it stopped his heart. It was unmistakable. Something truly terrifying had just happened.

In less time than it takes to blink, he'd dropped the mallet and was sprinting to the house. His foot slipped and he went down face first, but he hardly felt it. His heart was hammering out of his chest by the time he got around the corner of the house.

He saw Ma running to help Pa down off his horse. Pa's left arm hung limply at his side and a bloody spot on his shoulder was widening by the moment.

"Oh dear God!" she cried out again. "Luke! What happened?"

"No, Julia. Grab me on the other side," he winced as she helped him down.

"Oh dear God, help us!"

"Are you shot?" Jake shouted. "Who did this? Pa? What's happening?" Everything seemed to be going in slow motion.

"You've got to get hidden. They're coming ..." Luke

steadied himself. "Get hidden, I said. There's no time."

Down the road, a dusty smudge was getting closer.

Five year-old Summer stood wide-eyed and motionless inside the front door of the house, a mixing bowl still in her hands. Her long black hair blew in the breeze as she stood stock still, seemingly unable to process what was going on.

"You heard Pa, get in the house!" Jake shouted as he pointed to the door with his shaking hand. He was surprised to hear the ferocity in his own voice. She dropped the mixing bowl and cried out clapping both hands to her mouth.

"No. No, Jake." Luke's voice was gentle. He forced a tight smile and spoke unnecessarily slowly.

Julia watched him, amazed that he was managing to impart some sense of stability to an out-of-control situation.

"The house won't work, son. That's the first place they'll look." He put his hand on Jake's shoulder.

Jake turned and looked into his father's eyes. They were kind eyes—hazel in color and crinkled around the edges from days of walking a plow, squint-eyed, in the sun.

Luke went down on one knee and reached out with his good arm toward his little girl. "It's okay darling. Come here to Papa, Summer."

She hesitated only a moment and then came running. "Papa, who hurt you?" she sobbed as she threw her arms around his neck.

Jake felt a lump come up in his throat that he couldn't swallow. He blinked and furiously wiped hot tears out of his eyes. He gritted his teeth and willed no more tears to come.

Luke kissed his daughter's tousled hair. He squeezed her lightly with his good arm, but didn't answer her question. "I love you, darling. Now go to your ma." Summer scrambled over to grasp her mother around the legs.

Jake set his teeth and tightened his whole face as his pa stood again to face him. He didn't want his pa to see he'd been crying.

Luke put his good hand on Jake's arm and locked eyes with him for a long moment. Jake felt that his father was looking at him, not the way a parent looks at a 14 year-old, but the way one man looks at another. Jake felt he had aged in a moment.

"You take your ma and your sister and hide under the chicken coop."

"Pa, I'm staying!"

"No you are not, Son. There's too many. I know what I'm doing. Go! Take care of your mother and sister. Quickly!"

Ma put Summer on her hip, tears still streamed down her cheeks. *O Lord,* she prayed silently, *please help us!*

Luke watched as Summer realized she was being taken away. "No, no!" she screamed as she fought to get out of her mother's arms. "Don't leave Papa, he's hurt! Papa! Papa! Come with us!"

Luke could no longer watch them—it was enough to tear out his heart. *God protect them,* he prayed. Then he turned and headed toward the house as fast as he could go.

Jake ran ahead of his mother and sister and threw open the coop door. The chickens cackled and flew around the coop as Jake dropped to his knees, frantically brushing away hay from the floor until he could find the knothole.

"Ma, go back to Papa!" Summer sobbed.

Julia put her little girl on the ground and squatted to face her. "Summer, this is no game. You must be silent, *instantly.*" It hurt her heart to see how Summer's eyes widened in fear, but she couldn't be soft now. "If you make even one sound, you could cause things to be even worse."

Wide-eyed, Summer nodded slightly with understanding. She immediately clamped her mouth closed, scrunched her eyes shut, and stood there with her little hands in fists. Julia felt so proud as she saw how hard her little girl was trying to obey. She scooped her up and squeezed her tight, trying hard to keep herself from sobbing aloud.

Jake found the knothole and the trap door flew up. Part of the wooden floor was hinged here on leather straps. Below was little more than a large hole in the ground, and it was filthy from chicken droppings, but it offered a safe hideaway that only the family knew about.

About eight months ago, Luke had come home with some disturbing news. A family that lived only a few miles north had been robbed in their own home. The father, who wasn't the type to trust banks, had been badly beaten before he would tell the thieves where he had hidden the family's money. The family lost everything. Luke decided his family would have a safe hiding place, now well hidden under a new chicken coop.

Julia remembered how she'd thought Luke was overreacting when he dug out and built the coop. She had almost forgotten all about it—but now she was thanking God for this little hole.

Jake helped her down, then handed her Summer. He quickly climbed in, but instead of sitting down, he crouched, holding the door above his head so he could see out.

"I can't see Pa," Jake whipped his head around.

"God will take care of your pa, Jake." Julia hated to hear the way her own voice was shaking. "We must pray for him." Summer sobbed softly into her mother's shoulder.

Julia looked at her son, his wavy dark blonde hair was filled with sweat and dirt. He looked so much like his pa.

"Who *are* these men?" Jake whispered sharply. "Who shot him? What's going on?"

"I honestly don't know, Jake. Please just pray!" she said as she bit the side of her lip and thought, *Now that's not entirely true, is it? You have an idea, don't you?*

"Where is Pa anyway? I hope he's getting the gun." Jake felt so angry. *I should have stayed with him!*

"There he is!" He saw his father jogging painfully back to stand beside his horse. The first of the four men was riding up. He father stood unflinching next to his horse. Jake pounded his fist when he saw Pa did *not* have the gun.

I should be out there! Jake thought again. It took every ounce of control for him to keep from flying out of that dugout and to his father's side, but Pa's words came forcefully to mind: *Stay here and protect, Ma and Summer.*

He strained to see details, but he was just too far removed to see much. All four men on horseback surrounded his father, but he couldn't see much from this distance except basic details. All four were riding bay horses. The one with the black hat was tall, and Jake might have assumed he was the leader, but he wasn't the one doing the talking. The man with the white hat was. *He must be the leader,* Jake thought.

He could barely hear anything from his hiding place. The man with the white hat was asking his pa something. Pa answered. The man said something else, and his father spoke again. "They're talking … but … I can't hear!" he whispered to his ma in frustration. The panic was rising in his chest with every passing second.

He turned and looked at his ma. Her eyes were tightly

shut as her lips moved silently. Summer's face was still buried in her mother's shoulder.

He looked back to his pa. Whatever this conversation was about, it didn't seem to be getting worse. The man still spoke in a normal tone of voice and he could hear his father answering calmly. Maybe they would just leave. *Oh God, please let them just leave.*

"God, *please* take care of my father," he whispered as he ducked down a little farther. "If we ever needed your help, we need it now!"

The man asked another question and Luke answered. Jake started when the man put his right hand down next to his gun holster and fanned out his fingers in a peculiar way, like he was playing the piano in the air. The man said something else to Luke, and then did it again—fanned his fingers in the air. Luke said something back and the man seemed satisfied. He sat up a little taller in the saddle and began to turn. Jake felt himself relax slightly. Then before he could even grasp what was happening, the man grabbed his gun and a shot rang out.

Jake watched his father drop to the ground. *They shot him!* He watched in horror as the man calmly cocked his gun, aimed, and shot his father again.

Jake dropped down into the dugout hard and fast pulling the trap door down over his head. *They shot him! They shot him!* He locked eyes with his terrified mother. He could barely see her in the light coming down through the slats, but he watched as she clamped her eyes closed and bit her lip until it began to bleed. She held Summer so tightly that it looked like she was smothering her, but Jake could see that Summer was grasping at her mother with the same urgency.

"Now find it!" they heard one of the men shout.

Find what? What are they looking for? Jake could hear one of the men coming closer. The man stopped to yank the door of the coop open. The chickens were panicking. Dust and droppings were raining down through the slats onto their heads.

Oh God, I'm not ready to die. I'm not ready to die. Jake could see the man's boots through the cracks overhead. He got a glimpse. It was the biggest of all the men—the tall one with the black hat.

"What does he want me to do?" the man muttered under his breath. "Look under every stinkin' chicken?" He walked over to the nests and began throwing out the hay by handfuls.

The chickens had all run out the open door, so there was no more clucking to cover any sounds they made. Thankfully, the man above was making a lot of noise tearing up the chicken coop.

Suddenly the man stopped and was quiet.

Julia pulled her daughter closer. Summer was as stiff as a stick, but her breath was quick and panicked on Julia's neck. She felt her own heart beating hot in her cheeks and ears.

Jake tried to quiet his own breathing while the man just stood there, silently, as agonizing seconds passed. He flattened himself against the dirt wall, and held his breath, waiting for the ceiling to suddenly fly upward.

The sweat pouring off his head stung Jake's eyes.

Farther off, they could hear the crashing sounds of the house being ransacked. Jake and his mother both watched the ceiling even though they couldn't even see the man's boots anymore. The hay he'd torn out of the nests was now completely covering the floor.

Finally, the man coughed and then shouted to his companions, "It's not out here, it's got to be in the barn or the house." In a few steps, he was gone.

Jake's face was hot and his ears were buzzing. He relaxed slightly against the dirt wall.

They could hear the sounds of the house and barn being torn apart. Time seemed to be passing so slowly. It was both a relief and a horror when they finally heard the men riding away.

Jake stood cautiously. His arms trembled as he raised the chicken coop floor. He looked around slowly then quickly scrambled out and ran around the far edge of the barn. *Yes.* All four of the men were riding away.

He ran with all his might to his father's side. Before he even got close he could tell that it was too late. He felt as though his heart was wrenched from his body.

He dropped to his knees. He could hear his own breathing, and feel his own heart racing. This couldn't be happening—surely it was a nightmare. He felt that he was watching this happen to someone else.

"Oh God! Oh God!" He heard his own voice wailing. "God ... you let him die. I prayed ... and *you let him die!*"

He'd never felt more alone in all his life.

Somewhere far off he could hear his mother and Summer crying.

dirt

Julia held her daughter's small hand as the three of them stood beside the freshly dug grave. Summer held the wildflowers she'd picked in her other hand. Julia was disturbed at the hardness she saw in her son's face. Jake just stood there, motionless. She nodded to him and he looked down at the family's Bible he held in his hands.

He opened it to the passage she'd asked for and read, "Jesus said unto her, I am the resurrection, and the life: he that believeth in me, though he were dead, yet shall he live: And whosoever liveth and believeth in me shall never die."

Julia's heart was breaking at the bitterness she heard in his voice. He read because she asked him to, but he did not believe what he was reading. She felt at a loss. *Oh Lord,* she prayed silently, *what on earth am I supposed to say to him?*

"Your pa was the strongest of believers," she told them both. "He wasn't afraid to die. He often spoke of it without any fear."

Jake remained motionless. He closed the Bible and handed it over without looking at her.

Summer let go of her hand and knelt down in front of the open grave. She dropped her wildflowers in one-by-one. "Goodbye Papa," she whispered.

The three of them stood there silently for what seemed like a long time. Summer stood back up and took her mother's hand. "The flowers are much prettier in Heaven, aren't they Ma?"

"Yes darling," her eyes filled with tears. *Oh, the faith of a little child. God I thank you for this child of comfort.*

"And Papa gets to be with Jesus every day."

"Yes, baby."

"And that's a lot better than being here, right?"

"Yes, it is." She picked Summer up and held her tight. "Darling, your papa knew where he was going. In a way, I envy him. He's happier now than he's ever been. We are the ones who are sad, to be left here without him for a little while."

Jake wordlessly picked up the shovel and began to fill in the grave. His stiffness made her shudder. *Oh Lord, please show me what to do. I don't know how to reach him.*

She put her hand briefly on his arm. He did not react. Then she turned with Summer and began slowly walking back toward the house.

Jake stopped shoveling for a moment. He stared, transfixed, at the pile of dirt he was covering his father's body with. He lightly cut the spade into the dirt at the top of the pile. He watched as clods of earth rolled down into the grave. *Just like us,* he thought. *One minute we're on top of the world, then without warning we're knocked down. Things bigger than us, things we have no control over, come in and roll us down and crush us.* He stepped on one of the clods, smashing it flat.

He turned to look at the small figure of his mother, with Summer on her hip, slowly walking back to the house.

He leaned on the shovel and rubbed the back of his neck with his hand. Turning, he looked down into the grave. The white bed sheet sewn around his father's body was only lightly covered with dirt.

It was a wonder that his mother hadn't wanted anyone else here. Pa was extremely well liked around town. People had been coming to the house in a steady stream, bringing food and offering condolences.

Jake had heard his mother talking to one of the neighbors when she didn't know he was listening. She'd said, "I just think it will be easier for the children this way. We can say our final goodbyes privately. I hope you understand."

Yes, yes. The neighbor understood.

Yeah, Jake spat bitterly, *understood nothing.* Their lives were going on just as before. They went home and ate food and told jokes and laughed—for them, nothing had changed. They didn't understand.

He peered down into that dark hole once more. *Pa died for no good reason. The thieves didn't even take anything. It was senseless.*

Jake spoke to his father's lifeless form, "Pa, the last thing you said to me was to take care of Ma and Summer... and I'm going to do that." He scooped in another shovelful of earth.

charred

The wild horse felt delightfully alive beneath him. Jake couldn't believe Pa was finally letting him help to train one of the new horses. This was the best birthday present any ten year-old could ever have!

"Hold him steady, Son. You can do it." Luke smiled as he held the long reign and Jake circled around. Jake was beaming, he was that excited. He smiled so hard his face hurt and he threw back his head and laughed.

Pa laughed too. Then a shot rang out and Pa's face was frozen in pain. Blood gushed from his chest and he fell forward on his face. Jake jumped from the horse and ran toward his father. There was so much blood. It mixed with the dust into a hot, thick mud. Suddenly that's all there was, all around. Jake's couldn't even see his father anymore and the mud was coming up around his chest.

He fought with his arms, but more and more blood was coming from everywhere. It rose higher and higher. The mud was around his neck, it rose over the sides of his cheeks. He screamed and struggled, but he couldn't move. It rose over the edges of his lips, to fill his mouth...

"No!" Jake screamed and sat straight up in bed. The nightmare still held him with invisible threads. He jumped out of bed and wiped his hands over his face, assuring himself that he could, indeed, breathe. He was covered in sweat.

"Jake, what's wrong? Are you all right?" Julia came running down the hallway.

"Yes. Yes," he breathed. "I'm okay. Just a dream."

"Momma," Summer's sleepy voice could be heard down the hall. "Momma, where are you?" Summer had been sleeping with her ever since her father's murder.

"I'm right here, honey," Julia called to her.

She laid her hand on Jake's flushed cheek. "You're sure you're okay?"

"I'm fine. I'm just going to sit up for a while."

I wish he wouldn't stiffen every time I touch him. I suppose it's just his way of trying to be a man. Oh Lord, I don't know how to lead him through this time in his life. If Luke were here... She stopped herself. Nothing could change that now.

Lord, she prayed for the hundredth time, *please reach him.*

"All right. I love you, honey." She turned and went back to bed.

It had been three weeks and Jake was still plagued with nightmares. He could barely get to sleep in the first place. He seemed to jump awake with every sound, imagining the thieves had come back to find whatever they'd been looking for. When he finally did fall asleep—nightmares. They usually started with fond memories of Pa and then turned ghastly without warning. All night long—he felt he was getting no rest.

He walked out and stood in front of the fireplace. He wiped his face again with his hands. *When is this going to end? Is anything ever going to be normal again?*

He leaned over onto the mantle and his hand brushed the family Bible. He jerked away.

He stared at the Bible. He stared venom into it.

His anger and bitterness had been growing like a cancer. "God," he spoke out to the empty room, "why didn't you protect my pa? I pleaded with you. My ma pleaded with you. Little Summer pleaded..."

He continued to stare at the Bible. It just sat there on the mantle—stupidly, unable to respond. He grabbed it from the shelf and threw it to the floor. It landed at the edge of the ashes of the banked fire.

He watched it as it lay there. At first, nothing happened, and then a steady, smoldering sizzle began to sound as the edges of the leather started to bubble and curl. A thin ribbon of smoke began to coil upwards into the room.

He felt a little stab of conscience when he thought about how much this would hurt his mother. He kicked the Bible out of the fireplace.

For a few more moments, he watched the streamer of smoke rise until it finally stopped.

As he stared at its charred edge, Jake felt all the hatred, anger, and bitterness solidify into one immovable mass inside his chest. Strangely, he also felt a sense of relief. Something about this actually felt *better* somehow. *Yes.* He felt much better than he had in weeks. He left the Bible on the floor, went back to bed, and slept soundly the rest of the night.

chimney

Ten Years Later

"**M**a, it's got to be done." Jake climbed the ladder with a slight limp and continued to break off pieces of the stick-and-daub chimney top. "Don't stand right there or I'm going to drop something on you."

"Lucas Jacob Forester, if you fall again you might break your neck!" Ma was overwrought. She wrung her hands.

"I didn't fall that far and I'm fine, Ma." Jake rolled his eyes. "Now, I don't mean any disrespect, but I'm 25 years-old. I don't need a woman telling me how to do my work."

Julia stomped her foot and tears sprang to her eyes. "Son, you need to think about more than your pride. If something happened to you, I don't know what we would do."

Jake sighed and climbed down the ladder. "I'll try to be more careful, Ma, but this has *got* to be done, and it's got to be done *now*. It's mid-September. October... November..." He counted off on his fingers. "It may be warm now, but it's going to be getting cold soon and we're going need the fireplace again. This is perfect timing since the corn was early this year. I have this little bit of time here to try to get some things done. I can't imagine how I've let it go so long already. It's a miracle we haven't already burned the place down."

"I know." She furrowed her brow then sighed and threw up her hands in resignation. "I know, I know it has to be done." Her dark brown hair was a little greyer now. She pushed wisps of it back under her sunbonnet and turned to walk back to the vegetable garden. "God, please protect him," she prayed aloud as she went.

Jake winced at those words. It was really beyond him, after all these years, how she could still believe God protected people.

Yeah, He sure did a great job of protecting Pa, Jake thought as he climbed back up and continued to knock loose the old sticks and dried mud that made up the top of the house chimney.

He shook his head. He supposed it must just be part of a woman's weakness to believe in fairy tales like that. He shook his head. *No, that can't be it. Pa believed it too.* He thought for a moment more, *I don't know. Maybe it's just their generation.*

He shrugged, turning back to the chimney and used his hammer to knock out another piece. *I really don't know why I've let this go for so long. It's a wonder the house hasn't burned down around our heads! This job should have been done ten years ago.*

Jake's mind went back to the week before Pa's death. They were getting ready to tear out the stick-and-daub part and re-build it with stone, so they took an afternoon trip down to the creek bed with the wagon. It was a fun day.

Even Ma and Summer had come.

The scene replayed in his mind. There was Ma reminding Summer to keep her skirts out of the water while she waded. Pa was talking to him about how to pick stones that were the right size and shape. The two of them huffed and blew as they carried the stones to the wagon, and then went back to the creek to splash their faces.

Pa said, "I'm so thankful I have you, Jake. This is a job for two men, not one."

Jake smiled slightly, remembering. He had felt so proud, so grown up.

And now, here I am, doing the job alone, he thought as he tapped the hammer around the edge of the top layer of stones. He needed to get as much of the old mud off as possible.

As he tapped, he felt one of the stones come loose in his hand. *Oh no. I don't want to have to rebuild this whole thing!* He pulled the stone out and leaned over to examine the hole. *Maybe I can just re-mud this one... Hold on. What's that white thing?*

Jake reached in and drew out the last thing he expected. It was one of his father's handkerchiefs wrapped and tied around a paper and something hard. He sat down on the roof and tried to untie the knot. His hands felt so large and clumsy that he finally had to use his teeth to untie it.

As it opened in his hand, he was stunned to see two gold nuggets.

dragón

Catrina opened her eyes. She stared up at the ceiling for a
moment. By the light, she guessed it was probably nearly
noon. There was no real reason to get out of bed this
early except that her stomach was growling.

She sat up, swung her legs over the side of the bed and
stared at the dirty wallpaper. *What on earth am I doing
here?* She'd asked herself this a million times.

It was always the same answer: *I'm making a living. I'm
surviving.*

She took the looking glass from the side table. Her
glossy, black hair framed a slender face with high cheek
bones. Bright hazel, almost golden, eyes sparkled against
her pale complexion. The customers were always making
comments about her eyes. She blinked at her reflection. By
her looks, she guessed she could probably keep "working"
for many years to come.

But I don't want *to keep doing this. This is no way to
live. I've got to get out of here!* She looked again at her eyes
in the glass and examined the almost indiscernible crow's
feet starting around their outer edges.

Her stomach growled again. *Get out of here to where?*

Starvation? Get your head out of the clouds.

I could go back to Father. She looked at her reflection again, but had to turn the glass away. *No, I can never face him. It would be better for him to think I died. Just look at what I've become—a common harlot.*

"Catrina," she heard Garret calling from downstairs in the saloon, "I've got someone here I want you to meet."

Her shoulders slumped at the sound of his voice. *Oh no,* she thought, *not another one of those.* That "someone here I want you to meet" was a signal. Over the last couple of months, Garret had brought in several of what he called "business contacts." *More like sheep to the slaughter,* Catrina thought sadly.

Catrina would take the man to a specially prepared room down the hall. It was lavishly decorated, including a beautiful clock on one wall and a display of ornate hammered copper plates and decorative glass on the facing wall. What the "business contact" didn't know was that hidden amidst the copper plates and glass was the lens of one of the newest portrait cameras available. Catrina would watch the clock on the one wall and then exactly on the hour she would make sure the man's face was steadily pointed toward the camera. Unknown to the poor "sheep," that's when Garret would take the exposure.

That's why these always had to be done during the day, so that the intense daylight streaming in through the top half of the windows would make the exposure bright enough.

The idea that a portrait could be taken of someone in such moral compromise wouldn't even occur to most. People were used to having to sit still for several minutes if they wanted to have a portrait made, but now a brand new development process allowed a portrait to be created in as little as three seconds.

Of all the things she had done in her life, she was more ashamed of this than anything else she could think of. She knew Garret must be blackmailing these men with the portraits, but she didn't know for what. *This place sure is aptly named,* she thought. *"El Dragón Rojo."* She rolled the words around in her mind for a moment. *The Red Dragon. Garret is the dragon and he devours people alive.*

"Catrina?" he called again. She heard a waiver of impatience in his voice.

"Give me just a moment to freshen up," she called back, "I can't wait to meet your friend." She tried to make it sound as sincere as possible, but she groaned inwardly.

Sam Garret stood at the bottom of the stairs alongside an overstuffed peacock of a man who was nervously fumbling with his hat in his hands.

"She'll be right down," Garret smiled and winked. Internally his impatience with that girl was growing into a cold fury. "Believe me, she's worth the wait—I tell you she's got gold nuggets for eyes."

Garret prided himself on an unflappable exterior—only those who knew him best could detect the flicker of an icy shadow in his eyes. *That girl needs to be ready for work by 10. She should have been down here instantly. She's only been here a year, and she's already gotten far too sassy. I'm going to have to teach her a lesson.*

He smiled largely and clapped the man on the back, "Frank, come on over here and let's have a drink while we wait."

gold

Jake's mouth dropped open. One of the gold nuggets was about half the size of a hen's egg and the other was a bit smaller. The gold rush had ended nearly ten years ago, and as far as he knew, gold was *never* found this far west. But there it was in his hand.

He smoothed the paper it was wrapped in. On it, a hastily scribbled pencil message in his pa's unforgettable handwriting: "Jake, never sell this land—there's more gold. I love you. Pa." He couldn't believe what he was looking at.

Jake balled it up in his hand. "Ma!" he shouted as he came down the ladder, "Come here!"

"What is it?" Julia called back. She stood quickly from her work in the vegetable garden and looked back toward the house. Jake was stomping away from her and around the corner to go into the house. He seemed to be holding one hand with the other. *Oh no! He's cut himself!* She brushed her hands on her apron, hitched up her skirts, and raced to the house.

"What? What is it?" she shouted as she came through the door.

He stood with his back to her. Suddenly he turned and slammed the gold down onto the table, "You knew about this! Didn't you?"

"Oh no," Julia felt her spirits sink. She closed her eyes slowly and sat down, "It was in the chimney?"

"This is what those men were after, isn't it? You knew Pa had found gold and that he hid it," he shook his head in betrayal, "How could you lie to me all these years?"

Julia felt she'd been slapped. "I *never* lied to you, Jake. Never."

"You don't want to call it lying—fine. You *withheld the truth* from me, from Summer." He turned in a circle rubbing his hands through his hair, "All these years you pretended not to know why Pa was killed. I can't believe it."

Julia's conscience pricked her, "I never really thought of it as a lie, Jake. I'm sorry for the way this has hurt you..." She trailed off. "But I'm honestly not sorry for keeping it from you."

"Ma, I'm a grown man." He smacked his hand down on the table, "What possible reason could you have for keeping this from me? How could you let me scratch and scrape to keep this place together? How could you let me struggle so hard to make ends meet, when I could have been looking for the gold? This would solve all our problems!"

Julia folded her hands and looked down at her lap. *Oh Lord, how am I going to be able to make him understand?* "Your pa..." she trailed off, "You're not going to understand this, Jake, but your pa didn't want you to know about the gold."

"He *what?*"

"For the majority of your life, you were not raised to know the Lord."

He cursed under his breath, "Is this supposed to have something to do with God?"

"Please hear me out," she softly pleaded. "Your pa didn't come to know the Lord till you were eleven. You only got to see him as a Christian man for three years before."

He cut her off. "Before God *protected* him?"

She chose her words carefully and spoke them slowly, "Before God *chose* to let him die." She let those words linger in the air between them for a few moments, making no explanation or apology for God's decision.

"Your pa believed the Bible—he believed it with all his heart. And it says that the love of money leads people to pierce themselves through with many sorrows. Jake, you were raised in a godless home for so long. Your pa worried that you might never come to Christ. He prayed for your salvation continually. He must have told me a dozen times how grateful he was that God had not let *him* find the gold until *after* he had come to know Christ. Not telling you about the gold was his way of protecting you. And I felt that I needed to continue that."

Jake felt defeated. *How am I supposed to talk logic with someone who takes everything on faith? All this time, she's kept it secret to try to "protect" me? I guess, in her own peculiar way, she means well.*

He sighed. "You say Pa didn't want me to know. Well, what about this?" He handed her the crumpled note.

She read her husband's quickly scrawled writing. She shook her head. "I… I…" Julia searched her mind for an answer, but nothing came. "I don't know."

Holding that scrap of paper in her hand brought that day back in vivid detail. She ran her fingers over every letter and her eyes filled with tears. *This is the last thing he ever wrote. Oh Lord, why did you let this happen?* A thought suddenly sprung to mind, "Jake, was there anything else with this—a paper with an eagle at the top?"

He shook his head. "No, there was nothing else. What paper?"

"It's the title—the title to our land. I've not been able to find it since your pa's death."

"Why haven't you ever told me our title was missing?" he demanded.

"Because I don't really think it's anything to worry too much about," she replied, trying to sound more confident than she felt. "Besides, I'm sure there's a copy of it in San Francisco. Your pa took a special trip there right after California became a state to get it all settled with the Land Commission."

Jake sat down hard. He spent a few minutes in silence, staring at his hands.

Julia, who was used to his outbursts of anger, sat quietly waiting for another one.

Finally, he picked up the two nuggets from the table and rolled them around in the palm of his hand. "Ma, whatever Pa's intention was, one way or another, I know about the gold *now*. So I think you'd better tell me the whole story." He looked at the clock. "And unless you want Summer to know too, you'd better tell me quickly."

soup

The portrait made, Catrina quietly excused herself from the bedchamber. She was much hungrier now than when she first woke up. Her stomach was growling incessantly. She went downstairs and through the door behind the bar that led to the kitchen.

Rob, the barkeep and sometime cook, was standing over a pot of stew. He was a giant of a man who had to duck slightly as he went through doorways. He was a gentle as he was huge—a towering, jolly fellow with a round belly, neatly trimmed brown and gray beard, and a hearty laugh. He looked up and smiled at her as she came in the room. "Good morning, darlin'!" He called every woman "darlin'." She grinned back at him. He'd always been kind and friendly to her and he'd never made any advances. True, he was old enough to be her father, but that hadn't stopped other men.

"A bowl, please Rob." She sat down on a stool and cut a piece of bread from the loaf, "I'm famished!"

"Coming right up, darlin'," he chuckled as he slid her an empty bowl.

This was his idea of a joke, and it did actually make

Catrina smirk, "A bowl *of soup,* please." It smelled wonderful.

"It's oxtail stew, darlin'." He plunged in a spoon and scooped up chunks of tender carrots, potatoes, and bits of browned meat drowning in thick broth.

She took a moment just to breathe in the smell. She smiled back at Rob and dipped her bread in the stew. She was raising the spoon to her mouth when everything went upside down. She had a searing pain in the side of her head and found herself lying on the floor looking up at Rob. She saw an expression of sympathetic pain on his face, as if he wanted to help her, but couldn't. She didn't know what had happened. She tried to get her arms under herself and get up. However, her head hurt horribly. She fell back down and looked to her left. There stood Garret.

He was looking at her and his mouth was moving. But she felt so dazed, and she couldn't hear anything. She watched his mouth moving as the sound slowly came back to her right ear, "...don't understand this, then I'm sure I can come up with some other ways to teach you. This is the last I will say of it. In the future, you will be up and ready to work no later than ten." His face was entirely devoid of emotion. His voice was not even raised. He adjusted the cuff link on his right sleeve, turned on his heel and walked out.

Now she was beginning to feel the burning from the hot stew that had flipped all over her. Rob rushed to her aid with a cold, wet dishrag. He quickly wiped off the stew and lifted her back up onto the stool as if she weighed no more than a feather. She sat there for several minutes still feeling disoriented. As he busied himself with kitchen work, she heard him cursing under his breath about Garret's violent temper, and what a cowardly thing it was to punch a woman.

Rob gave her another bowl of stew and a piece of bread. "You may as well eat darlin'. It'll make you feel better." He put his warm rough hand over hers for a moment. She knew he was doing his best to comfort her. She looked up at him and tried to smile in gratitude. He nodded slightly and turned back to his work.

She reached up and tenderly felt her right ear. There was a small quantity of blood coming out. Rob saw it and gave her the washrag. She numbly took it and wiped off the blood. *I wonder if I'm going to be deaf in this ear?* She looked at the blood on the washrag. *For the rest of my life am I going to be paying for this?*

She looked down at the soup and remembered how hungry she'd been. She took up the spoon mechanically and sipped the broth. It should have been warm and good, but she felt she couldn't taste it properly. She tried taking a bite of bread, but her jaw felt strangely out of joint. She didn't feel like eating anymore. "Thank you, Rob." She got up and made her way upstairs to her room.

citro

"Jake," Julia said as she rose to make tea for them, "Tell me what you know about our family history."

"I know your pa was Mexican, but he made you learn to speak English. I know that your folks died in a fire." He tried to think of what else he knew. "I know Pa had a fight with his brother, and that's why he ended up coming here from England. And I know you and Pa met and married in San Francisco. I guess that's about all I can think of. What is it you think I need to know?"

She bent to put coal into the stove, "Jake, you're a grown man now and there are things about our family that you don't know. If I'm going to tell you all about the gold, then I'm actually going to start at the very beginning and tell you everything."

Julia dipped water out of the bucket into the kettle and sat it on the stove lid. "Everything you said is correct. My father was Mexican—Oracio Gutierrez Santiago. He was a well-educated, handsome man. He loved to learn, and he loved to teach. He really should have been a schoolteacher, but he was a storekeeper. He was always teaching me, making me keep my mind sharp. And you know I've often told you how he made my mother and me speak English in the home. He had a belief that it was going to become a more and more important trade language, and he was right, wasn't he?" She smiled at Jake.

"Most people thought my mother was Mexican too, but in actuality she was from Russia. Father was raised Catholic and Mother pretended publicly to be Catholic, even though she was actually Jewish. Father and Mother didn't want anyone knowing. Father thought it would be bad for business. I was told to tell others I was Catholic, but in reality neither one of my parents was serious about their religion. I really wasn't raised to be either.

"We moved to San Francisco when I was a young girl. Back then, it was called Yerba Buena. Of course, this was all part of Mexico at the time. The move was a good one for us—I got to go to school, and Father's store was doing very well—but it only lasted about six months. Late one afternoon, before I got back from school, Mother and Father were killed in a fire that started in the store. It was horrible. It spread across much of the town before it was put out by a rainstorm."

She walked over to the counter where she fiddled with a dishrag. The fact that his grandparents died in a fire had always just been a neutral piece of information, he'd never really put himself in his ma's shoes to try to understand what that must have felt like to her.

Her back was to him and her voice came out in a whispered crackle, "Today my heart is doubly crushed by the fact that neither one of them knew Jesus as their Savior." She wiped away her tears with her fingers, "I can't even think about it very long."

She stood with her back to him a few more seconds, then

seemed to gather herself together. She began to wipe the counter off as she continued. "I didn't have a single living relative. I was very alone. I lived as best I could on the streets for about a week. One night while I was trying to sleep, a drunken man grabbed me. He tried to take advantage of me but I was able to fight my way free. I just ran and ran. I can still remember that night so clearly. It was dark and cold and I was in absolute terror. I turned a corner and saw some light. There were two women loudly laughing together outside a saloon—the Citro. To me, at that moment, that light seemed like safety and warmth. Maria and Lola were the women's names. They took me in."

She walked over and resettled the kettle on the stove, "Within a few days they were both talking to me about becoming a saloon girl. I remember Maria saying, 'What's better; to be here, warm and well-fed with *some* control over what a man does to you or to be out there, cold, hungry, and running for your life from some drunk?' What she said seemed to make so much sense."

Julia turned to watch her son's reaction. She could see in his eyes that he'd already anticipated it. "Yes, Jake. I became a saloon girl."

Jake was reeling but he tried not to show it. He often visited the brothels on his trips to San Francisco, although he couldn't remember going to one called the Citro. For a split second, he wondered if his ma knew this and was making this whole thing up just to make him admit something. But no, she wouldn't lie. He felt restless with embarrassment. *Ma is so religious, I just can't imagine it. Why is she telling me this? I could have never found out on my own.*

Julia felt a mixture of humiliation and relief that Jake finally knew. "Looking back now, I know that if I would have tried harder that I could have found another way to survive. The first couple of times, after the man left, I cried until I made myself sick. But in time I got used to it."

Jake thought about the ladies he'd been with. He couldn't imagine any of them actually feeling that way. Faces flashed through his mind. It made him feel like some kind of a monster to think that they might have been crying and throwing up after he left them.

"At first I had such a strong conviction that what I was doing was evil, I actually felt terrified that God was going to kill me," she continued. "But that changed when I had a clandestine, backdoor visit from one of the parish priests. It was revolting. I lost my fear of God in the face of such hypocrisy. I figured he knew more about God than I did, and if he wasn't scared, then why should I be."

"It was about three years later when your pa sailed here from England. He and your uncle Jonathan had inherited the family's shipping business when their father died. For several years, they ran it together with no problems. Then something changed—your uncle Jonathan became a Christian. Not just a churchgoer anymore but a true *Christian*. He was genuinely re-born—he became a completely different person." Julia *so* much wanted her son to understand this. She looked into his eyes for any sign of comprehension.

Seeing none, she sighed and continued her story. "Jonathan began to put his foot down about shady things they'd been doing for years. Your pa just couldn't understand it. Plus, Jonathan was constantly talking about God, to the point that Luke said he just couldn't stand listening to it anymore."

Jake thought, *I know exactly how he felt.*

"Luke sold his half of the business to his brother, took the money and struck out for a new life about as far away from Jonathan as he could get. He ended up in Yerba Buena at the Citro."

She put her hand on the kettle to see how warm it was getting. "Luke liked me from the moment he first saw me. When he came in, he always asked for me, never any of the other girls. He was handsome, funny, and always making witty comments. He was a real charmer and I was very flattered by his attention. One night, he asked me to marry him. This may sound strange to say now, but I didn't say yes. I told him I'd think about it and I really did need some time. Where I was, I felt like I had independence, fine clothes, and a good living. At that time, my vision of a wife was of someone weighed down with endless cooking, cleaning, washing and mending, not to mention children. And all the while, the husband would be sneaking around having fun with the girls at the Citro. It took me a good long time to decide if that was a life I really wanted."

Again Jake felt surprised. He couldn't imagine Ma feeling that way or thinking those things. That sure wasn't the ma he knew. *I guess she's going to say religion changed her. That must be what she's leading up to.*

"We were married by a justice of the peace on January 18, 1841. Married life wasn't as bad as I had expected. It was actually fun—for about a year. But a little over a year after we were married, I found out that Luke was starting to frequent the upper rooms at the Citro again."

Jake was visibly surprised. He knew his pa used to be a drinker before he got religion, but never thought he would have been unfaithful. It made him feel a little angry.

"I was so hurt. But I told myself, 'It was inevitable,' and

'I should have expected it,' and 'He still loves me but a man has needs that just can't be fulfilled by one woman all his life long.' But something inside me didn't really believe all those things and I started getting more and more depressed. I wanted something to reassure me. I wanted some comfort. I thought religion might be the answer."

Here it comes, thought Jake.

"So I decided to go to Mass. But when I went in, there was that same old priest that had visited me at the Citro when I was only 14. There he was, standing up there all pious. He looked me in the eye for a second and then looked away quickly. I felt revolted again. He didn't even believe all the garbage he was spouting.

"It wasn't long after that the big brawl broke out. There was gambling at the Citro and apparently someone had been cheating. Luke was there and he jumped into the middle of it. He ended up saving the life of a wealthy Ranchero, Emilio Sergio Alvarado. Señor Alvarado was so grateful he carved out a small slice of his own ranchos and gave your pa the title to this land.

"Luke was so pleased, he was eager to get out here and start a brand new life. I was excited too. Out here, it takes more than two days by horseback to get back to Yerba Buena. I thought, 'No more Citro, no more problems!' And I was right—but only for a little while. You see son, wickedness is not something we can leave in another town. Your pa's, and mine, it traveled here with us, in our very hearts."

The kettle was boiling now. She took the tealeaves from the tin and added them to two china cups. Over this, she poured the boiling water. Then she carried both cups to the table and went back to the cupboard for the honey.

"I'm home!" came Summer's cheerful voice from outside. In another second, she was in the door. She took her sunbonnet off quickly. Even though she was a young woman now, she hated having to wear it. "Are we having tea?"

"We sure are," Julia said, grabbing another cup. "Tell me about school today, darling."

Jake felt frustrated. This was all interesting, but it had taken so long to tell and he still didn't know about the gold! Luckily, the nuggets were in his hand when Summer came in. He closed his fist quickly and stood up, putting them in his pocket.

"That's okay, Ma." As he put on his hat he shot her a look that carried his frustration. "You two have tea. I've got to get back on that chimney before it gets dark on me."

"We'll talk some more tonight, darling," she told him as he was going out the door.

portrait

"You dirty... filthy... blackmailer!" The little fat man's voice was pitched high with anger. He could not have been more outraged as he stood there in Garret's office holding a portrait of himself with that woman of ill repute. His eyes widened as a thought suddenly occurred to him. He took the portrait quickly and ripped it to shreds. Relief washed over his round face.

Garret poured himself another shot of bourbon whiskey. He kept the good stuff back here for himself. "Won't you have a drink, Frank," he said smoothly as he filled a second shot glass, "Another interesting thing about this new technology is that more than one copy can be made of the portrait." He pulled another copy out of his desk drawer.

The man's face went white with fear, "What do you want?"

"Now calm down. No one ever has to see this," Garret shook his head in a patronizing manner as he returned it to the drawer. "Sit, sit, please. Don't worry, Frank, I don't want your money. All you have to do to make this all go away, is just tell one simple lie."

The man sat. He grabbed the shot in his fat hand and downed it in one swallow.

broken

Hours later, downstairs in the saloon, business was starting to pick up. Catrina's ear hurt severely and a high-pitched ringing had started. She felt a cold stab of terror at the thought of what Garret might do if she stayed in her room.

Her ear had stopped bleeding a while ago, but she checked in the mirror anyway. *You've got to hand it to him, he sure knows how to hit a girl and leave no marks.* As she looked at the side of her head, the only evidence of her intense pain was that her ear was still a little pink. No one would notice. *Exactly the way he wants it.*

She adjusted her clothes and tried to put a smile on her face. Her reflection looked pained and she knew Garret wouldn't stand for that. She grimaced as another piercing pain shot through her head. And with the increase in noise downstairs, the ringing in her ear seemed to be getting louder and louder. She didn't know how she was going to function tonight.

She smiled wryly into the looking glass. *You've got no other choice,* she thought. *Let's get to it.*

She came out her door with a smile. "Hello fellas!" she

called with a sultry smile and a wave. A chorus of "Hello, Miss Catrina!" rose to greet her. She felt a little dizzy and nauseated but continued to force a smile as she headed to the stairs. As she descended the stairs, she was suddenly overcome with a terrible wave of vertigo. She missed her footing and fell. Her head smacked the banister and she saw a bright flash of white light.

The next thing she knew, she was at the bottom of the stairs. She saw Rob's kind face leaning over hers with a worried look. Other men were crowding around. Garret was even there on the edges, playing the "concerned" role for the sake of appearances. Rob looked round quickly to the door and shouted, "Is Doc coming or what?!"

"Yes, he's on his way," someone shouted back.

"Now you just lay still, darlin'," he said as he held a cold rag to her head. He looked very worried. His face was much paler than usual and sweat was rolling down his brow into his beard.

"What happened?" She tried to sit up but when she moved her head, the whole world spun. Then she saw her arm lying at an impossible angle. It was bent, but *not* at the elbow. She lost consciousness.

When she next awoke, she was lying on a padding of blankets across several tables. The saloon was empty and dark except for two lamps lit at either end of the bar. She felt peaceful, happy, and even a little like she was flying. She realized the doctor must have given her something for pain.

Her head was aching, so she moved it slowly and carefully to look at her left arm. It was cast in plaster of Paris and bandaged from her shoulder to her mid-forearm. The casting was giving off a gentle warmth. With her other hand she felt an enormous knot on her forehead. She could see that her right ankle was swollen and splinted. She felt bruised all over.

She closed her eyes. *At least the ringing in my ear isn't as loud.* She wondered if that was because it was getting better or because of whatever she'd been given.

She heard people coming from the kitchen. They were talking. One of them was Rob. "…saw how upset those men were, Garret. I can guarantee you if any of 'em ever found out you'd give her that box in the ear, you'd be lynched in no time flat."

There was a pause as Garret considered that. "It seems a shame to lose such a pretty face."

"Aw! There's plenty of other girls," Rob remarked. The two of them were closer to her now, but the pain medicine had Catrina feeling so calm that she didn't even open her eyes.

"Maybe you're right, Rob," he finally said. "Get her out of here. Tonight, if possible."

"I surely can do that, sir."

"I'll see you back here in a couple of days then." Garret's voice headed toward the front door. "Good night, Rob."

"Good night, sir."

Catrina heard the front door close.

"That filthy mongrel!" Rob growled under his breath. "He should be horse-whipped to death!"

Her eyes fluttered open a little. "Hi Rob," she said with a smile. "I feel great."

"Yeah, I know darlin'. That's the morphine Doc gave you," he patted her cheek lightly, "I'm afraid you're gonna be feeling a lot worse before you feel better."

"What happened to me?" her words were slurred.

"Well, your arm is broke clean in two. But Doc said if you're gonna break it, that's the best way to go." He winked at her and she smiled back. "Your head is pretty banged up, so we gotta watch you close for the rest of the night. Oh, and your ankle. Doc said he thinks that's just a bad sprain."

"What were you two talking to Garret about?" she felt the morphine was getting stronger somehow.

"I'm gettin' you out of here, Catrina, darlin'. I'm taking you to my sister's place in San Francisco. It's gonna take you some weeks to get healed up and I don't want you anywhere near Garret while you're doin' that." He smoothed his beard.

Oh no, not San Francisco, she thought with a stab of fear. *I can't take a chance of being seen by Father.*

"Besides..." he wavered. "You're such a nice girl. Wouldn't you like to have yourself a respectable job? Have a new start on life? Maybe even find yourself a handsome feller and settle down?"

She raised her eyebrows at him.

"Oh, no. No," he chuckled. "Not me! Darlin', don't you know I'm old enough to be your pa!" He laughed again, "No. You see, my sister owns a laundry. She just wrote me about how much business she has. I figure, once you're healed up, she might could use another set of hands. Now, launderin' may not be glamorous, but it *is* respectable work."

A laundry girl? Maybe that would *work,* she thought. *If she did happen to see Father, he could just believe she'd been a laundry girl all these years. Maybe she really could have a whole new start on life.*

"Why are you always so nice to me, Rob?" The morphine

definitely felt like it was getting stronger. She was starting to float away.

"Oh, I just think we should all try to be neighborly to each other. Don't you?" He put his hand over hers. "I mean, don't the good book say we should love our neighbors same as we love ourselves?"

"I didn't know you were a religious man," she said slowly.

"Oh I'm not!" he protested. "Now my sister *is*, God love her soul, but you'll have to forgive her for it." He smiled again. "No, I'm not religious, but I like to think I'm a *good* man. I'm not a fool. I know I'm gettin' older, and I'm gonna have to meet my Maker one of these days. I guess I'm just tryin' to get in enough good deeds to outweigh my bad ones." he winked at her and put his hat on. "So you just lay here and try to sleep a little. I'm gonna go home and get my wagon ready. I'll be back for you in a while."

"I can't thank you enough, Rob," Catrina said as she closed her eyes. As she lay there, she thought about what he said.

I wonder how many good deeds I need to do to make up for my bad ones? She sighed. *Probably so many that I'll never be able to get them all done before I'm dead*, she thought despairingly as she floated away into sleep.

press

The house was filled with the smell of chicken pie and green beans. Supper had been extra late because Jake had wanted to get the chimney top finished today. He had worked until the sun went down, but the job still wasn't quite done. He hated the feeling of leaving a job unfinished, but he was sure he could finish it up in a few hours tomorrow.

"Great supper, Ma." Jake took one last bite. The flakey layers of golden crust crunched ever so slightly as he chewed through to tender hunks of chicken and gravy. He pushed back from the table, immensely satisfied. "Jewel, *nobody* beats your chicken pie!" Jake never called his mother by her first name. He was repeating the words his pa had so often said after eating this, his favorite meal. Jake even used the same inflection. It was a special memory he and his ma shared each time she made this. She looked up at him and smiled, knowingly.

"That's what pa used to say, isn't it?" Summer asked as she cleared the table and began to wipe the dishes.

"Yes it is," Ma said, "This was his favorite."

"It's my favorite too, Ma. I wish we were well off enough

to have chicken every day," Jake said, with double meaning, as he looked up at her.

"Well, that's not very likely," she said, and started to laugh but got his meaning when she looked up. "Besides," she continued as she got up to put the kettle on for tea. "It's really too rich to have every day. You'd be perfectly sick of it sooner than you'd imagine."

When the dishes were all put away, Ma put two steaming cups of tea out on the porch as Jake carried out two chairs. Summer came out in her nightgown. She finished tucking her hair into her night cap, then leaned over and kissed Ma on the cheek, "Sleep sweet, Ma." She kissed Jake on his forehead, "Sleep *quietly*, Jake." She grinned widely at this nightly joke about his snoring. She'd been doing it ever since she was a kid and had kept it up, even though at 15 years-old, she really was a young woman. "I will thank God for you both before I go to sleep."

"Good night, Sum'," Jake said fondly as he began to fill his pipe.

"God watch over you tonight, child," Julia said to her retreating form. "I love you."

"I love you too, Ma," she called back.

Jake lit his pipe and Ma sipped her tea. They sat quietly together on the porch for some time. Aside from the crickets and the occasional warm breeze of a late summer evening, everything was utterly still. The stars in the Milky Way gleamed like diamonds on black velvet.

"Who do you suppose put those up there?" Julia indicated the stars, "One can't help but wonder, wouldn't you agree?"

What Jake couldn't help was rolling his eyes at her endless attempts to get him to talk about God, "Do you think Summer's asleep?"

"Yes," Julia sighed, "I think it's fair to guess she's asleep by now." *I can't seem to say anything right, Lord. Please reach my boy, because I certainly can't.*

"Can you finish now?"

"I've forgotten where I left off."

"You were about to tell me about the gold," he remarked, sardonically.

She laughed lightly, "Is that all you can think about? I'm filling you in on your whole family history here."

I knew it couldn't be that easy. Jake took a sip of his tea. It was already cooling. *She's got to try to use this opportunity to convert me,* he thought. "Well, go ahead then."

"I remember, we had just moved out here. I was thinking that since we were so far away from anything like the Citro, that I was going to have a whole new husband. Of course, there was Pureza Township only two miles away. But at the time there was nothing there but the mill and a general store." She turned to look at him. His pipe glowed red for a second.

"But about a year after we moved out here, Sam Garret came to town. He set up the Dragón faster than you can imagine. So your pa's greatest 'friends' were dropped down in front of him again—booze and loose women.

"Then came you. When I got pregnant with you, Luke made a really strong attempt to give up that old life, but it only lasted about six months. Then when you were born— oh, that's one of the few occasions in my life when I can remember your pa crying. He didn't even really believe in God, but when he held you for the first time, he just broke down crying and saying, 'Thank you, God,' over and over again. I remember that day so well. Luke promised to never take another drink again."

She was quiet for a moment, "Of course his promise didn't last. It couldn't. But it would be years before either one of us knew the reason why."

She paused. Finally enough time had passed that Jake knew she must want him to say something, "Um…" he groped blindly for something that would placate her. "Because he needed God, right?" He internally winced at even having to carry on this stupid charade. *Why can't she just skip to the end and tell me about the gold?*

"The reason he couldn't stop, even though he genuinely wanted to with all his heart, was because he was enslaved." She took another drink of tea and then began again dramatically, "Think about the tragedy that's going on in the South right now. Imagine you're one of those poor enslaved Negroes. When it comes right down to it, you pretty much have to do what your master tells you. You can choose to disobey but you're going to get beaten. Or you could try running away but there's a good chance you're going to get caught or maybe even killed for it.

"The Bible says that we are slaves to sin. The world, the flesh, and the devil are our masters. Your pa genuinely *did* want to get free, but the devil, the world, and the flesh kept beating him till he went back to obeying them. At that time, he didn't yet know how he could be bought out of slavery to become a free man."

Enslaved? He took another draw on the pipe and kept looking straight ahead. *What a bunch of hogwash. I'm certainly not "enslaved" to anything. I do what I want, when I want. I'm my own man. I make my own rules. I'm not "enslaved" to the Devil, my flesh, or some imaginary God like she is. I mean, sure, I've done my share of drinking and of enjoying the ladies but that's only* natural. *That's what it means to be a* normal *man. What does she think I should be, a monk cloistered in some monastery? And besides, I've always been respectful of her religiousness. I don't want to shame her, that's why I've always traveled to San Francisco for that kind of thing. For goodness sake, I've never even stepped foot in the Dragón! Heck, by the way I act around here, everybody probably thinks I'm as religious as she is!* The more he thought about what she was saying and what it implied, the more irritated he became. But he was intent on letting nothing show on his face. He didn't want to give her any encouragement.

Oh Lord, I'm such a failure, she thought as she watched him staring resolutely out into the darkness. *He's not even listening to me.*

"I'm sorry. I guess I'm just going on and on," she apologized. "I don't need to talk about that anymore, you remember how your pa was *before.* So, when you were eleven, not long after I found out I was pregnant with Summer, that's when we got the letter from your uncle Jonathan. He told us about this young preacher who was really turning England on its ear. You know," she said thoughtfully, "Come to think of it, I don't even know *why* your pa actually read the clipping. He usually just skimmed his brother's letters because they irritated him so. But for whatever reason, he actually did sit down with me that night and read the newspaper clipping out loud to us as we were having tea after supper.

"I've always kept it in the Bible." She got up to retrieve the Bible from inside the house. "And I tell you, I've thanked God *so* many times that you happened to be up the night the rat knocked it off into the fire. Otherwise it might have been lost forever."

Jake's conscience smote him again for the lie he'd told her so many years ago.

She put it on her chair and went back in to return with a lit coal oil lamp. She carefully opened the charred edge of the Bible almost exactly to the middle. There was a yellowed newspaper clipping. She picked it up carefully like it was a treasure of some kind and handed it to him.

He took it in hand awkwardly. On the one hand, he had zero desire to read it, and did not want to give her any impression that he was interested. On the other hand, he thought that if he feigned mild curiosity, she might actually hurry up and finish the story. Finally, he emitted a non-committal, "Hmmm."

Sensing his lack of interest, she took it gently from him and placed it back into the Bible. "Anyway, everything changed that night. Your father became a new person and by that, I don't mean that he 'turned over a new leaf'—I mean that he was entirely re-born. God gave him a new heart with new desires. The change was amazing—nothing short of a miracle. Jesus bought him out of slavery. He was a free man."

"Anyway, he dropped the saloon, and he dropped the ladies—instantly. And it wasn't really like the times he'd tried to quit before, it was different somehow." She stopped, trying to think of how to explain what she meant. "In his eyes, in his voice, I could see that there weren't any lies there anymore. No more cover-ups. It's hard to explain."

She sat back down and put the Bible on her lap, "I admit, even I didn't really understand it at first. It took me two more months before I actually came to Christ myself." She looked him in the eyes quizzically. "Maybe it's something no one can really understand unless it's happened to them."

Jake shrugged his shoulders at her. *How long is this going to take?* he thought. He tipped his chair back against the wall and put his feet up on the post.

"So when he stopped going to the saloon, his friends started chiding him. Sam Garret was the worst. Every time they saw each other in town, he'd laugh and say, 'So when are you going to get over this religion stuff?' Your pa would always smile, real friendly like, and say, 'Never, Garret. Never.' At first, Garret and all the others expected this change would be short lived, so it was all like a big joke to them. But as time continued to pass, Sam seemed to get more and more angry about it. Personally, I think it's probably because he lost one of his best customers.

"Finally Sam just stopped speaking to your pa altogether, even to the point of embarrassment. We'd be in town at the general store and your pa would say, 'Howdy Garret,' but Sam would act like he hadn't heard him and just walk right on out. A couple of different times I remember Sam saying 'Hello' to someone standing right next to your pa, but nothing to him as if he wasn't there.

"It would make me so mad," she clenched her fists. "I'd just be seething! And Luke would say, 'Jewel, what else do you expect out of someone who doesn't know the Lord?'" She laughed lightly. "The fact that your pa, who used to have such a fiery temper, was now so *forgiving*, so *compassionate*, it would just melt me. I got *so* convicted by him in that area. He really was growing more like the Lord all the time.

"When Garret started the town paper, your pa immediately saw the potential to reach people with the same newspaper sermon that had reached us. He decided to go try to talk Sam into printing the whole sermon series. I remember how nervous he was. It was a little over a year since he'd been in the Dragón.

"When he walked in the door he told me Sam's face looked shocked for a split second, but then he smiled real big, walked over, and clapped your pa on the shoulder. He turned Luke around to face the crowd and announced, 'The prodigal returns!' Everyone hooted and cheered! Your pa was so humiliated for him that he asked if they could talk privately in Garret's office.

"There Luke told him that he'd only come about the articles, and he showed Sam this one," she said, indicating the one in the Bible on her lap. "Sam didn't read far before he started getting really angry. He asked your pa if he was trying to put him out of business. He told him he wouldn't print that 'religious garbage' in a hundred years and told him to get out. Apparently, he really lost his temper because people were talking about how he had shouted Luke out of the saloon. It was strange behavior for him—he usually acts so emotionless.

"I think your pa was heartbroken. He saw so much potential for spreading the Gospel in the paper. Every evening for about two months he prayed that God would provide some way to print those sermons."

Jake dimly remembered Pa praying that, but he was not paying any attention anymore. He felt himself almost drifting off to sleep.

"And that's when it happened—he found the first gold nugget."

Jake sat up suddenly. He took his feet off the post and the front legs of the chair came down with a crack.

Julia wanted to laugh and cry at the same time. It was

such a funny reaction to see him so abruptly wide-eyed and now hanging on her every word. And she wanted to cry because she knew that this love of gold, this love of the world, could destroy him. *Luke had always said he didn't want Jake to know until he became a Christian. What on earth was he thinking when he wrote that note?*

"Your pa was absolutely elated!" She smiled, remembering. "He knew it was an answer to prayer. That's when he took that extra long trip to San Francisco."

"To get the printing press." Jake nodded his head slowly as he put the pieces together. "So that's how we afforded it. I remember thinking it was such a crazy thing to travel so far to get."

"He was so excited to get it, but he was killed before he had the chance to use it," Julia said sadly, "Your pa said he wasn't going to let *anyone local* know he'd found gold. He felt sure it would end up in bloodshed of some kind. That's why he was so insistent about putting the dugout under the chicken coop. When he heard about that family being robbed in their home, he realized we were in much greater danger than they had been.

"But someone found out, Jake." She looked him deeply in the eye. "Someone found out and they killed him. You and your sister grew up without a father, I've lived these last ten years without my husband, all because of the two little rocks you have in your pocket. Does that even make any sense?"

"But there's *more*, isn't there?" he said greedily, and then slowed down realizing how bad that must have sounded. "I mean to say, it's not just these two nuggets. There's more gold than this somewhere on the land, right?"

Julia startled at her son in astonishment. There it was—

raw greed flaming out of his eyes. She quietly gathered herself together, stood, and walked into the house without a word.

"You idiot!" Jake cursed himself.

laundry

The wagon jostled and bumped incessantly. At first, Catrina just set her teeth against it, but now, nearing the end of the second day of travel, she was so weary and sore she just wanted to be still for a while. The whole thing reminded her too much of the trip she'd taken as an eleven year-old runaway down south to Los Angeles.

Rob looked stalwart and a little sleepy as he sat with reigns in hand. He stopped the wagon as they came around a bend in the road and they could see all of San Francisco stretched out. He lifted his massive frame to climb down from the wagon seat to stretch, "We're almost there, darlin'."

Catrina looked toward the section of town where her father's jewelry shop had been. *What if he's not even there anymore? What if he's not even* alive *anymore?*

"So where's your sister's laundry?"

"Round about there," he said, pointing. Catrina felt relieved when she saw he was indicating an area of town that seemed a good distance from her father's shop.

"We've still got a ways to go, so tell me more about her," Catrina felt nervous about traveling all this way to be foisted on someone who didn't even know she was coming. But Rob had assured her, over and over again, that his sister would be thrilled.

He climbed back up. "Well, she's younger 'un me. It's just me and her, no other brothers or sisters. She's a great cook. Learned it all from our ma. Oh, I tell you, her dried apple pie will make your tongue slap your brains out!"

He burst out in a booming laugh. No one could hear that and not laugh too—it was contagious.

"Like I said, Rebekah never married. She's had this business for what must be goin' on ten years now. She's got a mind for business, she does. Just like a man that way. She got the idea to start the laundry back during the gold rush and, boy, I can tell you she sure made a bundle back then!

"I don't rightly know what happened to it all—the money I mean." He pursed his lips and scratched his beard. "I guess she must have given nearly all of it away. She's just crazy religious, always giving money to missionaries to get the heathen converted. I guess she figured she don't need much. She's always been a simple girl. Lives real simple. Always talkin' about God and Jesus. Just loves to go to meetin' and real strict about the Sabbath."

"But Rob," Catrina squirmed, "Don't you realize that if she's so religious, she's not going to want a... uh, someone like *me* living in her house."

"Oh," Rob said with understanding, "That's what's got you worried? No, no. She ain't like that. She's told me plenty of times how 'Jesus was a friend of sinners.' She's always got her home open to someone who's on hard times, who wants to get their life straightened out." He said this last part with a slight smirk, both in his voice and on his face, and turned to wink at her. Clearly, he meant she was going to need to play the part of the penitent sinner or listen to more than her fair share of sermonizing.

Oh well, she thought, *that's not so bad a price to pay, is it? I guess in the long run it's better than getting my head knocked off by Garret.*

"So, why haven't you gone to her to get *your* life straightened out, Rob?" she said, smirking right back at him.

He chuckled. "I don't want my life quite that straight, darlin'."

business

or two weeks now, the mood in the Forester home had been cool. Summer was used to the occasional shouting fight between Jake and Ma. Jake had a bad temper; there was no doubt about that. He would usually end up shouting. Ma would sit there and absorb whatever he threw out. Then hours or sometimes even days later he would apologize and everything would feel settled again. But this was different.

Ma was not acting like herself. She wasn't laughing or smiling as she usually would. She only spoke to Jake when she absolutely had to. And even then she seemed to be talking to him with her head turned away, as if she could barely stand the sight of him.

Jake was acting odd, too. He seemed to be trying to get Ma's favor by attending to all the chores she'd been nagging him about for years. Then around Ma he was unusually quiet and went around with his head down, as if he was deeply ashamed of something.

Family meals were tense and quiet.

Summer could not imagine what had happened but whatever it was, it seemed to be lasting way too long and she resolved to talk to Ma about it. Today they would be busy all day canning tomatoes side-by-side. Jake wouldn't be in for hours as he'd announced he was going to work on the barn roof.

They had been working together over an hour when Summer finally decided to bring the subject up. "Ma, what's going on with you and Jake?"

I knew she was going to ask, Julia thought as she slipped the peelings off the hot tomatoes, but she said, "What do you mean?"

"Well, the two of you obviously had a fight of some kind," she said matter-of-factly. "I'm a grown woman, Ma. It's impossible not to notice the way you two have been these past weeks."

"Has it really been weeks?" Julia felt her conscience prick her again.

"Yes it has," Summer verified. "And I want to know what Jake did."

"He didn't *do* anything." Julia asked herself, *Is a half-truth really the same as a lie?*

"Well, what did he *say* then?" Summer put her knife down. "It has to be something, Ma. And what's really got me confused is why you're holding it over him the way you are. He's obviously sorry for whatever it was."

"What makes you say that?" Julia turned away and stared at the wall.

"Look at the way he's trying to do everything right, Ma. Look how he walks around with his head down all the time. He's ashamed of whatever happened." Summer continued, "Why won't you forgive him?"

She has no idea what she's talking about! She's just a girl. She doesn't understand the situation. Julia clenched her fists. *She doesn't know that the same greed that got her pa killed is living inside her brother!*

"It doesn't seem right," Summer continued, picking the knife back up. "You've told me many times how we have to understand that Jake acts the way he does because he doesn't know the Lord."

Julia's conscience jabbed her again. *When is it that our children become our teachers?*

Slow minutes passed as she stood there staring at the wall. Just getting up the courage to admit she'd been wrong felt like trying to drag a boulder out of her heart. "You're right, Summer." She sighed long and hard. "I honestly haven't been close to the Lord these past weeks. I haven't been praying like I should. I haven't been reading the Bible. Down deep, I don't think I *want* to forgive your brother for this. Something in me wants to make him suffer for it." Julia had to grit her teeth just to get this confession out. "I know that's probably the worst thing you could ever hear your mother say."

"It's part of the wickedness that's in all our hearts, Ma. Mine, same as yours." She walked over and put her hands on her ma's shoulders. "But why don't you let me take over here for a while. It sounds like you have some business with the Lord."

When did my little girl turn into a woman of God? Julia was as proud of Summer as she was ashamed of herself. She wiped her hands on a dishrag. "You're right. I do." Taking the Bible from its place, she went back to her bedroom.

bounty

It was early evening when they finally pulled the wagon up to Rebekah's place. The dirt street was wide here and there were plank sidewalks going up and down in front of the shops. To one side was a sewing notions shop and on the other side a shop that sold leather goods. The sign hanging above the laundry door read, "Campbell Laundry ~ Shirts Boiled Here ~ Cleanest Duds on Orange Street."

There was only a little light left. The gas streetlights would soon be lit. But since there were several saloons and dance halls nearby, people in this section of town were just waking up.

"She's done quite well for herself," said Rob as he climbed down, "The downstairs is the laundry and her kitchen is in the back. Then she's got a real purty sittin' room, and two bedrooms, upstairs." Putting his huge hands under Catrina's arms, he lifted her easily out of the wagon.

Wow, she really is well off for a woman who's never been married, Catrina thought.

As they approached the open front door, Catrina could see Rebekah standing behind the counter. She was tall for a woman but not nearly the height of Rob. She was a plump, rosy-cheeked lady who had her light red hair pulled into a neat bun on top of her head. She wore a serviceable but plain light blue dress and a crisply ironed white apron with bluebirds embroidered on the hem.

She was laughing and chatting with a man who was obviously picking up his clothes, but when she caught sight of Rob coming in the door, both her hands went straight up in the air and she screamed with joy. The man she'd been chatting with quickly got out of her way and she came charging across the front of the shop like a locomotive. She grabbed Rob in an enormous hug and nearly lifted the Goliath off the floor all the while continuing to scream with glee. Rob laughed and laughed as he hugged her back.

The man who had been picking up his laundry smiled and tipped his hat as he left.

"Now Sis, you act like I haven't visited in a coon's age!"

"Well you haven't!" She swatted him with the corner of her apron. "When we're only two days away, you need to get out here more often. But who's your friend?" Rebekah grabbed Catrina's one good hand between two of hers and shook it warmly. Catrina couldn't help but notice how rough and red her hands were. *I guess that's what comes of working with laundry all day.*

Rob laughed. "This is my friend, Catrina, and I'm gonna tell you all about her over dinner. So what are we having?"

"Now, don't expect much," Rebekah said.

"Don't listen to her." Rob elbowed Catrina, "That means it's gonna be good."

"Rob, you're such a scoundrel!" His sister lightly punched him in the arm, "It's time to close up shop now anyway, so let's head back to the kitchen and get acquainted!"

Catrina followed the two of them. She didn't think she'd ever seen a more enthusiastic greeting and she was trying not to giggle out loud about it.

Rob had been right. Rebekah already had a kettle on, a pot boiling with potatoes, and a chicken, plucked and cut up, was waiting for flour and hot fat. Even the table, covered in its clean red tablecloth, already had three places set out. *This is impossible,* Catrina thought. *She couldn't have known we were coming. But it's almost as if she'd been expecting us.*

"You were expecting someone?" Catrina asked tentatively before sitting down.

"Well, I was, and I wasn't." Rebekah laughed as she deftly moved back and forth, and around the kitchen as if she was a woman of much less girth. "When I was praying this morning, I just got this real strong feeling like the Lord was going to send someone special today."

Catrina's eyes went as wide as saucers. Rob just sat there, as if he'd heard this kind of thing before and it was perfectly normal.

When Rebekah saw Catrina's reaction, she just chuckled. "Now don't you read too much into that, deary!" She placed two steaming cups of tea before them. "Sometimes I think it really *is* the Lord trying to tell me something. But a lot of other times, it's just me, talking to myself in my head with my imagination carrying me away."

She talks to herself in her head? Catrina thought. *Is she insane, or what?* Catrina continued to watch Rebekah flour the chicken when it suddenly occurred to her, *Wait a minute, I'm talking to myself in my head right now.* She almost laughed aloud at herself.

"I suppose," Rebekah said as she flopped down another piece of chicken into the sizzling fat, "the closer I get to the Lord, the better I'll get at telling the difference." She turned and smiled. "But it sure looks like it was Him this time, doesn't it? So tell me what's happening."

As Rob related the story of how they came to be there, Rebekah continued cooking. As she busied herself with all the kitchen duties she still managed to look Rob and Catrina both in the eye, as well as pat Catrina on the hand, shoulder, or cheek, no less than ten times as the story unfolded. Catrina winced a little at Rob speaking so plainly about her profession. She looked up to see Rebekah's reaction, not sure what to expect.

"Deary," Rebekah said, "The way you're lookin' at me, I can tell you expected me to be shocked. Well, honey, I tell you, you'd be shocked by what *I* was before I came to Christ. You know, the Bible even talks about it."

Rob looked out of the corner of his eye at Catrina, as if to say, See what I mean?

Rebekah jumped up and got the Bible from her pie safe. Catrina barely had time to think what an odd place that was to keep a holy book, when Rebekah opened it and placed it on the table in front of her. "See here, 'Know ye not that the unrighteous shall not inherit the kingdom of God? Be not deceived: neither fornicators, nor idolaters, nor adulterers, nor effeminate, nor abusers of themselves with mankind, Nor thieves, nor covetous, nor drunkards, nor revilers, nor extortioners, shall inherit the kingdom of God. *And such were some of you.*'

"See there," she said, her plump finger running back and forth under the words. "It says, '*And such were some of you.*'" She looked at Catrina and smiled, then continued reading. "But ye are washed, but ye are sanctified, but ye are justified in the name of the Lord Jesus, and by the Spirit of our God.'"

Catrina was not sure how to act. She didn't know what kind of response was expected out of her.

Rebekah folded the Bible closed and stuck it back onto the third shelf in the pie safe, then went back to beating the potatoes with a wide wooden spoon. They began to stand up, white and fluffy, in her mixing bowl. "That's why it don't shock me, deary, because I'm one of those *'and such were some of you.'*"

Finally, she loaded a plate with the crispy golden chicken, and put it in the center of the table. Next came the mashed potatoes now swimming in butter. Catrina's mouth was watering.

Rebekah sat down at her seat and bowed her head. Rob bowed his and Catrina did likewise.

Rebekah prayed aloud. "For this, Thy bounty, Lord please make us truly grateful. In Jesus' name, Amen."

Passing the bowl of mashed potatoes to Rob, Rebekah looked Catrina in the eye, "Catrina, you are most welcome to stay as long as you like. Everything I have belongs to the Lord, to do with as He wishes."

The next morning, Rob drove away with a smile and a wave of his hat. Catrina was eager to do something to help out, but Rebekah told her that she really needed to wait until her one arm was completely healed before she did anything.

"Just come out here and chat with me," Rebekah said.

Catrina sat in a chair beside the front counter. All day

long men brought their clothes and all day long Rebekah tended over two hand-crank wash tubs, filling and refilling them with boiling water and soap chips, then again with boiling water to rinse. She would then crank the clothes out between the rollers, and race outside to hang them up to dry. Then the iron was heated on the stove and she went to work with that. She was a whirlwind of activity and when she wasn't cheerfully chatting with Catrina, she was singing hymns. The shop seemed always filled with song.

Despite Rebekah's insistence that she needn't do anything, as the days passed Catrina began to find things to do to help out. Even with only one good hand, she could grate the soap cakes. She found she could take the dry clothes down from the line and bring them in for ironing. And she started to deal with the customers at the front counter. After a few more days, she really felt she was getting the hang of things.

The more she got to know Rebekah, the more she liked her. She was honest and hardworking. She was compassionate and funny. Catrina had never really had a friend like this before. Almost a week into her stay, Rebekah presented Catrina with a new dress right after breakfast. It was just like Rebekah's blue work dress, only in Catrina's size. And she gave her a crisp white apron.

"I think it makes us look more professional if we match don't you?" she said.

"Oh! You didn't need to go to such expense, Rebekah!" Catrina held the tailored dress up in front of her. She had been becoming more and more embarrassed about her saloon clothes. But she'd had no choice—they were the only ones she had. Until now.

"The left sleeve has some tiny hooks here on the

underside seam," Rebekah said, taking the dress from Catrina and demonstrating as she talked. "There's an extra little panel here so you can wear this over your cast, without having to take the seam out. You just fasten the hooks like this. Then after you're all healed up, you'll hook them on the tighter row like this. Then this little flap comes over to hide the hooks. No one will even know they're there."

Catrina felt even more in Rebekah's debt. She hardly knew how to say thank you for one more thing. "This was so thoughtful!" she said with feeling.

"Oh, and I also had a burgundy one made," Rebekah said as she finished putting away the breakfast dishes, "Just in case you decide you'd like to go to Sunday Meeting with me tomorrow. It's upstairs on my bed." Rebekah gave her a pat on the cheek and indicated the stairs.

Catrina smiled her thanks and headed up. When she opened Rebekah's bedroom door, she gasped. There on Rebekah's bed was not only a lovely burgundy dress, but also a matching silk hat with dyed feathers, a pair of black leather, spool heel lace-ups, and a new set of hoops. Catrina usually hated hoops, but these were moderately sized—not the outrageously large ones that a girl could hardly get around in. It was all so beautiful, so extravagant. She felt overwhelmed to the point of tears.

"Oh Rebekah, this is too much!" she shouted down the stairs. Rebekah had been waiting to hear her reaction at the bottom of the steps and around the corner popped her plump, red face. Her eyes almost disappeared into her cheeks when she smiled that widely.

"I'm glad you like it, deary," she responded. "But you'd better get dressed for today, it's almost time to get to work."

I think she's the nicest person I've ever met, Catrina

thought as she began to change into her new blue work dress. *How am I ever going to be able to pay her back for all this?*

A few more weeks passed and a local doctor removed the Catrina's cast declared her arm had healed properly. Catrina told him it felt weak but the doctor said that wouldn't last long. She also found her ear nearly restored. The ringing was hardly noticeable.

Catrina really did feel like she'd been given a whole new start on life. She had a respectable job. She was going to Sunday Meeting now, regularly. She listened to Rebekah read the Bible every night before supper.

She worked hard in the shop all day, eager to earn her keep by being as much a help to Rebekah as possible. Catrina was even starting to sing along with her as she learned the hymns.

One day, Catrina noticed her hands were starting to become rough and red like Rebekah's. But instead of feeling repulsed, the sight actually made her happy. She felt like her sins were being washed away by this respectable life she was now living. For the first time since she was an adult, she was becoming a good person.

power

"Jake, can you come down?" Julia shielded her eyes as she looked up at him.

"Uh... yeah." He laid his tools down on the barn roof and came down the ladder.

"Jake, I apologize for the way I've been treating you since that night." Julia bowed her head. "I shouldn't have been that way at all, it was sinful. I've asked God to forgive me and I need to ask your forgiveness too."

"I'm the one who said something so stupid," Jake offered. "I should be the one asking for forgiveness. I felt like such an idiot the minute it was out of my mouth. It made it sound like I care more about the gold than the fact that Pa was murdered for it. But I want you to know that's not true. I think the man who shot him should hang—all four of those men should hang."

It wasn't actually the response she was hoping for, but it looked like that was all she was going to get. "I love you, Jake."

"I love you too, Ma" The two of them hugged.

Jake stood there, looking at her expectantly.

Now the hard part, she thought. "I'll always love you.

No matter what. But I have to tell you that I have prayed about it and I've come to a conclusion. I'm not going to tell you where the gold is."

"What?" he shouted. He could feel his face getting redder by the second.

"Jake, I don't know why your pa wrote that note," she continued resolutely. "I don't know what his plans were or what he thought was going to happen. But I'm the only parent now and I have to make decisions that make sense to me."

The veins on his neck were beginning to stand out. "You're going directly against what Pa wanted! You *have* to tell me where it is!" He felt himself beginning to shake with rage.

"No, Jake. No I don't." She stood before him calm and resolute. "The same greed I saw, *and* see *now*, in your eyes tells me you're not ready to use the gold rightly."

"Rightly?" he shouted as he pulled off his carpenter's apron and threw it on the ground. "I've got to become religious before you'll tell me where the gold is? Is that what you're telling me? You've poked and prodded me all these years to get me to convert, and now, since you know I won't by any other means, you're trying to bribe me? Some Christian you are!" He finished his shouting with his back to her as he stomped his way into the house.

Summer came out to discard the tomato peelings. She looked at her mother wondering what all the shouting had been about. Ma was standing in the barn lot with her hands folded and her head down. The wind was gently blowing her skirts.

Before Summer could even cross to ask her ma what had happened, Jake came storming out of the house with a bag over his shoulder. He nearly bowled her over. "Out of my way, Sum!"

"Where are you going?" she called after him as he tramped out to the barn.

"I'm going to San Francisco for a few days," he bit back at her as he passed his ma to get his horse saddled.

Ma followed him into the barn and watched him as he threw the saddle blanket on and then the saddle. She stood quietly as he buckled straps and tightened the girth. "You may never understand why I'm doing what I'm doing, Jake. But whether you believe it or not, I'm doing it because I love you."

"You do *not* love me" he spat out. He spun to face her with all the hatred he could muster. "I'll tell you what you *love*. You *love* your imaginary God, you *love* your religion, and you *love* thinking you have power over me!"

He turned and mounted. "Well, your imaginary 'all powerful' God is some kind of sick sadist, if He exists at all. What kind of an 'all powerful' God would let an innocent man get gunned down right in front of his only son? No, you don't love me. You love what you think you can *make me into*—some kind of religious nut like you." He tipped his hat. "And I've got news for you, Ma, I'd rather go to hell!" He pulled up the reigns and rode off.

Summer came running to the barn just in time to see Jake riding away, and her ma collapse on the barn floor crying her heart out.

tiptoe

Catrina was out taking her walk. It was good to get out of the laundry and just see the sky for a while, even if it was only the slice between the buildings. It had been so long since she'd been in San Francisco and it seemed like a wholly different town.

As she walked, she realized she was getting a little too close to the part of town where her father's jewelry shop was. Each day as she took her walk she had found herself drifting this direction. She had been thinking more and more about the possibility of contacting him.

From carefully asking around, she had learned that Salterson Watch and Jewelry Company still occupied the corner of Kearney and Marketplace. Today, it was one of the best-known jewelry shops in San Francisco because it backed up to the Olympic Theatre. Anyone who was anyone coming to San Francisco would just *have* to see the variety show at the Olympic Theatre and thus, just about everyone she had asked knew right where Saltersons was.

She had confided a lot of her life story to Rebekah, but this part she didn't feel like she could share yet. Rebekah knew nothing of where she went on these excursions, except that she was just getting some fresh air.

She hadn't gotten the courage to make it all the way to the shop yet, but she watched the men in the area closely for any resemblance to her father. She wondered what would happen if she saw him. Would he recognize her? What would he do?

Today was the closest she'd been. She stood at the corner of Kearney and East, a mere two blocks from her past. She squinted as she stared toward the spot. Without realizing it, she was standing almost on tiptoe—as if that would help—her lips pressed together and her hands clasped in front of her. An invisible barrier kept her from crossing this street. She continued to stare although she could really make out nothing from this distance.

"You need some help, ma'am?" The voice seemed to come from nowhere and startled her. She looked down and to her right. It was a boot-blacking boy. His small dirty face looked up at her as if she might be mentally deficient. She wondered how long she'd been standing there.

"Oh! No, no, no. I'm fine." She began to walk backwards away from him. "Fine. Just fine. Thank you." She turned and began to walk swiftly back toward the laundry. *How embarrassing.*

overboard

Julia walked up the steps and into the store. "Good afternoon, Kylie."

"Well, you don't look like it's too good," she replied from behind the counter, "What's wrong, Julia."

"Oh, nothing to speak of." She *really* did not want to discuss this with Kylie. And if she didn't absolutely *have* to have those lids and rings, she wouldn't have stepped into the store for a million dollars. She wished she could have sent Summer, but the girl was so broken up about the way her brother left that she was still crying when Julia left. She quickly indicated a shelf and tried to change the subject, "Came in for more lids and rings. We had a bumper crop of tomatoes in my kitchen garden this year. You know, I don't know if I'll ever get the hang of farming. Corn *early* this year and the tomatoes come in *late*. It doesn't make any sense to me."

"I'll get your lids and rings but don't change the subject on me," Kylie interrupted. "What's happened? You don't look like yourself at all."

Julia looked away.

"This isn't about the kids going up to San Francisco, is

it?" She blew it off lightly. "Yeah, Dan came in giving me some lame excuse that they were going to look at new plows. Makes me laugh. Do they think we were born yesterday?" She stepped around from the counter and chucked Julia on the shoulder. "They're good boys, they've just got to sew their wild oats. It's only natural. Nothing to worry about."

"Kylie, I know you're trying to help and I really do appreciate it." Julia knew Kylie considered herself a Christian, but in all the years they'd known each other, Julia just couldn't see signs of a true conversion. Kylie didn't seem to have an internal hunger for holiness, a desire to please God, or to read His Word. Julia wasn't sure how she could ever bring up the subject with her but for years she had wondered if Kylie was genuinely born again or not. It was statements like these that made Julia believe she probably wasn't. "But you *have* to know what you're saying is dead wrong."

Kylie tipped her head to the side, as if she didn't understand.

"We've talked about this before. They're not 'good' boys any more than we're 'good' girls. You know the Lord's word says that none of us are good: 'no one is good but God alone.' Secondly, 'sewing their wild oats' is not 'natural'—it's absolute rebellion and wickedness in God's eyes. And it *is* something to be worried about. We should be cut to our very hearts with fear for our children's souls." Julia ended with her hand fluttering up to her throat and tears starting to fill her eyes. She wished she could talk less emotionally.

"I'm so sorry." Kylie walked over and put her arms around her. "I can see how upset you are. I always say the wrong things. Don't even listen to me. What can I do for you, honey?"

Julia returned her hug, and then pushed away gently. "Just the lids and rings. I've got to get back home to finish the canning. Thanks."

"You just want that on your tab?" Kylie's hand hovered over the ledger.

"Yes, thank you."

"Look, why don't you and Summer come over for supper tonight? Since the boys are gone, we can all have supper together," she said as she finished writing.

"That sounds really nice, Kylie." Julia put the lids and rings in her basket. "We'll bring some of the tomato preserves we're putting up today."

"We'll see you tonight." As Kylie waved goodbye to Julia, she thought, *Poor Julia, she just goes a little overboard sometimes. After all, doesn't the Good Book say, 'boys will be boys'?*

knife

Jake had been friends with Dan O'Neill since childhood. Neither one could remember a time when they didn't know each other. The thing that seemed to seal their friendship, as young men, was that they both had to go through their father's deaths around the same time. Both were suddenly expected to be the "man of the house" much earlier than their peers. No one else seemed to understand them the way they understood each other. Going through that pain and growth together gave their friendship an unbreakable quality.

Ever since they'd been sixteen years old, the two of them had been making excuses to head off to San Francisco. Although neither one of them believed in God, they both kept up appearances in town for the sake of their mothers.

When they reached San Francisco, Dan immediately went to look at the new line of plows so he wouldn't be "lying" to his mom. While he did that Jake went to cash in the smaller of the two gold nuggets. He ended up with an enormous wad of bills. Dan was astonished. Even as a storekeeper he'd never seen so much money in one place. "What did you do, rob a bank?"

"No," Jake told him. "This money is mine. It's always been mine. My pa gave it to me."

After some time and many, many drinks in the Barbary Coast district, Jake finally told Dan everything. "And now she won't tell me where the gold is, unless I become a religious man. So, you know what I told her?" he slurred, gesturing with his drink. "I told her where she could go!"

"No!" Dan's eyes, which were a greatly unfocused from so much liquor, went wide. "You didn't tell your ma to go to."

"You're right," Jake garbled, and then belched. "But I sure wanted to. Actually, I think what I said probably hurt her even more. I told her I'd sooner go to hell than become religious."

The two of them sat looking into their beers.

"But I'm not going to think about that right now!" Jake slammed his beer down on the table. It sloshed up and over the sides to soak the table as well as his pants and shirt. "I'm here to have fun! So let's bring on the fun!" He stood up and hooted, "Let's bring on the ladies!"

Jake would not have been surprised at all to see his very brains running out into the street. His head felt like it had an ax through it. The sunlight was intolerable. He shielded his eyes as it shot through his skull like cattle brands. He sat up slowly and then came the nausea. He threw up and groaned. Then it came again, although there was hardly anything left in his stomach at this point. He dry heaved a couple more times. *I'll never drink again,* he promised himself. And then, *I've got to go get another drink to settle my stomach.*

He was laying on a part of the board sidewalk between two buildings. He couldn't even remember how he got here. He wondered if he had any money left and felt his pocket. Amazingly, there was still a little cash. *It's a miracle I wasn't robbed while I lay here,* he thought. *I wonder where Dan is?*

He got to his feet shakily and started walking. He stumbled along like a newborn foal on quivering limbs. He caught sight of a drunken vagrant on the other side of the street. He grabbed his pocket instinctively, thinking of protecting what money he had left. But the drunk grabbed his pocket too. It was him—his own reflection in the window of the saloon across the street.

The sight took him aback. He looked down at himself. *What a disgusting mess.* He stunk of stale beer and urine. *Oh no, could this get any worse? I've got to buy some clean clothes and get a wash somewhere.*

A few hours later he was stepping out of a hotel, clean and dressed in a new pair of trousers and a dark blue flannel shirt. His hair was still wet and it was a little breezy for wet hair. He smoothed it back and put his hat on. *If Ma was here, she'd tell me I'll catch my death walking around with a wet head like this.* He smiled slightly then his face twisted as he thought about what he'd said to her. Thinking about it now, he cursed his own bad temper. He couldn't believe the things he said sometimes. He felt just awful.

What was it Ma had said? That the love of money makes people knife themselves with grief? Or something like that. As he thought over the last evening and this morning he realized he could not have proved her *more* right if he had set out intending to do so. He sighed internally knowing that he would have to find some way to apologize to her.

Maybe I can get her something?

But first, I've got to hook up with Dan. Another little wave of nausea rolled over him. *At least those headache powders seem to be working.* His head still hurt but not nearly so badly. He felt he probably needed to eat something but couldn't imagine what he could keep down at this point. He turned and began to walk back down to where he and Dan had parked the wagon the night before.

He visited several different saloons before finding him. Dan had obviously had a very different night. He was still living it up. It was only a little past noon and he was already, or perhaps *still*, three sheets to the wind with a beer in one hand and a blonde saloon girl sitting on his knee.

"Oh!" Dan stood suddenly, knocking the girl off his lap. "Oh, my friend!" He stumbled toward Jake and embraced him. "This is my friend, Jake. My friend, Jake. Jake, Jake, Jake, where have you been?" At this last sentence, he poked Jake in the chest with his index finger, hard. "You've been gone *all* night!"

Jake thought about how idiotic his friend looked. "Come on, buddy. We gotta get you sobered up. We need to be heading back."

"Oh, no, no, no," he shook his finger in Jake's face. "He gestured to the blonde saloon girl who was now standing by his table, "Dolly and me, we got plans. We do. We got plans for tonight." He turned and winked largely at her. She provided a courtesy giggle and wave. "We'll go home tomorrow morning, okay? Okay?"

"All right," Jake replied, "I'll meet you at the wagon in the morning."

"Where you going? Stay here and have a drink!" He stumbled toward Jake and got right in his face to whisper loudly, "I've still got a big wad of those bills you gave me!" He clandestinely pulled open his pocket.

"Well, give me a little. But I think I'm going to head downtown for the day."

Dan took out the bills and split the stack with him. "But didn't we come here to have fun, Jake? There's still plenty of fun to be had! Come on, stay!"

"Nah." Jake turned to go. "I think I've had enough fun for this visit. Besides, I think I'll head down near the Olympic. There's plenty of places to get a gift around there, and I'm going to need something to apologize to my ma with. See you in the morning."

"Okay, Jake." Dan returned to his seat and Dolly returned to his knee, "See you in the morning."

Jake had been going back and forth, in and out of the shops that lined Kearney street, looking for something he could get for Ma. It seemed that every third shop sold nothing but liquor and cigars. There was a music box in the window of the jewelry shop on the corner. But he was afraid Ma would see it as too much of an extravagance and ask him where he'd gotten the money for it.

He winced to think of what Ma would say when she found out he'd cashed in one of the nuggets and completely blown the money. He didn't know how long he could keep it from her.

He finally felt like he could eat something and went into the first little restaurant he came across. He ordered tea, bread and butter, and country ham. They seated him by the window. He sat and watched the people, the wagons, the buggies all going back and forth. Up and down the street they went, unstopping. There seemed to be no meaning in what he was watching—all these people running around, endlessly. *Where are they all going?* he wondered as he took another bite of bread. *For all I know, they could just be going around and around in circles just like a clockworks getting nowhere.*

Then a woman caught his eye—probably because she *wasn't* moving. Her light blue dress and white apron made him think she must be a worker of some kind. She was stopped at the corner across the street.

She had beautiful long black hair that was not braided or pulled back, but just flowing softly down her back. It was so unusual to see a woman out without a hat or bonnet of any kind, that he puzzled at it for a moment but she didn't seem to care. As he looked at her he felt he was staring at the antithesis of the gussied saloon harlots with their layers of powder and pins. He found himself struck by her natural loveliness.

He waited for her to cross the street or go wherever it was she was going, but she just stood there, looking. Every once in a while she seemed to check around herself to see if anyone was watching her. But then she would go back to just looking straight ahead. Jake took another bite of the ham and craned his head around at the window to try to see what she was looking at. It was impossible to tell.

She just went on standing there looking. Then, at last, she seemed to make a decision. She turned around and walked in the other direction. He watched her until she disappeared into the crowds. He wondered if she'd been waiting to meet someone who didn't show up. At any rate, her leaving seemed somehow sad.

finished

The next morning was cool and hazy. Catrina got plates from the cupboard as Rebekah pulled the table a little closer to the stove for warmth. Sausage gravy was bubbling in a pan and white flour biscuits were browning in the oven.

"It's a chilly one this morning," Rebekah commented. "Not too much longer and we're going to need a fire going in the fireplace." She rubbed her hands together and checked the biscuits. "Just to let you know, it will be getting harder in the winter. Takes longer for the clothes to dry and we really have to watch the skies for rain so as to get stuff in off the lines."

Catrina poured them both a cup of tea. She added plenty of sugar to hers and warmed her hands on her mug. "I imagine it gets harder on your hands, too." She looked at hers—they were rough, but not so red anymore. The beeswax and lard mixture she'd been putting on them at night seemed to be keeping them from getting worse.

"Yeah, it's always been hard on the hands," Rebekah replied looking at her own. "But you're right, it does seem *more* so in the…"

A loud rumbling noise began. Both women looked at each other in puzzlement. The table began to jar and shake. Catrina quickly lifted her tea off. Suddenly the front window of the laundry exploded into a million jagged fragments and the room began to sway violently back and forth.

"Earthquake!" Catrina yelled. Rebekah immediately abandoned the stove. Catrina dropped her tea and both women ran out the back door and into the middle of the back lot.

All around them in every direction buildings swayed like fishing poles. Glass could be heard shattering, wood breaking, popping, cracking. Other people were screaming and running out of their homes or places of business, some only partially dressed. In one direction, a thunderous crash was so loud that they both instinctively crouched, grabbing their ears. It already seemed like an enormous amount of time had gone by, but the ground was still rocking.

"Why is it going on so long?" Catrina yelled.

"I don't know," Rebekah shouted back. "I never knew one to last this long."

Jake was waving to Dan as he crossed the street. But he could see Dan was trying to calm the horses. Something had spooked them. He started to jog over to help when both mares began to buck and kick. Then the rumble started. The ground began to shake and they could hear people screaming from all directions.

A booming crack came from one of the city's firewalls directly across the street, and it fell like the ton of bricks it was. Mortar dust rose in an enormous cloud.

People were flying out of the businesses all around them,

and one man in the middle of the street began to scream that it was Judgment Day. They heard another massive crash just down the street. Everything around them was complete pandemonium.

The longer it went on, the more they could hear people screaming in all directions. One man out on the street began to shout that it was Judgment Day. Catrina looked at Rebekah in terror, and Rebekah looked like she was about to speak when a large cracking sound came from the chimney next door.

As both women gasped, it fell away from its building coming directly for them. Rebekah grabbed Catrina by the shoulders and flung her backwards but she was only able to take half a step herself before the pillar of bricks crushed her into the ground like a dishrag. The rest of it nearly cut the laundry in half. Boards splintered and flipped in every direction. Broken bricks and bits of mortar bounced off the springy turf and pelted Catrina all over.

As soon as the shower stopped, Catrina screamed. She frantically began trying to pull the bricks and lumber off Rebekah, "Help me! Help me! Someone help me!"

Rebekah was still moving, but as she pulled the bricks away she saw a deep indention on the back of her skull. Her hair was matted and blood was beginning to pool in the gash. "No! No! Rebekah! Rebekah!"

She gave a mighty heave on Rebekah's shoulder but she was only able to roll her on her side. Most of her body was still covered with bricks. Her round face was covered with dirt and blood, "Rebekah, Rebekah! What do I do?" Catrina was crying so hard she could barely see.

Rebekah's voice was barely a whisper. "I'm okay, deary. I'm going to go be with Jesus now. Don't worry, I'm not afraid,"

"No, no! You can't!" Catrina shouted at her. She couldn't believe this precious friend, the only *real* friend she had ever had, was going to die right before her eyes. She frantically looked around for someone who could help.

"I just didn't think I was finished yet," Rebekah sighed as she began to close her eyes.

"Finished? Rebekah, what are you talking about?" Catrina thought she must be going delirious from the head injury.

"Oh, you know," she spoke softly and slowly. "Finished with the work God had for me. I... I didn't think I was finished yet." Her eyes closed slowly. "Oh well. God knows."

"No, no, no! Someone help me!" Catrina stood, but slipped in the rubble and fell on her face, "Someone help! Help!" She screamed through her tears, "Someone help me!"

Jake and Dan heard another terrific crash and then a woman's voice screaming for help. They abandoned the wagon and ran down the street toward the sound. Here a chimney had broken loose and fallen onto the building next to it.

Two women were in the debris. A young woman was trying to dig a big lady out from under the brick and mortar. Jake realized in a flash that it was the same woman he'd been watching yesterday while eating his lunch.

Dan and Jake exchanged glances before running in to

help. The larger woman was unmoving and they could both tell there was no hope. Nevertheless, they went to work with a will and soon the woman was uncovered.

Jake rolled the body the rest of the way onto its back. Dan smoothed the lady's skirt down to her ankles, while Jake tried to arrange her arms in a way that would appear normal. They looked at each other from across the body. Dan indicated with his eyes and a shake of his head that *Jake* was going to have to go tell the girl.

Catrina was standing with her back to them in the middle of the back lot. She had not stopped crying, even for a moment. Jake held his hat in his hands as he approached her. She turned just as he reached her. She looked awful. His heart broke for the pain he saw in her face and tears sprang to his eyes, "I'm so sorry, Miss," he hoarsely whispered. "She's gone."

Catrina knew it already in her heart but she let out a wail of grief. Jake thought she looked like she was going to fall over so he came forward and grabbed her. She clung to him and sobbed uncontrollably into his shirt. He just stood there holding her.

He opened his mouth but he didn't know what else to say. All the idiotic things people said to him when his pa died jangled back and forth in his head like a bunch of marbles bouncing down a hill.

Maybe the best thing to say is nothing at all.

The sound of her sobs were so much like the sounds his own mother had made when pa died that he felt transported in time. Tears fell down his cheeks as he stood there with his arms around her.

religious

Catrina was exhausted from so much crying. She sat on the edge of Jake's wagon box. The few things she owned were sitting in the bag next to her and Rebekah's treasured Bible sat on top of that.

She had learned that Jake and Dan were from Pureza. It seemed providential that they had met because Catrina was going to have to take the body back to Rob.

And then what? she thought hopelessly. *Nowhere to go. Nothing.*

They would be heading there shortly. Jake and Dan had gone for food and water, they would be back soon.

She found her mind wandering to Jake. She'd never seen such a compassionate and gentle man. He was handsome and strong too.

What am I thinking? She cursed herself. *How can I sit here on the same wagon with the dead body of my only friend, and be thinking about men? What is wrong with me? I have to be the biggest sinner who's ever lived. I hate myself!*

She turned to the head of the wagon where Rebekah's body was wrapped in the white window curtains from the front of the laundry. She wondered again if she should have tried to re-dress Rebekah's body in her Sunday Meeting clothes. But she just couldn't think about doing that right now. She just couldn't bring herself to look at that still face again. Not yet.

As she sat looking, it occurred to her that there is nothing in this world more still than a dead body. *It is more still than a rock, or a table, or any inanimate object. Oh Rebekah. I never even told you 'thank you.' You saved my life.*

She quickly looked away. Grabbing her bag, she pulled it close but did not open it. She couldn't even look at the beautiful burgundy church dress or the hat with the dyed feathers. She couldn't even think of them without her throat closing up, *Oh God, why? Why did you let this happen? I should have died. Rebekah was a good person. Why did you let* me *live?*

Another thought flew through her mind: *Could God have been punishing Rebekah for even being around someone as bad as me?* She honestly didn't know. *Why didn't God let me die instead?*

Oh God, why?

As Jake guided the horses back over the hills he thought about what a contrast this was to the ride he and Dan had taken out here just days ago. He had been so angry, and felt so justified in taking the gold and whooping it up for a couple of days. Now he and Dan sat side-by-side on the wagon seat in somber silence transporting the body of a dead woman and her grieving friend back to Pureza.

Nothing puts things in perspective like death, he thought. The seriousness of the situation made everything he'd done for the last few days seem completely idiotic.

The girl, Catrina, was in the back of the wagon box, her bag and Bible beside her. He and Dan had offered to let her ride up on the wagon seat, but she said she *wanted* to ride back there. Jake decided that was probably because it was a little bit more private. *Grief is a private thing*, he thought.

As he guided the wagon, hour after hour, he took many occasions to look back at her. At first he tried not to, it felt like an invasion somehow, but then he found he couldn't help himself. The more he looked at her, the more he wanted to. As far as he could tell she held onto that Bible all day long.

She must be a very religious person, he surmised. At all times, she seemed to either have it in her hands or opened on her lap. And when she cried she would hold it to her chest, embracing it and pulling her knees up like a shield. Then her long black hair would fall like a curtain on the sides hiding her face.

The sound of her crying broke his heart. She seemed so small and alone. It made him think of Summer when Pa died.

————•◦•————

They stopped for the night and it was a welcome relief from the constant jolting. Catrina sat a moment longer in the back of the wagon box embracing Rebekah's Bible. It seemed like all she had left of her beautiful friend but she knew it rightfully belonged to Rob and she was dreading giving it over to him. She had tried to read it a couple of times along the way, but she just couldn't understand it. It just wasn't the same as when Rebekah would read it each night before supper. She wished she had Rebekah's religious faith but she just didn't seem able to muster it up.

She saw that Dan was unhitching the horses and getting them ready for the night. And she could also see that Jake was gathering wood to make a fire. She felt she should get up and do something to help, so she put Rebekah's Bible back on top of her bag, swung her legs over the edge of the wagon box, and hopped down. She went to gathering wood as well.

Jake noticed her and thought it said something about her character. She wasn't the type to be lazy or ungrateful. She seemed to be willing to pitch in to get a job done. That was a very important character quality, at least in his opinion.

As the two of them walked back and forth together, she was still completely silent. He didn't know what he could say to try to start a conversation with her. He was very relieved that she spoke first.

"So," she began, "how long have you lived in California?"

Her voice was flat and emotionless. Jake could tell she was just making conversation to be polite and he knew what an effort that must be for her. He remembered. He felt such a kinship with her pain. He wished he could just blurt out his entire life story so that she would *know* he really understood what it was to go through a death. But since he couldn't he tried to communicate his understanding in his face and eyes when he looked at her.

"I've lived in Pureza all my life," he replied. "I was born there."

Catrina wasn't expecting that response. *All his life?* She was a little shocked. She'd worked in the Dragón for a full year and had *never* seen him before. She figured she'd seen every man in that entire town at least once even if they were only down in the saloon for drinks.

What kind of a man never *steps foot in the only saloon within a two day ride?* Then it popped in her mind: *Could he be religious like Rebekah?* She thought about it, and it seemed to make sense. She wondered if that's why he seemed to be so caring, so compassionate.

He had finished putting all the wood down in a blackened circle where there had obviously been a fire before. *This must be a regular overnight stopping point between the two towns,* she thought. She tried to remember if this was where she and Rob had stopped on the way out to San Francisco, but it was all too fuzzy, probably because of the morphine at the time.

"How long have you lived in California?" he asked her as he put the match to the kindling.

"Oh, I was born in San Francisco," she replied. She knew she was misleading him to believe she'd lived there all her life and she did feel a tiny bit guilty. But if he was a religious man, she certainly didn't want him knowing she'd worked as a prostitute in his hometown for the past year. Some things were better left unsaid.

Jake put the kettle on for coffee. She watched him as he moved. He had a ruggedly cut jaw with a three or four-day beard. She thought perhaps he'd cut it off and was re-growing it. He took his hat off and his wavy brownish and gold hair seemed to stand up in every possible direction. It was a little comical and made her smile.

She thought he was very handsome but that wasn't really what made him so fascinating—it was that every time he looked at her in the eyes she saw there such a depth of gentleness and concern. His eyes, which were dark brown, seemed to look right into her soul so penetrating was his glance. When he looked at her it seemed as if he was feeling the loss of Rebekah just as deeply as she was. She'd never met a man like that before—a man who seemed immediately so connected to her heart.

I wondr? Is this just how religious people are? Are they all just naturally sweet and caring? But then she realized she didn't actually *know* if he was a religious man or not. She was just making assumptions.

Suddenly she had an idea. Rebekah had always read the Bible just before supper. Maybe that was something all religious people did. *Why not?* she thought. *I don't have anything to lose.*

She went back to the wagon and got Rebekah's Bible. She walked over to him, held it out and asked, "Do you usually read the Bible before supper? If you do, you can use this one if you want."

Jake took the Bible before he really even realized what he was doing, "Oh, sure. Sure." He opened it. As he flipped the pages his thoughts screamed at him, *Why did you do that?*

He hadn't opened a Bible since the day his ma had made him read at the graveside. He realized that he must be trying to impress Catrina. *What am I, twelve years old?* he thought as he continued to flip through pages.

Okay, okay so maybe I am *attracted to her. But aside from that, it's just common decency to try not to offend someone. Especially someone who's just had such a terrible loss. No matter what* my *feelings are, it's just too cruel to knock someone's crutch out from under them at a time like this.*

He suddenly remembered the 23rd Psalm and turned there. He could hardly believe it himself when he began to read aloud, "The Lord is my Shepherd, I shall not want. He maketh me to lie down in green pastures…"

Dan who had just finished with the horses walked up with a quizzical look on his face. Jake tried to ignore him as he continued, "…Yea though I walk through the valley of the shadow of death I will fear no evil…" As he read he couldn't help but notice how much his own voice sounded like Pa.

He finished and closed the Bible. As he handed it back to her, he put his own hands over hers for a moment in a gesture of comfort.

Well that clinches it, Catrina thought as she took Rebekah's Bible back from him. *Only a religious person would know right where to find something so beautiful and so comforting for our situation.*

earthquake

The following day, they pulled into Pureza. Catrina had not told them where Rebekah's body would need to be taken. Jake and Dan were both surprised when she asked them to take the wagon around to the back of El Dragón Rojo. Jake felt awkward at the thought of a nice girl like her going into a place like that, so, he offered to go in for her.

Catrina felt so miserable about the task she was facing that she actually considered it for a moment.

"No," she finally told him, "I owe it to Rebekah to tell her brother face-to-face. The two of them have done a lot for me."

She felt she was literally dragging her whole body as she walked in through the back door. *Dread* weighed her down like a lead cloak. She *dreaded* seeing Rob's cheerful face. She *dreaded* how his face would change when she told him. And on a whole other level, she *dreaded* the prospect of perhaps accidentally bumping into Garret while she was here.

She went through the kitchen and to the door that lead into the bar. She stood there staring at the door, trying to get up the courage to open it. But suddenly it burst open in her face and there was Rob, filling the entire doorway.

"Oh!" he grabbed at his heart in shock, and then his face blossomed into his usual jolly smile. "Catrina, darlin'! It's so good to see you!" He was about to hug her, but the expression on her face stopped him cold, "What's wrong? What's happened?"

"Rob," she closed her eyes. "There was an earthquake…"

"Rebekah?" he asked, but his face had already turned ashen.

"She threw me out of the way. She saved my life." Catrina had been crying so much that her eyes were already stinging and they smarted terribly as the tears came again. "A chimney fell and she saved me. I don't know why I didn't die instead."

Rob let the door close behind him and grabbed Catrina with both arms. His massive head came down on her small shoulder and he bawled like a child.

Catrina cried with him. She cried her heart out again.

———•••———

Jake thought he'd never seen anything so pitiable as this hulk of a man, hunched nearly in half, shaking with grief as he wept over the body of his sister. Tears sprang to his own eyes again. Catrina stood next to the man, crying along with him with her hand on his back for support.

They had learned that the people here in Pureza had actually felt the earthquake although very mildly. And the town had received some spotty news about it over the telegraph.

Dan excused himself to head home. His family's store and home were just down the street and he was understandably eager to get home to tell his mother he was okay. Jake would take the wagon back to him later.

As Jake watched Catrina comforting this man, it occurred to him that she probably had nowhere to stay in Pureza. He found himself fiddling with the idea of inviting her to stay at his house. He realized his mother and Summer would insist on it, considering her situation. Plus, they would probably like her instantly since they had religion in common.

He watched Catrina walking the big man back to the door they'd entered. She seemed to be telling him to go inside and that she would take care of things. The big man went back into the Dragón as meekly as a lamb.

She returned to the wagon. Jake jumped down to help her up. Her eyes were red and swollen and her nose looked the same.

"I have to have a coffin made." she stated plainly. "Will you please help me?"

"Of course I will, Catrina," he replied quickly. "But why don't you just let me take care of the whole thing. I can take you back to my house and you can rest for a bit while I see to it."

She looked puzzled and he instantly felt awkward. *She must think I'm insinuating something inappropriate*, he thought. He quickly added, "I live with my mother and sister."

Catrina was puzzled over such extended kindness but she reminded herself that it was because he didn't know what kind of girl she really was. He probably thought she'd been a laundry girl all her life—just a nice, pure, laundry girl.

"Thank you," she replied, clearly spent. "I really could use a rest."

Not long after, the horses were pulling them down the lane to the farmhouse. Jake stopped just past the barn. Still a little way from the house, he jumped down and jogged toward it.

Catrina watched as the front door came open and a slim dark-haired woman came out wiping her hands on a towel. When she saw Jake, she looked about ready to cry. She ran down the front porch steps toward her son with her arms out. As the two embraced, a younger girl came out of the house. She also ran up and hugged her brother, but then stepped back and allowed the two of them to talk.

They talked for what seemed like a long time and Catrina was starting to wonder if her staying was going to be an imposition. But when she saw them hug again and start walking toward the wagon she saw no hint of that on the mother's face.

"Catrina Salterson, this is my mother, Julia, and my sister, Summer." Jake helped her down out of the wagon.

"Miss Salterson, I am so sorry for your loss." Julia grasped her hand warmly. Catrina could see in her eyes the same depth of compassion she saw in Jake's.

"Thank you, Mrs. Forester," Catrina said. "And please, just call me Catrina."

"Then you must call me Julia." She put her arm around Catrina's shoulders and began to lead her to the house. "Please come in. You will be our guest as long as you would like to stay."

Jake jogged around to the back of the wagon. He took up Catrina's bag and her Bible and brought them into the house behind her.

The weather the next day was gray and blustery. Dan and Jake had dug the grave the day before and brought the coffin out to the graveside early that morning.

It was a small group that huddled around the hole in the ground. Dan and his mother were there. Julia, Summer, and Jake stood beside them. Catrina had walked from town with Rob. The wind whipped the ladies' skirts and the sky spat cold mist.

The previous evening, Catrina had asked Jake if he would agree to speak. The question seemed to fluster him, perhaps, Catrina thought, because he was not used to speaking in front of groups. He had suggested his mother would be a better choice.

So Julia stood at the head of the grave with her family Bible in hand. She had picked out several different passages of Scripture and simply read them, one after another. There was something both beautiful and simple about it. Catrina felt that Rebekah would have approved.

Rob's face was haggard and tears streamed non-stop from his eyes down into his beard. At the end of the Scripture reading, he got down on his knees, leaned over and embraced the coffin resting his head on the lid. He seemed oblivious to everyone around him. He kept his head down for several minutes, then finally kissed the coffin lid and stood.

The man had a lost look about him. For a moment he was seemingly even unsure of which way was back to town. Catrina caught a glimpse of his eyes as he slowly turned and began walking back alone—they looked vacant, hopeless.

potential

Catrina had only been staying with the Forester's for a couple of days, but already she found herself becoming attached to them. She couldn't imagine how any family could have been more kind to her. Not only had they offered her food and board for nothing in return, she even had a room all to herself as Jake's little sister had offered to room in with her mother while Catrina was staying.

One evening as they sat together around the fire, Julia began asking questions about Rebekah. At first, Catrina tried to answer the questions with as few words as possible. It just felt too painful to talk about. But Julia kept asking and Catrina kept answering. As she continued to talk reluctance seemed to melt away and a flood of reminiscing came pouring out of her.

She began telling funny stories—there were *plenty* of them. Rebekah always seemed to be laughing about something. There was the time the water pump had gotten jammed somehow and Rebekah climbed up on top of the roof herself to try and see what was wrong with it. Just as she stepped off the ladder onto the roof, a big breeze had caught under the front of her skirts and blew them completely over her head. Oh, what a laugh they had about that. She'd given the whole block a great look at her bloomers!

Then there was the man who came into the laundry absolutely reeking of pigs. Rebekah was in the back of the store, but swore she could smell him coming from all the way down the street. The moment the door opened, she had come charging from the back shouting, "No, no, no, no, no! I don't do pigs!" The man had been indignant saying he'd take his business elsewhere. To which Rebekah had replied, "Please do." And when he left, she proceeded to open all the windows in the laundry and put cloves on the stove to boil as she tried to air out the smell.

As Catrina talked, every story she told seemed to remind her of two more and she laughed and cried through the memories of the past month and a half as though it were a lifetime. She found it felt good to tell someone else about Rebekah's compassionate spirit, her humor, her generosity, and her love of God.

As she talked, however, she was careful not to reveal anything about her *own* past. The more she got to know this family, the more important it became to her that they like her, that they accept her. She dreaded the thought of them finding out what she really was.

Julia had tried to be careful and tactful in how she posed the questions but she felt compelled to try to find out if Rebekah had been a genuine Christian or simply someone who *professed* Christianity.

Thankfully, intermingled with the funny stories Catrina had told them, Julia heard all kinds of things that pointed to authentic salvation. Even Rebekah's final words were incredibly appropriate. As far as she could tell, Rebekah seemed to have all the scriptural signs of being a born-again believer.

This gave Julia a tremendous feeling of relief. Now that she "knew" Rebekah a little better, she wished she could go back in time and speak at the graveside again.

At the time, not knowing if Rebekah was saved or unsaved, Julia had felt it her duty to choose Bible passages that would apply to her either way. So, despite the possibility of insulting Catrina or Rob, she had felt led to read the sections about Christ separating the sheep from the goats on Judgment day. Had she known at the time she was speaking about a fellow Christian, she would have done things differently. She would have read verses about Heaven and the hope of the believer.

But then again, she thought, *maybe God led me to read* those *passages for the benefit of Jake.* She pondered it a moment longer. *And obviously Rob. Oh, also Dan. And now that I think of it, possibly Kylie and maybe Catrina too.* As she considered it, she realized God obviously had a purpose. *Oh Lord, use your Word to penetrate hearts. Your Word never returns void. Thank you for leading me even when I don't have any idea where I'm going.*

———

The next day was laundry day and Catrina's blue work dress really did need a good washing. It was dingy, especially around the hem and sleeves, with dirt and mortar dust from the earthquake. Since she didn't have anything else to wear she had to put on her beautiful burgundy church dress to do laundry in. It felt a bit silly to be wearing it during the middle of the week, and, of course, she didn't put her hoops on under it. She did find herself hoping that Jake would say something.

She brushed her hair until it shone glossy black and lightly pinched her cheeks to make them rosy. Finally she checked her face in the looking glass once more and opened the bedroom door.

Jake was just sitting down to his tea and toast when a vision stepped out of his little sister's room. Catrina seemed to be absolutely glowing with unadorned beauty. He could scarcely take his eyes off her. He knew he must be gawking when he heard Summer stifle a giggle. All at once, he could feel his mother and his sister looking at him looking at her. He felt himself begin to blush.

Then he saw that Catrina was also looking at him. Her eyebrows were raised and her lips were parted, ever so slightly, as if she were waiting for him to speak.

He suddenly realized he should stand, out of respect. He stood quickly and reached to take his hat off but then realized he wasn't wearing his hat yet this morning. He ran his fingers through his hair instead.

"I've never seen you in that. Well, of course, I haven't… I mean," he stammered. "That is to say… it's quite a lovely shade of… I mean to say you look very nice this morning." He sat down abruptly and buried his face in his cup of tea. *Is there any way I could make myself look* more *like a blithering idiot?*

"I hope it's not too forward to say," she replied with a smile and a downward glance, "but I was hoping you would like it." She flashed a quick look at his eyes to see what his reaction would be.

"You look like an angel," he said, looking back into her eyes much more confidently now. And he meant it.

Julia and Summer exchanged hidden glances and suppressed smiles as Catrina came to the breakfast table. Clearly there was the potential here for something more.

walk

It wasn't exactly cold outside, but it was brisk and the gray clouds were threatening rain. So the three women worked together in the kitchen on the laundry. Summer was boiling water, while Julia and Catrina were on their knees with the two tubs and washboards.

They chatted about this and that while they scrubbed the clothes. Catrina started out by telling them again about the more modern washing machines that Rebekah had used in the laundry.

"You barely have to get your hands wet," she continued. "But you do build up your biceps with all the cranking."

"But does it honestly get the clothes as clean?" Julia asked.

"For the most part," Catrina answered. "But you still have to use a brush on stains. It's also nice to use the rollers rather than wringing the clothes out by hand. It really does save your hands when you're doing a volume."

"This dress is really beautifully made," Julia said as she picked up Catrina's blue work dress from the pile of clothes. "Was it done on a machine?"

"Yes, I think so," she replied as Summer poured some

more hot water into her tub. "Thank you. Yes, Rebekah had it made for me at the tailor's shop down the street from her place. I don't think they make hardly anything by hand anymore. The machines are able to make such nice even stitches."

"Huh?" Julia was paying special attention to the hem and sleeves where it was dirtiest, but she'd stopped on the left sleeve, "Isn't this funny. Why is this sleeve made like this?"

Catrina was startled. The extra row of hook-and-eye closures in the left sleeve had become so commonplace to her that she'd wholly forgotten about them. She was instantly afraid that she was going to have to explain everything and she just wasn't ready to.

"Oh, Rebekah had these dresses made special for me." She hesitated as she tried to decide what to say. "Um... I had a broken arm." *Maybe that will be enough. Maybe she won't ask anything more.*

"Oh my," Summer said, clearly intrigued, as she filled the pot again on the stove, "How did you do that?"

Julia could sense that this was an area Catrina didn't want to talk about. "Dear, now, we don't want to pry."

"No, it's okay." Catrina didn't want Summer to feel bad for asking. "It's only a natural question. I broke it when I fell down a flight of stairs." *Oh* please *don't ask me what caused me to fall,* she thought with all her might.

"That must have been awful!" Summer replied, "What happened to make..."

"I know this is a change of subject," Julia purposefully interrupted, "but I just have to tell you that it comforts my heart greatly to hear that your friend knew the Lord."

Catrina breathed an internal sigh of relief. Summer,

although she didn't really understand why, took the hint from her mother and simply dropped the subject.

Julia continued scrubbing the hem of the blue work dress, "One of my favorite passages on that is in First Thessalonians. It says, 'But I would not have you to be ignorant, brethren, concerning them which are asleep, that ye sorrow not, even as others which have no hope.' I just love that. We don't sorrow like those who have 'no hope.'"

"Yeah, that sounds nice," Catrina agreed, although she wasn't exactly sure what Julia was talking about.

"If the person we love dies in Christ, we never have to mourn like we have 'no hope,'" she smiled as she continued. "Our sorrow lasts, sometimes for a very long time. But with my husband, and your friend, what a comfort it is to know that their sins were completely paid for by the blood of Christ. What a blessing to know they are with the Lord *today*. I personally don't know how people cope when they lose someone outside the Lord. Because then there is no hope left. None at all." Julia couldn't help thinking about Jake and how terrified she had been when they heard so many people had died in the earthquake. She had feared that the Lord's patience with him had finally run out. Her throat constricted at the thought.

"Yeah, I wish you could have known Rebekah," Catrina continued washing three aprons in the tub. "Believe me, if anyone ever deserved to go to Heaven, it was her."

Julia internally grimaced. While it seemed clear that Rebekah had been a real Christian, it seemed equally clear that Catrina didn't understand salvation at all. She wondered if it was the right time to go into it.

"If you don't mind me asking, how did your husband die?"

Julia was a little taken aback. "Luke was shot. He was shot and killed right here on the farm."

"Oh my!" Catrina exclaimed. "Who would do such a thing?"

"We still don't know," Julia finished. *At least not for sure,* she thought.

The conversation languished. Both women scrubbed in silence.

"The rinse water's ready," Summer proclaimed.

The two women wrung the clothes out by hand and laid them aside on the floor. Then they each heaved up their tub of dirty water and carried it out the back door.

When they came back in, Summer wanted to loosen things up, so as she filled Catrina's basin with clean, hot, rinse water, she asked a shocking question, "We're all girls here, so I'm just going to come right out and say it. Catrina, have you set your cap for Jake?"

"Summer!" Julia tried to twist her face into a stern look but could hardly do it. "The things you say sometimes! You don't need to answer that, Catrina." She waved it off.

"Oh, Mother!" Summer sighed exasperatedly. "I don't have enough girlfriends to talk to about things like this. It's fun to talk!" She looked eagerly at Catrina to see how she would reply.

Catrina was amused by Summer's girlish innocence—it was so pure, so sweet. She couldn't help but smile. "I like Jake very much, if that's what you're asking. I'd really like to have the opportunity to get to know him better."

"Because, if you two end up sparking..." Summer's mother cut her off.

"Sum, you know I don't like that new word," Julia said sternly.

"I mean to say that if you two end up *courting*, then I could be your chaperone," Summer announced. "And I wouldn't be like *some* chaperones, staying too close, not even letting you talk privately. I would stay across the room, or far enough away, so that it would be *almost* like you were really alone!"

Summer said the last part with such girlish delight, Catrina laughed lightly. To Summer the idea of even being *almost* alone with a man was enough to make her heart skip. Catrina envied her that purity. *She's what I would have been if Mother had lived. No...,* she tried to be more honest with herself. *No, that's not right. She's what I would have been if I had made different choices.*

Jake came in just as the women were trying to decide if the clothes should be hung outside or draped inside to dry. As soon as he came in the door, Summer began grinning at him like a maniac. He could see his ma was suppressing a smile and Catrina actually chuckled out loud.

"Okay," he said looking side-to-side, "Are you two telling stories on me or what?"

"No," his ma said. "Of course not."

"Nope." Summer continued to grin.

"All right then..." he waited a moment to see if someone would explain. When no one did, he went on. "Catrina, I know it's a bit of a gray day, but I don't think we're going to have any rain at least for a few hours. I was wondering if you'd like to take a walk with me, just down to the creek, before lunch."

"That sounds nice, Jake," Catrina replied.

"I'll be your chaperone," Summer spouted suddenly.

"What?" He held himself back from saying what he really felt, remembering that Catrina was a religious girl. "We need a chaperone just to take a walk down to the creek?" He looked at his ma.

"I think it's a good idea. You know the Bible says we should avoid even the slightest appearance of evil," Julia replied. "A chaperone preserves a lady's honor, unquestionably. And," here she winked at Summer, "it will be *almost* like you're really alone."

The three ladies laughed and Jake knew they were sharing a private joke. He simply took Catrina's arm and led her out the front door.

forward

Sam Garret sat at his desk feeling more satisfied than he had in a very long time. In his hand, he held a gold nugget around half the size of a hen's egg. It was worth a fortune. He rolled it around in his palm.

All the pieces had been in place for some time now. If only Catrina hadn't shown back up in town. With the company she was keeping, she could potentially wreck everything. He had to figure out how to get some leverage over her to keep her quiet. Either that or he was going to have to kill her.

He looked again at the nugget in his hand. *There's plenty more where this came from. It's time to go forward.*

title

Catrina and Jake spent a very pleasant hour or so walking back and forth together at the edge of the creek. Summer had turned out to be a very good chaperone. Keeping to her word, she had stayed far enough away that they could talk completely privately. It had actually been *almost* like being alone.

Catrina had begun by launching a volley of questions at Jake about himself. She really *did* want to get to know him better but at the same time, she didn't want him getting to know her better. On some level she knew this was ridiculous—as soon as this family found out what she really was, it would all be over.

He told her about his childhood, about growing up on this farm, and growing up in this town. Then he got to the part *he* really didn't want to talk about.

"Then when I was about fourteen, my pa died." He went on quickly, "Dan's pa died during the same month and the two of us really understood each other because of that. He and I have been best friends ever since. I'll probably never have another friend like him as long as I live. We've had so many great times together…"

He trailed off. He was thinking of a hundred funny stories, things that he and Dan had done together over the years, but every single one that came to mind was completely inappropriate to share with a girl like her.

He decided to change the subject, "But I've been going on and on. Tell me a little about you."

I wish you would keep *going on and on. I don't want to tell you anything,* she thought. But she had to reply, "Well, there's not much to tell really." She chose her words carefully. "I was born, and grew up in San Francisco and you know I worked in the laundry with Rebekah."

He looked at her, waiting for more. Finally he chuckled, "Well, what about everything in between?"

"In between?" she peeped. Her heart raced a little, but then she calmed herself. He didn't know anything—he just wanted to hear about her life.

"Yeah, tell me about your parents, your friends, your life…"

"Well," she cleared her throat, "my father is a jeweler. My mother died when I was eleven." She didn't want to go on.

Jake understood, "I'm sorry, I know how hard it is to lose a parent."

He stopped walking and put his hand on her arm but she didn't look at him and he sensed that this was a very painful subject for her. He began walking again and asked about her father. "So, your father is a jeweler?"

He tried to inject a little humor by smiling and asking, "Well, I have to say I wouldn't expect the daughter of a jeweler to be working in a laundry."

He turned to see she was not walking with him. She stood staring at the ground, "I…" She faltered. "I… have some things in my life that I regret."

Jake had no idea what she could be talking about. "Well, I think we all do."

"When my mother got sick... when she died... I know it doesn't sound reasonable ..." Catrina sighed. "I blamed my father. Of course, it didn't have anything to do with him. Mother died of the influenza. It wasn't like Father gave it to her or wished it on her." Catrina fiddled with her hands nervously. She did not want to go on with her story.

Can't people turn over a new leaf? she thought desperately. *Can't I choose to start all over again? Can't I change? If I don't ever tell him, it will be like I'm starting a completely new life. Maybe that's even what it means to be "born again."* She looked up at him. He looked at her intensely. He was waiting for what she was going to say next.

I could start a new life with Jake.

A life of lies? her conscience nagged her.

No. I won't lie to him, she decided. *But... that doesn't mean I have to tell him every single detail.*

After a long pause, she continued, "I ran away from home. I haven't seen my father since I was eleven."

"Oh." He felt the bond between them deepening as she shared this obviously painful regret. "That must have been very hard."

"It was," she said truthfully. "I've thought about trying to contact him again. But so much time has gone by."

She looked out across the creek as she spoke. For a moment, it was as though he was seeing her again for the very first time, standing at the corner staring down the street as if waiting for someone.

"But I don't know how he would react. He could hate

me for what I put him through." A gust of wind blew her hair over her face. "He would have every right to hate me."

Jake didn't respond. He wanted to say that if her father hated her for it, he wasn't any kind of father in the first place. But he didn't feel he knew her well enough yet to say something like that on such a sensitive subject.

"Or, a man in his position, with a successful business, might end up being…" she faltered, "…shamed… in the community by a daughter like me returning." She looked at the ground again and furrowed her brow. *For more reasons than you know.*

Now *that* started to make Jake angry. He was about to say that there was nothing shameful about doing a fair day's work for a fair day's wage. That if her father was ashamed of his daughter working in a laundry, he wasn't worth anything at all! But before he could speak, she continued.

"But then again," she went on with a lilt of optimism in her voice, "maybe he's been just waiting and hoping for me to come home all these years." She turned to face him and the intermittent gusts of wind blew her hair around her face. "The problem is… I just don't know."

She gazed into his eyes for understanding and found it. In all these years, she had only confided in a small handful of people but it came so easily with him. He seemed to listen with his whole being. She found herself teetering on the edge of telling him her whole story when she involuntarily shivered.

The wind had been getting colder and when Jake saw Catrina shudder, he felt like an idiot. "What's the matter with me? Keeping you out here in the cold!" He didn't even have a coat to give her. "I'm so sorry. Let's get back to the house." He shouted over his shoulder, "We're going back to the house, Sum."

"Oh good," she hollered back with a laugh as she wrapped her arms around herself. "I'm starting to freeze!"

———•••———

A few days later, Julia was kneading at the kitchen countertop. It was baking day, and she was covered in flour. The day was beautiful, the sun was shining, and it was warm enough to have the windows open.

Jake and Catrina were taking yet another walk by the creek with Summer chaperoning from a distance. Julia smiled. She was pleased with the relationship that was developing between the two of them.

The only thing that would have made it better is if Catrina was a Christian, she thought.

No. No. She had to stop herself. *If Catrina was a Christian, she'd have no business courting with my son. Light has no part with darkness.*

She flipped the dough again. *I just wish they both knew you, Lord.*

Julia was surprised to hear a horse coming. She looked out the window and her eyes widened. It was the sheriff. She quickly wiped her hands on her apron and came out the front door.

"Sheriff Morrell?" She wondered what could be wrong.

"Mrs. Forester." He tipped his hat as he came down from the horse and walked toward her on the porch. He had an apologetic look on his face, as if he was dreading what he was about to do.

He pulled some papers out of his vest pocket, "I'm real

sorry to have to be the one to serve these papers on you."

Julia took the folded documents and began looking through them, "What are they? What's happening?"

He took his hat completely off. A line of sweat ringed his grey hair. He shook his head. "It seems Sam Garret is making a claim on your land."

"What? What does that mean?" Julia felt her face reddening as she continued to piece through the papers. Off to the side she could see Jake jogging up to her. He must have heard the sheriff ride up.

"Sheriff," Jake said in greeting as he arrived.

"Jake," he responded with a nod.

"What's going on?"

"I was just telling your mother, here, that Sam Garret has made a claim against your land."

Jake thought this must be a joke. He would have laughed if the sheriff had not looked so serious, "What? How can he do that?"

"I'm afraid it's perfectly legal," he replied. "He's gone to some attorney in San Francisco to draw up these papers. He's claiming that your family has no title to this land. That you've been squatting here all these years."

A spear of cold fear went through Jake's heart. Ma had said the title was missing. He covered it with bluster, "Well that's completely ridiculous! My family has lived here for more than thirty years. You've known us forever, George! You knew my pa. We're not squatters!"

"I know." The sheriff shook his head in disbelief. "I can't figure it. When the circuit judge comes through, all you have to do is bring your title in, and it will be over— just that quick."

Jake couldn't help looking at his ma. She looked back at

him. Something in their glance translated to the sheriff. "Is there some problem with that?" he asked.

"Of course not," Jake lied.

The sheriff brushed his hat off. "You've got a little over a month before Judge Spence is back to this part of the circuit. I don't know what else to say except I'm real sorry about this."

"We know it's not your fault, George," Julia reassured him.

He replaced his hat and mounted his horse. "Rachel and I will be praying for you all."

"We sure do appreciate it," Julia responded as he turned and began riding back down the lane.

They stood together and watched him go.

"We've *got* to find it," Jake stated simply as soon as the sheriff was out of earshot.

Catrina and Summer arrived at the house about a half-hour later. When Jake had left them at the creek, he had said he would be right back so it had taken them some time to figure out his plans had changed.

When they came into the house, they were shocked to find Julia and Jake turning the place upside down. Every drawer had been taken out, every box opened, even the mattresses had been taken off the beds. The place was in complete disarray. Julia had climbed into the loft and was handing parcels down to Jake.

"We'll have to do the barn next," he was saying to her as he stacked the things she was handing down.

"What on earth is going on?" Summer exclaimed as she came through the door.

"Nothing you need to worry about," Jake snapped at her. He immediately regretted it as he watched Catrina react.

"When are you going to stop treating me like a child?" Summer came back. "I deserve to know what's happening."

Jake was so frustrated he almost swore at her. Instead, he raked his fingers back through his hair and shot out the door toward the barn.

Julia leaned over from the top of the loft to explain. "The sheriff came by to serve papers on us," she said to her daughter. "Sam Garret is trying to make a claim on our land. We have to find the title. The problem is that it's been missing ever since your pa died."

Catrina sharply took in a breath at the mention of Garret's name. She covered it by feigning shock and disbelief about the whole situation.

"Oh no, Ma!" Summer cried out in fear. "What if we can't find it?"

"There's no need to panic." Julia smiled as she came down the ladder. "There's a copy in San Francisco with the land commission. The worst thing that can happen is that Jake will have to make a trip."

Catrina felt physically sick. If this family was going to have contact with Garret, there was *no way* she was going to be able to keep her secret.

papers

Several hours later, Julia went out to the barn. The girls had spent that time getting the house put back together and working together to get the rest of the week's baking done. She expected to find Jake working himself into a fury but what she found was very different.

He was sitting on a stool with his head in his hands. Next to him was the press, its oil cloth cover removed for the first time in years.

It was shiny black cast-iron and the top was decorated with an ornate impression of a sea creature. The sides had impressions of winged poles with snakes wrapped around them. There were some other pieces to it as well, including a long bar and an eagle counterweight, but pa had removed them years ago and they were gathering dust on top of the type cabinet.

"Oh!" she said in excitement, "I didn't even think about the press! What a good idea! Did you find anything?"

He stood up. "Well, yes. But not the title." He took a sizeable stack of yellowed papers and handed it to his mother. "These must have been the articles Pa was wanting to print up."

Julia began to page through it, secretly hoping that he'd just missed it, that it was stuck to the back of one of the other sheets.

Jake must have known what she was thinking. "Don't bother. I can't even count the number of times I've already been through it. There are newspaper clippings, letters from his brother, even a couple of pages that Pa wrote himself, but the title's not there."

Jake counted on his fingers. "I've been down under the chicken coop. I've been up a ladder on the back of the house checking and re-checking every single stone in the chimney. I've been all over this barn. I even went through every case in the cabinet of type and those boxes of frames and wooden blocks that came with the press." He put his hands in his pockets. "I tell you, it is not here. It's not here *anywhere*."

Jake said all this with a calm that was strange for him. She would have expected him to be flying into another temper by this time. She waited for it, but nothing happened.

He kicked at the dirt around the base of the press. "I've even dug up a little of the dirt floor here, thinking that maybe it fell off the press and somehow got covered. Nothing."

"I see," she replied.

"Looks like there's no way around it," he stated simply. "I'm just going to have to make a trip back out to San Francisco to get a copy from the Land Commission."

"Okay then." Julia felt like she must be talking to someone other than her hot-headed son.

"I'm going to go have a cup of tea," he said as he began walking back toward the house.

Maybe Catrina is having an even better effect on him than I would have hoped possible, she thought as she looked back down to the stack of papers.

She continued paging through them until she came across one that was in Luke's handwriting. It was small and had marks from having been folded and carried in a pocket for a long period of time. He had written "Temper" at the top and below that he had written out a page of Bible verses:

An angry man stirreth up strife, and a furious man aboundeth in transgression. – Proverbs 29:22

He that is soon angry dealeth foolishly: and a man of wicked devices is hated. – Proverbs 14:17

He that is slow to wrath is of great understanding: but he that is hasty of spirit exalteth folly. – Proverbs 14:29

He that is slow to anger is better than the mighty; and he that ruleth his spirit than he that taketh a city. – Proverbs 16:32

It went on and on. She could tell that verses toward the bottom had probably been added at later times. He had underlined and circled certain words and obviously had unfolded and refolded this paper many times. She smiled as she thought back to what a different man he had become after he had been born again. The shouting, the unreasonable ramblings—all of it had melted away.

She held the paper close and then began to flip through the rest of the stack as she started to walk back to the house. Suddenly she stopped. Her eyes widened as it occurred to her that Jake had just been going through this as well. Could *this* be the explanation for the lack of his trademark temper? She thought back through everything and it seemed to make sense.

She felt a surge of hope. She quickly took the stack of papers back over to where she'd picked it up. She *had* been planning to bring these back to the house, but if Jake was actually going to read them.... She put her hand on them and prayed, *Dear God, please use something in here to bring Jake to you.*

Her hand was almost shaking as she lifted it from the stack. She composed herself and then walked back to the house.

businessman

Julia walked in as Summer was slicing a loaf of bread that had finally cooled down enough to handle. Jake was finishing his tea at the table with Catrina sitting across from him.

The rich smell of molasses and the tang of onion and salt pork filled the house. Julia walked over to check inside the oven. The pan of baked beans was bubbling nicely.

"I think we're about ready to eat," she said as she closed the oven door and turned to get her potholders.

"Ma, I was just telling Catrina and Sum that I'm going to go ahead and make the trip to get the title copy." Jake drained the last of the tea in his cup. "But it's just occurred to me that it might be better for me to just go and talk to Sam Garret about this. Try to figure out just what this is all about."

Julia had been about to say she thought that was a good idea when Catrina blurted, "No! Don't do that."

Everyone turned to look at her.

"Why shouldn't I?" Jake asked.

Catrina could not believe she'd almost shouted that. But now she had to say *something*, "Do you... do you *know* this man, this Sam Garret?"

"Only by reputation. Oh, and more recently by what Ma has told me. He and my Pa used to know each other." Jake stood to take his cup back to the sink. "But no, I've never actually met him."

"What does his reputation tell you?" Catrina didn't really have any idea what Garret's public reputation was, so she had to skirt around this carefully.

"I'd say he's known as a shrewd and somewhat ruthless business man." He thought a little more. "And I guess there has been talk, now and then, about shady dealings."

"Well then…" Catrina started, "don't you think there's a possibility he could be dangerous?" Since her main motivation was keeping him from finding out the truth about her past, she almost felt like she was deceiving him. However, she reminded herself sternly, Garret really *was* a dangerous man. Down to his core.

Julia pulled the steaming pan out of the oven. "Sam Garret is very lost—a man given over to wickedness."

If Catrina hadn't been looking right at him, Jake would have rolled his eyes at this. "Even so, I think we need to find out more about *why* he's doing this. What's motivating him?" Jake looked at his ma. "I think it's important that we know."

Jake rode up in front of *El Dragón Rojo,* dismounted, and after securing his horse, walked in through the front door. He saw immediate recognition from Rob who stood behind the bar. It hadn't been long at all since they'd buried his sister and Rob still looked like he was taking it rough.

"Hey there, Rob."

"Hey," Rob replied, but there was no attempt at a smile.

Jake felt for him. Every time he saw someone else suffering, somehow he felt he was looking back in time at himself as a boy. He felt he should say something. "How have you been doing?"

Rob bowed his massive head. When he looked back up there was a momentary flash of anger that quickly gave way to sadness. His eyes started to fill with tears. He wiped them away almost instantly and cleared his throat. But he didn't answer the question. "I've never seen you in here before."

"Well, I'm here to try to see Garret." Jake had the papers in his hand and lightly shook them.

"He's in his office as far as I know." Rob came around from the back of the bar. Only when he stood briefly right next to Jake was his size shockingly apparent. His hands were the size of hams. He was, at minimum, at least a foot and a half taller than Jake. It was easy to see why Garret kept him on—no one wanted to start trouble in a place where the bartender looked like Goliath.

Rob walked around to the far wall. Jake watched as he knocked on a door, waited, and then had to duck his head as he leaned inside to deliver the message. In a minute, he was back behind the bar.

"He'll be out," Rob said flatly and then went back to working as if Jake wasn't there.

"Umm... thanks." Jake felt brushed off and awkward. He wasn't sure if he'd done something specifically to offend Rob or if this was just part of the man's normal grieving process.

Several minutes passed before the door finally opened and Sam Garret emerged. The first thing Jake noticed was that he was solidly built in the shoulders and that his dark hair was heavily-oiled and combed completely smooth. The second thing he noticed was that the man had a very unnatural gate. The lower half of his body moved but the top didn't. It was an overly controlled way of walking that made the man appear to be gliding like a specter. It was just plain odd. Jake smirked internally.

Then suddenly when Garret was about half way across the room, Jake experienced the sensation of being splashed all over with icy water—it was the adrenaline rush of fear. He tried to blink it away. It was ridiculous. He had no reason, whatsoever, to fear Sam Garret. For one thing, the guy was smaller *and* older than him. If it came down to a fight, there would be no contest. Not that he was anticipating a fight.

He tried to shake off the feeling. He told himself it was completely ridiculous. But his stomach went into knots and that feeling just kept niggling at the back of his mind.

"Jake Forester, is it?" Garret smiled and extended his hand. "I'm afraid you couldn't deny it if you wanted to. You really are the spitting image of Luke."

Jake shook his hand.

"What can I do for you, Jake?"

"Well, Mr. Garret, you can explain what this is all about." Jake indicated the papers.

"Ah, yes." Garret pressed his lips together and nodded. "Shall we sit down?"

They sat across from each other at one of the tables.

"I'm sorry for the inconvenience this is going to cause you and your family, but I've really put it off for as long as I can. I'm sure you can appreciate that I'm a business man, Jake." Garret started to turn to Rob at the bar. "Can I offer you a drink, on the house?"

"No. Nothing," Jake replied. "Thank you."

"Very well." He turned back fully to Jake. "I'm not sure if your mother ever told you, but Luke and I used to be pretty good friends. That is, before he got religion."

"Yes, I know that," Jake started, "but that has nothing to do with this."

"Actually it does." Garret seemed earnestly sincere as he looked into Jake's eyes. "I've known for *years* that your family has been squatting on that land. I could have come in at *any time* and placed a claim on it but after your father died I had sympathy for your poor mother. There she was, trying to raise two children, with no father…"

"Wait a minute!" Jake had to force himself to lower his voice. He wanted this to be a civil conversation. "We are *not* squatters. My father was given this land by a Mexican Ranchero for saving his life in a bar fight. Then when California became a state, Pa had the title ratified by the Land Commission in San Francisco."

"I'm afraid that's only what your father wanted your mother to believe." Garret shook his head. "The *truth* is that Señor Alvarado allowed your family to live on the land. And I *do* remember Luke telling me the man had promised to give him a title for it but the trouble is, he never got around to it. So then when California became a state, Luke had nothing to take to San Francisco with him except that Ranchero's broken promises. Without any proof, without any documentation, he was unable to get a title from the Land Commission. I remember the night he came back, he was so depressed and he ended up so drunk that…"

"That's a lie!" Jake half-stood and shook his head. "That can't possibly be true! Ma has *seen* the title, she described it to me!" Jake swallowed bitterly when he realized that in his idiot temper, he'd just revealed that they couldn't find the title.

"I'm not sure what your mother saw." Garret shook his head sympathetically. "But it wasn't the title to that land. There is no title, Jake."

Jake sat back down at the table. He stared into Garret's eyes. It was uncanny. The man seemed to have all the outward signs of sincerely telling the truth, but Jake had the eerie sensation that he was looking at a mask instead of a man.

"Even if what you were saying was true, why now? Why would you wait all this time?" Jake narrowed his eyes as scrutinized Garret's face for any sign of falsehood.

"As I said, Jake, I'm a businessman. I feel like I've given your family more than enough time to recover from the loss of your father. You're a grown man now, capable of supporting your mother and your sister." Garret folded his hands on the table. "It just seemed like the right time."

Jake stood. "You realize this will all be over the moment I show the title to the Judge."

"There is *no title*, Jake." Garret also stood. "Again, I'm sorry for what this move is going to mean for your family. But I do want you to know I have a property on the other side of town that I would be more than happy to rent to you, very reasonably, while you make this difficult transition." He pressed his mouth together into a thin-lipped but understanding smile.

"That won't be necessary," Jake tipped his hat and walked out.

A spear of wicked joy shot through Garret's heart as

he walked slowly back to his office. He could have almost skipped with glee, but he didn't. His ability to entirely conceal his true feelings was masterful, *They don't have the title! They don't have it! I can't believe it! This is going to work out better than I could have possibly imagined!*

———•———

"That is not possible," Julia said, sitting down on her bed. She and Jake were talking privately in her bedroom. "I've handled the title myself. I've held it in my hands, many times. It's on light yellow paper with an eagle at the top."

"Did you ever actually *read* it?" Jake asked. "Is there *any* way it could have been something else?"

Julia shook her head. "No, it wasn't anything else. It was the title to this land." She felt exasperated. "Are you going to believe Sam Garret over your own mother?"

"No. No, of course not." He sat down on her dressing chair, "It's just that I wasn't expecting him to come up with this long complex story about how we've supposedly never had a title to the land."

"Well, what *were* you expecting?" She crossed her arms over her chest.

"I don't know." He shook his head. "I guess I was just hoping for something easier to explain away."

"Child, Satan never works that way."

"Ma, I'm not a 'child' anymore! And I'm not talking about 'Satan,' here… I'm talking about Sam Garret—a very flesh and blood man."

"I'm sorry, Jake." She rubbed her temples. How could she explain this in a way that he would accept? "What I mean is that evil—*real evil*—usually comes in the form of very easy to believe *deception.*"

A long pause hung between them.

"I do have to admit that there was something about him" He looked down at his feet. "I mean there *is* something about Garret that's not..." He sighed, almost ashamed to admit it. "As he was walking across the room to me, I suddenly had this really... It sounds stupid to even say... I got this really *bad* feeling..." He didn't know how to express it, but he wondered if that's what she meant by "evil." He looked over to her for some kind of clarification.

She shrugged, unsure of what he was asking, "Sam's always given *me* a bad feeling."

He just shook his head. She obviously didn't know what he was talking about. He went on, "I guess you'd better tell me all you can remember about when Pa went to get the title."

"I've been thinking about it. Now, the Land Commission was set up in March of '52. I remember your father was really anxious to get it taken care of right away, so he went to San Francisco toward the end of that month." She thought a moment. "If it wasn't the end of March, I can tell you it was no later than very early April. He was only gone a couple of days. He said it all went smoothly. We were one of the very first families in the area to get the whole title issue settled."

"Well, knowing the approximate date should make it just that much easier," Jake replied. He stood and opened the bedroom door. "I'll plan to take a trip up to San Francisco toward the end of next week. Then we can put this all behind us."

temper

Later that week, around dinnertime, Jake was in the barn. He had just finished mucking out the horses stalls for the night and sat down for a minute to rest. The pile of papers still sat there on the printing press. He had expected Ma to treat them like they were some kind of treasure, but she apparently didn't really care too much because she hadn't even brought them into the house.

He picked up the stack again and began to thumb through it. The third paper was the one he'd read last time, in Pa's handwriting, about "Temper."

Boy, you were right about that one, Pa. He sighed and shook his head. If it hadn't been for his stupid temper, he wouldn't have blurted out to Garret that they hadn't been able to find the title.

Stupid. Stupid. Stupid, he scolded himself. *Just one more in a long, long, nearly endless line of stupid things I've done because of my temper.* He held the worn paper carefully in his hand. *How* did *you get control over yours, Pa? What? Did you just say these Bible verses over and over again to yourself? Is that what did it for you?*

He huffed. That didn't make sense.

He saw an envelope from his uncle Jonathan. Inside was a letter and a clipping.

Luke,
I was there when this sermon was preached. It opened many people's eyes to their need of God's forgiveness.
Love,
Jonathan

Jake quickly looked over to the barn door. He didn't want his mother to see him looking at this stuff. He was just curious as to what the clipping said. He began to read:

Will you dare to say you have never taken the name of the Lord your God in vain? You have never sworn profanely, yet surely in common conversation you have sometimes made use of God's name when you ought not to have done so.

Jake sniffed at this. He had used God's name in vain so many times he couldn't even count them. But what did he care.

"Thou shalt not kill." You may never have killed any, but have you never been angry? He that is angry with his brother is a murderer; you are guilty here.

The word "murderer" grabbed his attention. He read that again.

What is this preacher saying?

He screwed up his face and read it softly aloud, "He that is angry...with his brother...is a...*murderer?*"

Everything in him balked at the thought. *That's ridiculous. That can't possibly be true.*

The more he puzzled on it the more his eyebrows began

to furrow. *Is he trying to say that just being angry is the same as* murder *to God?*

No.

So, because of my temper I'm supposedly as bad as the men who shot Pa? He could feel heat coming into his face. It seemed so unjust!

God counts me *as a murderer?* He noticed he was clamping his teeth down so hard it was beginning to hurt.

That can't be right. What kind of God is this?

"What! What is it, Jake?" Catrina's voice startled him.

"What?" he shouted back at her, looking around sharply in all directions.

She began to laugh at having startled him so but she covered her mouth to hide it. "Oh! I'm sorry! I'm *so* sorry. It's just you." She motioned back to the house and then to him. "I mean, I came around the door and your face! You looked like you're getting ready to tear the barn down with your bare hands! I thought something must be wrong." She pressed her lips together and tried not to smile.

He realized what he must have looked like, took a deep breath and smiled back. "It's okay. Nothing's wrong." He raised one eyebrow and wagged his head. "Well, that is to say, nothing *else* is wrong. I just got myself a little overheated reading some of my Pa's old papers."

"Oh?" She walked into the barn. "What papers?"

He realized quickly that this could lead to some conflict, so he tried to brush it off, "These? Oh, they're just some letters and papers..." He tried to trail off, but she was looking at him to finish the sentence, "and sermons." He went on quickly, "They're just some things that my Pa wanted to print up and give away to people. I guess you could say it was kind of a dream of his."

She walked over to him. "You came across them when you were looking for the title?" He nodded as she sat down on the stool. "So what was getting you so upset?"

He wanted to answer truthfully but didn't want to alienate her, "It was just a few things this certain preacher was saying." He flipped back to see the header on the clipping. "Spurgeon is his name."

She raised her eyebrows slightly and cocked her head. "So, you think he's a bad preacher?"

Jake wondered for a moment if this was a trick question. Maybe all religious people knew this Spurgeon and thought he was wonderful or something. After all, why would his father have kept these clippings and even gone to so much trouble to try to reprint them?

Still this guy had to be off his rocker if he thought that anger was the same as murder. No one really believed that, did they?

He wasn't sure what to say. "Why don't I read a little to you and you tell me what *you* think." That felt like a safe answer. He could watch her and gauge her reaction. Maybe that would give him a better idea of whether or not he should take any of this seriously.

He opened his mouth to begin reading the part about anger and murder but then realized that if she did agree with this Spurgeon, then he would be as bad as a murderer in her estimation. So he pretended to scan for the right spot but randomly picked a different section to read.

Has no lascivious thought crossed your mind? Has no impurity ever stirred your imagination? Surely if you should dare to say so, you would be brazen-faced with impudence.

Oh, that's a great *choice!* Jake saw Catrina jolt slightly at the words and he wanted to bite his tongue. *What in the world is she going to think of me saying such things to her?* He hurried to read the next part.

Catrina felt ashamed and looked quickly down at the dirt floor. She had made herself the object of "lasciviousness," for so many years. She was soaked to the marrow of her bones with "impurity." But surely he didn't know anything, did he? She chanced a quick glance upward. He was simply reading. She searched his face, but saw only a hint of slight embarrassment about the subject matter.

And have you never stolen? 'Thou shalt not steal.' Surely there have been times in which you have felt an inclination to defraud your neighbor, and there may have been some petty, or mayhap some gross frauds which you have secretly and silently committed, on which the law of the land could not lay its hand, but which, nevertheless, was a breach of God's Law.

As Jake finished the words, guilt poured into his gut again about cashing in that smaller nugget and blowing the money.

"Secretly and silently committed"…" breach of God's Law"…"Thou shalt not steal." His eyes scanned and rescanned.

Am I really a thief? After all, the note was addressed to me. Doesn't that mean pa gave them to me?

But he knew he was only justifying himself because he still cringed at the thought of his mother finding out. And he couldn't even imagine what Catrina would think of him if she had seen how he'd spent those two days.

He looked up slowly to see what her appraisal would be.

Her head was still tilted down and she traced her foot around on the dirt floor. She didn't really want to answer, but as badly as it made her feel about herself she had to admit, "I'm no expert, but he sounds like a good one to me."

"Yeah," Jake admitted regretfully. On some internal level, he knew she was right. Somehow he knew it. She was right, and this Spurgeon fellow was right. He could hardly believe he was even thinking this way.

"Anyway," Catrina began, looking up at him again, "I came out to tell you it's time for supper."

"Thanks," he said, stepping closer to her. He just looked at her for a moment, cocking his head just slightly. Her long lashes framed those unblinking golden eyes. *Maybe there really is a God. And maybe He sent you to me.*

Catrina waited. He looked like he was getting ready to say something but he didn't. After what felt like an awkward pause, she followed up with, "Well, okay then." She began to turn but then remembered to say, "And thanks for reading to me."

Jake broke from the spell as he watched her back retreating toward the house.

"Catrina," he called after her, "what would you say to a picnic tomorrow?"

"That sounds lovely." She turned briefly to reply.

Jake smiled widely as he hung up his barn smock and followed her up to the house.

picnic

Jake packed the picnic and although it was only cold chicken sandwiches and a jar of his ma's watermelon rind pickles, he was rather proud of himself. He even packed Summer her own separate lunch since she would be following along behind them.

At first, this whole chaperoning thing had seemed ridiculous to him, but now he had to grudgingly admit that it wasn't such a bad idea. Although he had *been* with many women he had never gotten to *know* a woman this way. It was amazing what you could learn when there was nothing to do but talk. And he really enjoyed talking to her.

He knew just the place for their picnic. It was a little bit of a walk but it was worth it. As they finally reached the spot, he had to lead her by the hand through some scrubby brush. But he knew he'd done well when he heard her take in her breath at the site.

"Oh, it *is* beautiful," she sighed. She saw that the stream fell a little here. It wasn't a waterfall, but the water did make a beautiful sound as it slid over a little shelf of smooth, gray stones. There were three large trees growing here, two on this side of the stream and one larger one on the other. They provided a perfect canopy and the sunshine was dappled all over the ground and the water.

"I used to come here as a kid." He smiled as he began to spread a quilt out on the mossy ground. He watched Summer come through the scrubby brush farther downstream and sit down on a big gray rock in the sun.

Catrina sat down carefully on the quilt. "It's so peaceful!"

"It was a great place to come when I was feeling sad, or alone—or even angry."

She gave him a sideways glance. "Yeah, I've noticed you do seem to have a little bit of a temper problem."

"You noticed that, huh?" He chuckled and rubbed the back of his neck with his hand and sat down. "Well, it might have been easier to hide if we weren't living in the same house."

"Nope," she countered, "it's better that I know now. It tells me what I might be getting myself into."

"Well, I came by it honestly, you know." He opened the picnic basket and took out the jar of pickles. "It runs in the family. My pa used to have a terrible temper." He twisted the jar open with a liquid pop.

"'Used to?' So how did he get rid of his?" She reached into the jar as he offered it and pulled out one of the crisp slices. It smelled strongly of cinnamon. As she bit into it, it was at once crunchy and sweet and juicy. "Oh, these are fantastic. I've never had them like this before. Why, it's better than store bought candy!"

Jake was relieved for the change of topic. "Yeah, it's a shame Ma only makes them once a year. She tries to get us to go slow on them, but they never last very long."

"So, back to your pa," she continued, "how did he end

up getting rid of his temper?"

Jake looked at the stream as if it would provide an answer. That was the very question that lead him to start reading Pa's stack of papers the other day.

So, how did pa get rid of his temper?

He knew that Ma always said Pa became a "new man" when he was "born again." But Jake had always rolled his eyes at such assertions. He knew that his father had finally just mustered up the self-control to get a reign on it. And he'd always believed that he would too one day.

But what if there were more to it than that?

His previous day's admission that God might be real after all brushed against his mind like a falling leaf.

Maybe Pa really did somehow get changed by God.

He realized Catrina was still waiting for him to answer. "Ma says that God took it away."

"Oh," she said thoughtfully, "I bet you wish that would happen for you, huh?"

He was somewhat surprised that he could honestly answer, "Yeah. I do."

They sat in silence, enjoying the sound of the water.

He looked at Catrina out of the corner of his eye. She was really beautiful. But even more than that, she brought out the best in him. He could see that so clearly. He lifted his hand from where he was leaning, wanting to touch hers, but he didn't want to risk offending her. Instead, he reached into the basket and took out the two sandwiches wrapped in ironed white handkerchiefs.

"So when are you going to San Francisco?" she said as she took one.

"Actually I'm thinking about heading out right after our picnic." He took a bite. "I can't wait to get that title in my hand. It's going to be such a weight off my mind."

"Yeah," she replied sincerely. *It will be such a weight off my mind, too. When that's done, no more contact with Garret!*

"I kind of wish I could go with you," she said between bites. "I know Rob went back to take care of the shop and all Rebekah's things, but…" she went silent.

He saw that vacant, mournful look in her eyes. "But you don't feel settled…" he offered. "And you don't know why. Sometimes the whole thing comes back to you in a vivid flash and other times it seems like it was a dream; something that never happened at all"

She looked at him with gratitude. "How can you know my heart like that?"

"I don't know." He stared into her eyes. "I've never felt as close to any other woman in my life, Catrina."

He felt his hand reaching up to touch her face. It seemed to be moving with a will of its own. "I've never known anyone… so beautiful…" She was looking at him and his hand was almost touching her cheek. "So pure…" She suddenly flinched away.

"I'm sorry," he said instantly. *Stupid! I should have never tried to touch her!* And as he sat there waiting for her to turn back, he realized just how important it was to him that she did. He had really become attached to her. He thought for a moment and realized he was already to the point where he couldn't really picture a future without her—he had begun to anticipate a life together.

She continued to look in the other direction. Hearing him say that made her feel more filthy and ashamed than she ever had in her life. *There is* nothing *pure about me,* she thought hopelessly. More than anything else that had happened thus far, this solidified the fact that she could never let him find out about her past. *Never.*

She had already fallen so completely in love with Jake that the thought of losing him was more than she could bear. Her heart felt squashed and small in her chest. If she didn't speak soon, she was afraid she might start to cry.

She desperately tried to think of something to say and only one thought sprang to mind. "I was also thinking more about the possibly of looking up my Father." She felt even lower for lying to him but it was the only thing she could think of at the moment.

"I see." He thought for a moment. "Well, if that's important to you, then maybe we could all go together?"

"Oh no, no." She was careful not to put all the panic she felt at that suggestion into her voice. "It was just a thought." *Oh horrors!* she thought. *What did I almost get myself into?*

"Are you sure?"

"Yes." She turned to him. "Besides you'll go much faster alone and you can finally have the whole title situation under control." She hoped that giving him that additional logic would seal the subject from ever being brought up again.

She needed to change the subject. "Could I have a drink?"

"Right!" Jake jumped up with the two cups. "I'm sorry I forgot." He walked over to the stream and caught the icy, clean water in the cups.

"Thank you," she said as he handed it to her.

For some reason Jake felt suddenly bold. "Can I ask you a very forward question?"

She raised her eyebrows. "I guess so."

"What are you looking for in a husband?" The moment he said it, his heart was suddenly pounding like he'd run a mile. He couldn't believe he'd just asked her that.

She looked away for a split second to try to tamp down her extreme joy. She looked back at him with a smile. "You really want to know?"

"I wouldn't have asked if I didn't," he grinned back at her. He was so glad she was smiling!

She stood and held out her hand to help him up. "Then come here."

This time the touch of her hand was electrifying but he was confused as to what she was doing. He stood up and walked behind her along the edge of the stream. When they reached a spot of still water, she let go of his hand and put her hand on his shoulder to lean him over. She then pointed down into the water and his reflection shone back at him.

Back at the house, Jake saddled up and started the two-day trip back to San Francisco. All three women waved goodbye as he started down the dusty lane.

As Catrina watched him go, she was so filled with bubbling joy that she could barely suppress her own giggling. She had never felt so light, so radiant.

Now she knew that Jake intended to "court" her all the way to marriage.

Julia and Summer were eyeing her and sharing secret, grinning glances with one another. They knew from her expression, and from Jake's, that something significant must have happened during the picnic.

Julia put her arm around her daughter and started walking back toward the house, while Catrina continued to stare, transfixed, at Jake's retreating shape.

Just look at her. I wonder if Jake proposed? Julia smiled. She turned to Summer, "You know, we've all been cooped up in this house much too long, don't you think?" She raised her voice and half-turned to Catrina. "It's such a beautiful day let's all take a walk into town. Besides, Summer's about to grow out of her best dress and I think it's time to look at some fabric. So let's get ready girls!"

"Oh, great!" Summer exclaimed, just as the two of them went into the house.

Catrina was so filled with happiness that at first Julia's proposal didn't register. Then just as she turned, understanding suddenly descended. She felt like she'd been thrown off a mountain top.

She couldn't go into town! She couldn't take a chance on seeing Garret. Not now. Not ever! She was suddenly like a trapped animal. She wanted to sprint to safety, but where?

How can I be so naive! She began to panic. *This family is going to find out exactly what I am!*

She spun on her heel away from the house and gripped her hands together to stop the shaking. *Calm down!* she chided herself. *You're being so melodramatic! This is not a problem. We're going to the General Store not the Saloon! A woman like Julia wouldn't be seen within 1000 feet of such a place. Besides, it's the middle of the day. There is no way we're going to see Garret. It will be okay. I will be careful. It's going to be fine.*

She kept encouraging herself until Julia and Summer emerged from the house with their shopping baskets.

"Do you need to do anything, Catrina, or are you ready?" Julia called as she closed the front door.

"I'm ready." She was proud that the shaking had subsided and there wasn't even a tremor in her voice. "Let's go."

town

The walk into town was different than Julia had expected. Catrina had become more sober and even seemed slightly troubled. Julia could not fathom what on earth had happened in the few minutes it took for them to get their shopping baskets.

After they had been walking in silence for some time, Julia said, "So how was your picnic?"

"Oh?" Catrina had been thinking of so many things. Julia's voice pulled her back to the moment. "Oh, it was wonderful."

She smiled and allowed herself to feel a little of that joy again. "Jake picked a beautiful spot next to the creek." She took a few more steps, just looking dreamily at the horizon. She thought about the depth of his eyes, the tenderness in his voice, how well he knew her heart and how wonderful it would be to be his wife.

She became aware of the lag in the conversation and looked around to see that Julia and Summer were both looking at her expectantly. She wondered what else she should say. "Your watermelon pickles were wonderful too, by the way."

Summer snickered.

"Oh, yes." Julia smiled too. "I'm sure my pickles were just the highlight of the afternoon."

Catrina couldn't help but laugh.

"Okay...okay...So out with it! What happened?" Summer cut right in.

"Summer!" Julia scolded. "We really must work on your manners!"

"Well," Catrina said shyly, "nothing really. It's just that Jake asked me what I would be looking for in a husband."

Summer let out a "Whoop!" and Catrina couldn't stop her lips from turning up at the edges.

"Summer! When are you going to learn how to behave like a lady?" Julia swung around and put her hand on Catrina's arm. "Well, I think that's *wonderful*! What did you tell him?"

"I pointed to his reflection in the water," she answered simply.

"Oh! What a beautiful memory that will be for the two of you throughout your lives together!"

"Well," Catrina cautioned, "he hasn't really 'officially' asked for my hand. We were just talking, you know." Then she realized she was smiling so widely her cheeks were beginning to ache but she couldn't help it.

"We're going to be sisters!" Summer threw her arm around Catrina's back and gave a squeeze. "I *knew* it! I knew it the moment I saw your face on the walk back from the creek. I just knew it. I always wanted a sister!"

Catrina saw they were nearing the edge of town and sobered slightly but tried to cover it. "I really hope so Summer. I can't think of anyone who would make a better sister than you!"

———•———

At the General store, Kylie pulled open bolts of fabric for them. Julia and Summer were having a wonderful time, chatting away as they looked at all the different patterns. Catrina was trying to appear interested but found she was a bundle of nerves. She couldn't help scanning out through the front windows.

A man was coming. Catrina recognized him instantly from the Dragón. She was sure he had been up to her room at least once, maybe more. She immediately became intensely interested in a bolt of light brown fabric with thin yellow and red stripes which allowed her to turn her face from the door.

The bell rang as he opened the door. He tipped his hat and wished Kylie a good afternoon. Then he told her what he needed: a bag of nails, a tin of tea, a small sack of white sugar. Could she please put that on his tab? Well, yes she could. And how was Doris? Well, she was fine and he'd be sure to tell her Kylie said hello. The bell rang again and he was gone.

Catrina felt herself swaying on her feet as a rivulet of sweat came down her temple. With slightly shaking hands, she put down the bolt of fabric. She had to get out of there.

Julia saw her. "Catrina, you look as pale as a flour sack! Are you okay?"

Catrina wiped her brow. "I'm not feeling so well." *And that is no lie!* she thought. "I think I just need some fresh air." She started for the door.

"Summer, go with her." Julia motioned with concern.

"No, really." She lifted her hand to object. "I'm okay.

I'm just going to have a seat over here by the side of the building. I'm fine. Really."

"All right," Julia said after a pause. "We won't be too much longer."

Julia watched as Catrina walked toward the door, scanning right and left cautiously, then quickly went out and around the side of the building.

Is she looking for someone? No, Julia realized. *She's afraid of someone.* Julia looked out the front windows, and up and down the street, *That must be the reason she changed so much when I suggested we walk into town. I wonder who it could be and why?*

Catrina rounded the side of the building and went right past the bench. Farther down, behind a couple of barrels was a keg of nails. She sat down on it and pulled her knees and skirts back to where she was reasonably sure she couldn't be seen from the street. She let out a sigh of relief but then realized she needed to come up with a passable explanation to Julia and Summer as to why she was back here.

She was toying around with different ideas when her heart skipped a beat. Garret himself was standing out back behind the General Store with Dan O'Neill. The two of them were peering into a wooden box as Dan put the lid on the ground.

She could hear Dan: "Mr. Garret, *we* can't be held responsible for broken bottles in your shipments. You're going to have to go after the *company* for not packing them properly."

She heard the edge in Garret's voice. "If you weren't paid up in full, I might not be so understanding."

She could see the veins pop out on the side of Dan's neck as he clenched his jaw. Without a word, he turned and went back into the store. She wondered at the look of deep regret across his features.

Garret watched him go. "I'll have Rob over here to pick up the other cases a little later today," he called after him.

He was going to come down the alleyway. She really was trapped this time. There was nowhere to go. Her heart pounded so hard her vision began to jump with each beat. She dug her shoes into the dirt and pressed her back into the wall, trying somehow to become invisible.

Then he saw her. His face almost betrayed emotion for just a flash—but then it was gone. He stopped suddenly, as if thinking, then glided purposefully down the alley toward her.

It's her, he growled inwardly although his exterior remained composed. *She could ruin everything. She's the only other one who knows. If she breathes a word to that family, it all goes down the river.*

As he passed the store's woodpile, he spied a club-sized log and considered his options. *It would only take one carefully placed blow. No one is in the alley. I can take care of it quickly.*

Then he noticed something. She wasn't looking at him smugly as he had expected. In fact, she looked terrified.

What a perfectly lovely little idiot. She doesn't even know what she knows.

Then he watched her eyes dart back toward the front of the store and it only took him a second longer to put it all together. *That's it!* This struck him as the greatest kind of joke. *The Foresters don't know she's a prostitute.*

He relaxed his grip on the walking stick. *She's afraid of them finding out!* He could see it now. It was written all over her face.

There's my leverage. Oh, this couldn't get any better! Had he not had such mastery over his emotions, he would have laughed aloud. Now he knew exactly how to play it.

"What are you doing here, hiding in an alley?" he asked as he hovered directly in front of her. His voice was like a bottomless, black void. Nonchalantly, he brushed a bit of dust from his shoulder. "Afraid your precious new 'family' will find out what you really are?"

Catrina's eyes and mouth were wide with fear. She almost sobbed aloud.

fire

Two days later, Jake found himself standing in line at the U.S. Surveyor General's Office. By the time he made it to the front of the line, almost a half hour had passed and he was more than ready to get this over with. "I need a copy of a land title."

"What's the family name?" The pudgy man behind the counter didn't even look up. He was busy flipping through a file.

"It's under Forester."

The man looked up slowly, but said nothing.

Jake continued, "Lucas Jacob Forester. It was filed by my father in April of 1852." He wondered what other information the man needed. "It's near Pureza Township."

"Ah...yes." The man seemed to become nervous. He wouldn't meet Jake's eye, "I'll go see if there is one." He nodded quickly and headed out of the room.

"Wait a minute...what?" Jake called after him, but the man was already gone. He furrowed his brow. *Why did he say that? What was that supposed to mean?*

Long minutes passed. Finally the man returned, empty-handed.

"There does not appear to be a title, sir."

"There what?" Jake's blood pressure was on the rise. "What are you talking about? Of *course* there's a title!" He smacked the counter with his open hand.

"I'm very sorry, sir, but I have checked *twice*."

"You look here!" Jake reached across and grabbed a fistful of the little man's lapel. "There *is* a title to that land. You go look *again*! It's in the name of Lucas Jacob *Forester*. It was filed in April of *1852*!"

The man's double chins did a little dance as he tried to maintain his footing and keep from being pulled across the counter. "That's the problem. That's the problem!" He squawked nervously. "There was a fire in '52—May of '52!"

Jake loosened his grip and the man continued. "It was exactly one year to the month after 'The Great Fire.' Didn't you hear about it? It nearly destroyed fifteen buildings. Caused more than three million dollars in damage. Please let go of me. I'm just a simple clerk."

Jake let go and looked around. Twenty to thirty people had all stopped what they were doing to stare.

The now perspiring clerk stepped back from the counter and wiped his forehead with his pocket-handkerchief. "Bring in your copy of the title and we will be happy to re-file it."

Jake felt badly for grabbing the man like that. "I'm… uh. I'm sorry about…" He motioned to the man's jacket. Painfully aware that everyone was still watching, he straightened his own hat and said loudly enough for anyone nearby to hear, "Yes, I'll just get it and bring it in to be re-filed. Good day."

About halfway down the front steps of the building, he

stopped and took his hat off. He watched the people going by, going in and out of shops, coming from here and there.

He glared at the sun. There it was, shining in the sky, as if this were just another beautiful day. It didn't even have the respect to be covered with clouds. Gray and gloomy, that's what it should have been.

We're going to lose it. We're going to lose it all.

"Excuse me," a voice came from behind. "I couldn't help notice what just happened inside."

Jake turned to see an older man in a wide-brimmed hat. He had a bushy white moustache and a half-smoked cigar sticking out from one corner of his mouth.

"It's a terrible thing to find out that your title is just gone." The man cocked his head slightly. "I mean, it's *their* fault the title burned in the first place, right? Just ask yourself 'Why didn't they have those records in a fireproof safe?' It's a shame. A real shame. It's just not right that a piece of paper like that holds so much sway over a man's life." The man shook his head sadly.

Jake wanted to agree but he held back. There was something greasy, something untrustworthy that just oozed out of this man. He was like a snake leading up to a sales pitch. Jake just eyed him and waited.

He took a slow draw on his cigar and shot a stream of smoke out the other side of his mouth. "You know you *could* have someone make one up for you if you knew the right person and you had the right price."

Jake started to object but the man quickly continued, "I mean, it's not like the land's not rightfully yours anyway. And if the Land Commission had done its job, they'd have the copy you need, wouldn't they? You're just righting a wrong. No harm in that, is there?"

It clicked. It settled. It just made sense. Jake *needed* to do this to protect his family.

"No," Jake replied slowly, "no harm in that." Then he smiled.

Everything was going to be all right after all.

jewelry

Today was the fourth day since Jake left for San Francisco, the day he was due back, but Catrina was still not herself. Julia thought back to the day at the General Store, when Catrina had excused herself. She and Summer had been surprised and even a little worried when they'd come around the side of the building to find she wasn't there. Of course, they were greatly relieved to find her back at the house asleep in her bed.

Catrina explained that she'd left on her own because she felt suddenly ill and needed to get into bed as fast as she could. And she *did* spend most of the next day in bed as well, so it *might* have been some kind of a fainting sickness but Julia felt unsettled about it. She replayed it in her mind and was sure she had seen genuine fear in Catrina's face.

As the three women stood in the kitchen getting supper prepared, she wondered again if she should bring it up. Catrina was ironing the fancy white tablecloth for Jake's special 'welcome home' dinner, but her eyes were distant and disturbed.

"It was good for you to learn how to make this, Catrina, since it is Jake's favorite," Julia said cheerily as she peered into the open oven door at the chicken pie. "It was Luke's favorite as well." She closed the oven door. "I expect Jake will be able to smell it all the way down the lane."

Catrina brightened a little at the mention of his name which was, of course, Julia's hope.

"I'll be so glad when he gets home," Summer said as she walked over and peeked out the window. The sun was low in the sky. "It won't be long now."

"No. It won't," Julia echoed as she looked out as well. "Let me take care of the rest of that." She took the iron away from Catrina and scooted her toward her bedroom, "Now you go get yourself prettied up!"

Catrina smiled gratefully as she took off the work apron and headed toward the bedroom.

"Wear the burgundy dress!" Summer called after her. "He loves that on you."

Catrina smiled back at them as she closed the bedroom door.

Summer picked up the rag rug by the front door and took it outside to shake it when she thought she caught movement out of the corner of her eye. The light was getting low and maybe her eyes were playing tricks. She stood still with the rag rug draped over her arm and she saw it again. Something moved just past the edge of the barn.

More curious than startled, she stared at the spot as she took the few steps down off the porch. There it was again, but now she could see it was Jake's head. He bobbed it quickly around the corner. She started to squeal and wave but he began waving his arms and fanatically shushing her. She giggled quietly and ran out to him.

Minutes later, Catrina emerged from the bedroom to find the table set with the Forester's best, along with Julia,

Summer, and Jake standing side-by-side in the middle of the
room. Summer's face was fairly bursting with some secret.

"Oh!" she lightly exclaimed, "I didn't realize you
were here yet." She smiled at him. "I'm so glad to see you,
Jake."

He returned the smile. "I have a little surprise for you,
as you might have guessed." Here he nudged Summer, who
erupted in girlish giggling. Julia's smile just continued to
beam.

"Sit down here." He indicated a chair and as she sat he
walked around behind her. "But first a little blindfold," he
said as he proceeded to place a folded dishcloth over her
eyes and tie it around the back of her head.

She began to laugh. "What is this?"

"That's for you to guess," he retorted. "Now, I've
brought you back a surprise from San Francisco. What do
you think it is?"

"Um..." she began. Of course, she was desperately
hoping it was a ring—an official engagement. But she said,
"Is it candy?"

"Nope. You'll have to guess again." Jake was having fun
with this.

"Could it be a new hat?" She continued to guess as far
afield as she could muster.

Summer giggled and even Julia laughed lightly.

"No. You'll have to be hatless," he continued with a
mixture of humor and cruelty. "I'll give you a hint: it has
something to do with jewelry."

When she heard the word "jewelry", she knew it must
be a ring, but she continued to play the game, "Is it a
necklace?"

"You're just not very good at guessing today, my dear

Catrina." She could hear the smile in his voice. "I guess we'll just have to take this off."

As the blindfold came off she expected to see him holding a small box with a tiny golden ring a symbol of their future together. Instead she saw a second man.

He wore a dark blue suit coat and a white collared shirt. He was gray at the temples, but he still had his full head of hair. His moustache was heavily waxed, just as she remembered, even though it was mostly silver now. And his golden eyes, although now surrounded by crow's feet, still snapped with vigor as they spilled tears of joy down his shaven cheeks.

Time stopped.

As she looked into his face, so loving, so full of acceptance, she could only ask herself, *Why did I stay away so long?*

Finally she whispered the question, "Papa?"

He surged forward and lifted her out of the chair. "Oh, my precious girl! I feared I would never see you again!" He sobbed into her shoulder. "You're alive! You're alive! Thank you, God! Thank you, Father! Oh, thank you, thank you Jesus!"

"Oh, Papa." Catrina covered her face with her hands as he still held her in the air. "I'm so sorry. I'm *so* sorry. How can you ever forgive me?"

The two of them continued to cry and embrace. Summer, face flooded with happy tears, wrapped her arms around her mother, almost lifting her off the floor with glee. Julia both cried and laughed softly as she hugged Summer. Jake stood by, his eyes brimming, hands on his hips, grinning from ear to ear.

After several moments, Jake cleared his throat. "Mr.

Salterson?" Edwin looked around, smiled at Jake and sat his daughter, still crying, back down in the chair. He took a step away and wiped more tears from his eyes.

Catrina's face was behind her hands as she continued to cry softly.

"Catrina?" Jake knelt down before her, and tenderly took her hands away from her face. "I have one more question to ask you tonight."

Her eyes were swollen and stinging as she tried to open them and look. She saw him bring something from behind his back and he opened it before her. She would have recognized it anywhere—it was her mother's wedding ring. She let out a little gasp and looked back and forth between her father and Jake. Edwin smiled and nodded lovingly. Her father must have given it to him with his blessing.

"Catrina," Jake's voice cracked with his own tears, "will you be my wife?"

"Oh yes, Jacob," she whispered between her sobs. "Yes." She threw her arms around his neck and they shared their first real embrace.

<hr/>

The two of them walked, holding hands now, along the bank of the creek. Summer sat not far away on the big gray rock. She was trying to skip stones.

"It was easy enough to figure out when I remembered the block where I had seen you staring off into space. It was just a block down from Salterson Watch and Jewelry Company." He smiled and picked up a smooth stone with his other hand. "Catrina *Salterson*, father owns a *jewelry* store, staring that *direction*. I may not be the swiftest, but even I could figure that one out." He tried to skip the stone but it went straight in.

"I'm so glad you did." She squeezed his hand. It was so nice to feel how small her hand was in his. She felt safe with him. "I just don't understand why you have to go right back to San Francisco. Even Father isn't going back for several days. Couldn't you wait and go back with him."

"No." He felt his jaw tighten. His mind was resolute. "I've got to get this whole land title settled. The sooner, the better."

"But I don't understand," she countered. "What happened? Why weren't you able to…"

"Don't worry about it," he interrupted. "It will only be a few more days and I'll be back for good. Besides," he changed the subject, "don't you have a wedding to be planning?"

He grinned at her and she grinned back, "As a matter of fact, I do."

stormy

Jake had everything packed and he was ready to head back to San Francisco. He needed to cash in the larger of the nuggets so that he could pay for the forged title, but he had been assured that it was the best one money could buy. It would be on the exact right paper with all the proper seals and even the signatures would be duplicated with precision. But to get that level of excellence it would have to pass through a lot of hands, and each one of those hands needed a little greasing.

He went into his bedroom and closed the door. He put his chair up against it to make sure no one walked in on him unannounced. He had to get down on his back to reach under the bed.

Jake was so glad he hadn't blown *both* the nuggets. This one was much larger and he was sure it would cash in for a small fortune. He thought about thanking God but then figured God wouldn't be too pleased with the idea of a forged title. Oh, well.

He reached across, underneath, and felt around for it. When his pa had made this bed, he'd done it with saplings about three inches in diameter. And when he was eight or nine years-old, he had made his own little contribution to the design.

He had spent many nights under here carving out this little hiding place. It had taken a good long time to gouge the five-inch by two-inch hole in the underside of this log. Then, using bits of scrap lumber, he'd made a small, open topped wooden box that fit perfectly in the opening.

This was a lot easier to reach when I was a kid, he thought. But he'd found it and now only needed to turn the pin. The little box came loose in his hand.

But immediately he noticed it didn't feel right. It wasn't heavy enough! He tipped it and it didn't rattle. He pulled it out and sat up. The gold was gone!

He groped around under the bed then stuck his head under. Nothing. He panicked, stood and in one swift motion heaved the bed over upside down. He'd been hiding things in this spot since he was a young boy. He was *sure* neither his mother nor Summer knew anything about it. And yet it was gone.

It was *gone*!

His brain went around in furious circles until…

His eyes narrowed. He felt fury starting like a hot rock in his stomach and flooding over the rest of his body. He was so enraged that every fiber in his neck stood out like a gnarled tree trunk.

He said a name half under his breath.

That…that… He couldn't think of an expletive traitorous enough!

He threw open the wardrobe and pulled something down from the top right hand corner. *This will put the fear of God into him!*

The three girls were taking laundry down off the line as Edwin stood by telling a funny story. They heard the front door slam and moments later they could all see Jake on his horse in a full gallop down the lane.

They all looked at each other with puzzled expressions.

"But I didn't iron his other shirt yet. And we were all going to eat lunch before..." Catrina took a few steps toward him as he rode away. "He wouldn't leave for San Francisco without saying goodbye, would he?" She turned toward Julia who was also in the process of taking laundry down off the line.

"He has a very stormy disposition," Julia tried to answer lightly, but internally she felt afraid.

Jake rode up to the General Store, he leapt off the horse and burst through the front door.

"Where's Dan?" he nearly shouted at Mrs. O'Neill. She was alone in the store, up on a step stool, arranging cans on a shelf.

"Oh, Jake!" She almost lost hold on a can. "I think he's over at Garret's place. There was another shipment that came in this afternoon."

Jake left his horse at the General Store and stomped his way across the street and around the corner to the Dragón. As he was almost to the front door he caught a glimpse of Dan's wagon through the alley.

There was Dan, standing in the back of his wagon handing out crates to Rob, the barkeep. When Dan saw

Jake he started to smile, but stopped when he saw Jake's expression.

"You *stole* from me?" Jake growled out. It was an accusation, not a question. "You were my best friend and you came into my house and *stole* from me? From *me*?"

Rob backed away toward the building with the crate. Dan backed up a step or two on the wagon. "I have no idea what you're talking about," he said, but his face and voice screamed *Liar!*

"What's this?" Jake pulled out the small wooden box. As he held it up, almost crushing it in his hand, he watched full realization flood over Dan's face. It was as good as a confession. He threw the box with such force that it pinged up off the wagon's backboard and hit Dan in the small of the back.

"Aaa!" he called out, as he bent backwards in pain.

"You're the only other person in the *world* who knew about that spot." He took a step forward and drew out a gun. This was the gun his father *should* have taken when he went out to face those men that day.

Dan looked like he was going into shock. "You're not going to shoot me!" He held his hands out in front of him, "Jake! Jake, I didn't have any choice! This would kill my mom! No, please!" Dan sat down in the wagon and scooted as far back as he could go.

Jake's arm dropped slightly. His mind went back in time to when Dan's father had been murdered. He remembered Mrs. O'Neill becoming thinner and thinner almost starving herself to death out of grief.

He gritted his teeth and raised his arm again. "After all we've been through together? How could you!"

"I was so behind." Dan's fear turned into sobbing.

"Garret was going to take our store, our house, everything." He put one hand over his face. "I couldn't get any more credit with the bank. I didn't know what else to do…"

Jake tried to raise the gun again, but the consuming anger that had driven him this far had been cooled by Dan's pleas. He shouted, "You took away *our* last chance to save *yourself*? *We're* going to lose everything now—because of you! You…"

Then his mind recalled the face of his own mother as they hid in that hole so many years ago. The sound of the gunshots, her eyes paralyzed with fear, the blood that trickled down from her lip. The memory of that man as he stood coldly over his pa's body and shot him a second time came back with such clarity that Jake gasped.

I'm that man. It's me now.

Did that man feel as angry as Jake did now?

Did he feel as *justified* as Jake did to hold a gun out and squeeze the trigger?

"What's going on here, gentlemen?" It was Garret.

Rob had apparently gone in to get him.

"This is none of your business!" Jake turned to him. He was beginning to shake, "Stay out of it!"

"It's my business since it's happening on my property." Garret took a step forward and made a curious motion with his hand. He fanned his fingers out in the air as if he was playing the piano, right over his holstered pistol.

That hand motion.

Jake dropped his arm. An icy wash of childhood fear rolled over him.

That day at the saloon when he had brought the papers. Garret had done it then too. He could see it in his mind now.

He was a young boy again. He could feel the weight of the trap door over his head. He watched as the man in the white hat put his right hand down next to the gun holster. His mind zoomed in like a telescope and there was that motion. There was Garret's face. The sound of the shot came back to him with a roar.

Jake's arm rose up again, slowly, deliberately. This time his pistol was aimed squarely at Garret's head. Even Garret had not anticipated this. He put both hands out in front of himself. "Now if this is about your land, we can..."

"It was *you?*" Jake was astounded. He barely noticed Dan taking advantage of his distracted state to scramble out of the wagon to the opposite side.

He couldn't believe that the murderer of his father had been right here in town under his nose all these years!

"It was me, what?" Garret asked with genuine confusion as he took a step backwards.

"*You* shot my father." Jake watched him intensely. A hardly noticeable ripple of concern flashed over Garret's features but then it was gone, as if it had never been there at all.

"That is absolute nonsense," Garret countered in his logical, monotone voice. He continued to back around to his right.

For some reason, Garret's denial threw fuel on the long dormant fury. "I was *there*. I *watched* you do it."

"That's impossible. You..." Garret continued backing.

"I watched you, you *monster*! You shot him from your horse. Then you got down and shot him again."

That stopped Garret in his tracks. His eyes slightly widened before jerking almost imperceptibly to the left.

This was the moment Jake had been waiting for all these

years. He had his father's murderer in the sites of his gun. He'd played it out a million times in his mind—he had longed for it with all his soul!

He opened his mouth to say something but all his carefully rehearsed speeches were long forgotten.

Nothing else mattered now. This was justice.

Jake squeezed the trigger, but in the same instance felt his right arm being ripped out of the socket. He spun around and fell like a ragdoll. Incredible pain was spreading from the right side of his chest like he'd been set on fire.

He knew Garret hadn't drawn his gun. *Who shot me?*

He was on his side in the dust but his arm was useless so he had no way to get up. He couldn't even seen if he'd gotten Garret.

Glancing down at his shirt he saw blood soaking and spreading like an out of control fire. It was flowing out and pooling in the dust. There was a thumb-sized hole in his chest that was foaming and buzzing.

My lung is gone. I'm as good as dead.

Dan ran around to him and screamed, "Get the Doc! Get the Doc!" He ripped off his own shirt and pressed it against Jake's chest.

With each breath, the pain was growing more intense. His chest felt like a giant barrel had rolled on top of him. He was being crushed! His face and neck were bulging with effort. Dan's face was starting to get smaller and smaller down a long, black tunnel.

Now I'm going to die.

Now I'm going to die just like Pa did.

No, another voice within his mind said. *Not like Pa at all—I'm going to hell.*

The horror of it spread over him.

I'm going to hell.

In that instant, not only did he know it was all true but he also realized with crystal clarity that he had *always* known.

Of course, God existed.

Of course, every man would face His Judgment.

He had lied to himself.

He could now see the flimsy nature of the arguments he had erected around himself—all of them together were no more substantial than a cobweb blowing in the wind. Each "reason" he'd ever dreamed up could now be seen clearly for what it was: a paper-thin excuse to live in rebellion to God. Now all those slap-dash, superficial pretexts had melted away in an instant.

He knew he was doomed and that he deserved it.

Oh no!

I'm going to hell! He gulped at the air and began to fight his way back up as if from the bottom of a pond. *I can't die now! I don't want to go to hell!*

Oh God! Oh God, give me another chance! I don't want to go to hell!

His vision became more and more clouded as he struggled to hold on to consciousness. The buzzing in his chest was intolerable and the pain was getting worse by the moment. He felt like his head was going to explode and he couldn't breathe!

"Don't let me die!" he choked out to Dan.

Doc Thomas came running with his medical bag but Jake was gone.

room

Where am I?

Jake sat up in an unfamiliar room. It was quite large and yet this bed was the only piece of furniture in it. The walls were austere and there were no windows. Only a single door at the extreme opposite end of the room marked the walls.

Why am I in this bed?

A bald man in a black coat stood at the foot of the bed looking down.

Who is that?

Jake started to ask the man, but something stopped him. This did not feel natural. The man didn't look up. He didn't speak. He just stood there.

The man's hands were clasped in front of him. The long, spidery fingers were laced and still, ending in jagged, cracked and torn nails, filthy with black soil.

Who was this man? What had just been happening? Why was he in this room?

Jake cleared his throat, hoping the man would look up. He didn't.

Something was very wrong here. Jake's heart was

beginning to race.

"Um…Excuse me?"

Nothing.

"Excuse me, sir?"

Jake felt a growing terror as the man slowly lifted his head. His cheeks were sunken, and his pale, waxy skin was stretched thinly over his skull. Eyes, so dark they nearly appeared black, stared out motionless…soulless. They stared directly into Jake's eyes…piercing him. However, those eyes were *not human.*

His heart was pounding. He had to get out of here! He tried to clamber backward to get the whole bed between him and that thing but something was wrong. He couldn't move. He tried violently to kick, but neither of his legs would move. He went to rip the blanket off, but he couldn't move his right arm.

He ripped the blanket off and to his horror he saw that his legs had sunken into the bed and taken hold like tree roots. And perhaps even worse, his right arm had grown into his chest.

"No!" he screamed out. Deep down, some logical part of his mind realized this had to be a nightmare. "Wake up!" he screamed at himself.

He began to slap his own face. "Wake up! Wake up!"

The figure at the end of the bed unlaced its fingers and started toward him. The jagged nails reached toward his hands. It sealed around his wrist like a block of frozen meat. Now he couldn't move at all.

"Wake up! Wake up!" he screamed even more frantically.

The door at the far end of the room slowly opened and another one of them walked in. More followed. They were all carrying firewood. They brought it close and stacked it around his bed. The original phantasm continued to hold his wrist in its immovable, icy grip.

Jake was in hysterics. He screamed. He squirmed and writhed to get free.

Another one of the monsters grabbed the back of his neck with its frozen fingers, and held his head like a vice as it poured a cup of kerosene into his mouth. The odor was toxic. He gagged and spit, swallowed, and gagged again. The rest of the kerosene was poured all over him and the bed.

He heard something then he smelled it. It was the crackle of a newly lit fire. They were going to burn him alive in this bed!

"I'm in hell!" Jake screamed. "I'm in hell!"

Julia lowered his head back onto the pillow. "Thank God, not yet," she whispered. He had knocked the water all over himself but she thought she had gotten at least a little bit into his mouth.

"Can I let go of his hand now?" Summer asked.

"You can try. But if he starts hitting himself again, we're going to have to hold him," she replied.

"It's really not hard," Summer said sadly as she carefully lay his arm back down. "I've never seen him so weak."

Jakes eyes were frantically jerking around the room. He alternately moaned or cried continuously. She could only imagine the horrors this burning fever was inventing.

Julia's eyes stung as she wiped her own tears. She had cried so much over the last several days that her eyes felt like dry, scratchy saltblocks. How she still had any tears left, was beyond her understanding.

Dear Father, she prayed for the millionth time, *please have mercy on him. Please restore him to health, or if not, then please get him to his right mind long enough that he might repent and place his faith in the Savior.*

I don't know how I can possibly go on if he dies in his sins. Please Father, have mercy!

She continued to cry as she put another cold cloth on his burning head. He shuddered and screamed at her, "God help me! God help me!"

The terror in his eyes was palpable and shot through her own heart. She wondered what he was seeing. Could God actually be using this somehow? As much as he had been screaming these past few days about being in hell, she *did* wonder if there might not be some spiritual aspect to this.

Whatever you need to do, Father, whatever you need to do to bring him to yourself. She sat down beside the bed and wept, *Lord have mercy!*

———•—

He opened his eyes again. Time didn't seem to be passing properly. It was excruciatingly slow and unbelievably fast in the same moment. The window on the wall grew to the size of a barn and his feet at the end of the bed shrank down smaller than pebbles. His mother, sitting beside his bed remained the normal size but suddenly the bed was ten feet tall. He turned his head. Without warning, his ma had turned into Catrina asleep in the chair.

He awoke again. He was freezing, his teeth chattering. It must have been ten below! But Summer was pulling the blanket *off* him and his mother was putting an icy wet rag on his head. Were they trying to *torture* him? Their faces were pinched with concern. He wondered why they looked that way.

He kept waking and sleeping...so many times. The

doctor was there and then he wasn't. Ma was standing over him at night then Summer was wiping his forehead, now Catrina was spooning broth into his mouth. He had no idea how much time was passing. It was day, it was night, it was day again.

Monsters. Devils. Loved ones transforming into hideous creatures. This was like a long, drawn out nightmare from which he was unable to completely wake.

thirst

Thirst. He was *so* thirsty. He felt like he was dying of thirst.

"Thirsty," he croaked out.

On the floor, someone stirred then sat up. It was Catrina. She had been sleeping on a pallet of blankets next to his bed.

"Thirsty."

She began to cry. "Yes, here." *Thank you, God,* she thought as she held the cup of water to his mouth. He swallowed gratefully.

"I'll go get your ma and Summer!" She put the cup down and ran out of the room.

He had been ready to ask where they were, but as soon as the door opened and he was able to see out into the room beyond, he recognized they were in Dan's house.

Why am I here?

He felt disoriented, everything mixed up in his head. For some reason, the thought of Dan didn't sit well with him. He had a vague feeling of anger but nothing to connect it with.

Ma came in still in her nightgown and shawl, smoothing

her hair. Her eyes were so puffy and her nose was bright red.

Have we all been sick? Is that why we're here?

"Thank God!" his ma cried out. She came forward like she wanted to swallow him up, but only placed a light kiss on his forehead. She put her cheek on his forehead a moment longer. "It's gone down, thank God!"

He tried to move his right arm to push himself up, but it was stuck. He used his other hand to lift the sheet. His whole chest was bound in white linen bandages and his right arm was bound across his waist.

Did I hurt myself somehow? What's going on?

He moved both feet—they felt fine. He felt around with his left hand—his face and neck seemed fine.

"What's happened?" he spoke in a whisper. Everything seemed dim and shadowy. He shakily tried to push himself up with his left hand.

"No!" all three of them said in chorus.

"Summer, get dressed and go get Doc Thomas."

"Yes, ma'am!" she ran out of the room with a grin that went to her ears.

"You don't *move* till the doctor gets here," Catrina said firmly, but happily. She held a trembling hand above his chest, as if she were determined to hold him down in the bed. "I'm so glad you're alive." Happy tears were pooling in her eyes and flowing over even before she blinked.

She got down very close to his face. "I didn't tell you before, but I want you to know..." Tears came out of her eyes, and landed on his cheek. "I love you Jacob. I love you."

She had thought about it so many times while he was writhing in fever. She knew he couldn't understand her but she had told him anyway, in whispers, whenever he was still.

The doctor had said he had come through the surgery very strong. She had felt so encouraged, but a few days later, everything changed. The wound had started draining a thin, watery, foul-smelling liquid. After the examination, Doc Thomas had said that meant the wound was "malignant."

She remembered him taking his glasses off and looking Julia in the face. "I'm so sorry, Mrs. Forester, but Jake will not survive this," he'd said.

At the sound of those words, Catrina had begun to faint. Her father stepped up behind her and had to nearly carry her to a nearby chair.

Her whole life...this new life she'd been given...was *dying* in front of her. First her mother, then dear Rebekah, and now her very heart and soul was going to die.

She realized Jake had become her life. She couldn't live without him. Even as her father stood behind her, lovingly patting her shoulder, she was contemplating suicide.

Then Julia turned back to the doctor as Summer grasped her and cried into her shoulder.

"With all due respect, Doctor...*God* will make that decision, not you."

Doc Thomas acquiesced, "Quite right, dear lady." He put his glasses back on and then put his hand on her shoulder for a comforting moment.

Catrina came back to the present and looked over to Julia across the bed. She had her eyes closed and her hands clasped to her chest. She was rocking back and forth and whispering her prayers of thanksgiving into the air. The joy in her face was transporting.

"What's happened to me?" she heard Jake ask again.

"...and the bullet went in next to your shoulder blade and came out here," Doc indicated the spot on his chest. "Your lung collapsed and if it hadn't been for Dan plugging up the hole with his shirt, I believe your other lung might have collapsed as well."

I guess he owed me that much after sneaking into my house and stealing from me, Jake thought bitterly. As he had climbed out of that initial fog, his memory was coming back to him.

Doc Thomas put the stethoscope against his chest again and had him do some deep breathing. "It's astonishing really. I cleaned up the wound as best I could in surgery but I honestly didn't expect you to live through the fevers."

The doctor packed his things into his bag and snapped it closed. "But as Mrs. Forester reminded me, it is God who ultimately holds those decisions in His hand."

Catrina sat close by him holding his good hand as his ma walked the doctor out. Hearing that he was going to have to stay in bed for at least a *week* before he would even be allowed to stand up was like getting a prison sentence. The doctor said the healing seemed to be going well, but if he didn't remain nearly immobile, he would re-open the wound.

Now that the doctor was gone, he could see his ma and Mrs. O'Neill talking in hushed tones near the doorway. She handed Ma a tray of soup and bread and Ma carried it to his room.

It made him angry just seeing the interaction. There was his ma thinking the O'Neill's were so nice when she had no idea what had really gone on. He didn't want to stay another minute under the same roof with Dan.

As soon as she placed the tray in front of him, an idea occurred, "Ma, I'd like to find out if Doc Thomas thinks I'm well enough to go home. It's not that far and I'd be much more comfortable finishing out this waiting in my own bed."

Catrina and his mother exchanged looks. "Would you mind if we talked alone?" Julia asked Catrina.

"Of course not." Catrina squeezed Jake's hand lightly and left.

His ma closed the door behind her.

Julia knew this was going to be hard for him to hear. "Jake, we can't go home."

She sat on the side of his bed and began to explain. "The circuit judge came through while you were in the fevers. I had to go to the hearing in your place. I had to tell the judge we hadn't been able to find the title. And I can tell you it didn't help matters when Garret told the judge you tried to shoot him over this whole thing."

"I didn't shoot him over the land!" Jake sat up straighter but felt a spike of pain in his chest. "He's the one who murdered pa."

"What?" Julia was shocked. "How do you know?"

"It's this hand motion he does. I guess he does it just before he draws his gun." Jake demonstrated. "For some reason, when I saw him do it the other day everything just connected. I remembered seeing the shooter do it the day pa was killed. And when I confronted him with details it showed on his face. I *know* it was him."

Julia sighed and looked off in space.

"I almost got him," Jake muttered under his breath.

"Well, thank God you didn't!" Julia stood up, clearly

appalled. "You'd be going to jail for murder!"

"Who shot me?" Jake demanded right back.

"I don't know. I don't think anyone knows for sure."

"Do you know it was probably *Dan*?" he growled at her.

"That's ridiculous. He…" Jake cut her off.

"You have *no idea* what he did! Why do you think I took the gun in the first place?"

"Oh yes, I *do* know what he did," she countered, her own temper on the rise. "And I'm a *hundred* times more ashamed of what *you* did! You took your father's gun—the one he bought to *protect* his family—so that you could *shoot your best friend*! And all that over a stupid rock!

"Yes, you heard me!" She felt she was going to spiral out of control, but she was almost to the point that she didn't care. "A *stupid rock*! You think some dumb rock is more important than a man's *life*? You're no better than the man who murdered your pa! Do you hear me? You're *no better* than Garret!"

She stomped over to his bedside. "Don't you see your father was *murdered* over the *same* dumb *rock*!" She almost overturned the tray on him in fury, but stopped herself just short and stormed out.

Julia felt disgusted and furious with her son. Her gratitude to God for saving his life had seemingly flown out the window.

How could he do this?

If she had known how desperate the O'Neill's were for money, she would have given them the nugget herself. Oh, how different everything would be right now if she could have done that.

Why couldn't God have allowed that *to happen instead?*

The O'Neill's had done so much for them by giving them a place to stay when the judge ordered them off their land. Yet living in their home was a tremendously uncomfortable situation.

It didn't seem to matter how many times Julia told them all was forgiven. It didn't seem to matter how many times she explained how ashamed she was that Jake would merely *point* a gun at Dan, much less threaten him. She tried to express how grateful she was that they had opened their home but nothing helped.

Dan was cut to the heart with grief over what he had done and he was trying every way he knew how to make up for it. Single-handedly, he moved all their things from their home to the building his family had used for storage. He had even nearly broken his back trying to move the printing press as well, but at over two thousand pounds, it just wasn't possible for one man. So he'd chained their barn doors closed and padlocked them.

He worked himself to death to get everything just right but he could barely look Julia in the eye. And he never ate meals with them. He seemed to be trying to expunge his sin through penance.

Kylie was deeply ashamed. She knew that Dan had paid off their debts and their home, with what he had stolen so she was acting as though it wasn't even her home anymore. She wore her work apron all day long and wouldn't even sit down to relax in her favorite chair. Several times, Julia had seen her in the back hallway sitting on a wooden stool as if she were a servant waiting for her next assignment.

Whatever friendship might have existed between Kylie and Julia, was gone. "The lender" and "the debtor," or maybe "the thief" and "the jailor" had replaced it.

Julia felt ashamed every moment of the day and then she felt angry at having to feel ashamed. She was beginning to take all that anger and shame and pound it like a wedge between herself and her Savior.

murderer

is mother's words wounded him like a blow.

She was right.

Even now his mouth could formulate a thousand justifications for what he had done and he could shout them all back at her. But he knew she was right.

I am no better than Pa's murderer.

He languished on that thought. A deep despair began to fill his breast. He reached up with his left hand and felt the dressing over his wound. *I shouldn't even be* alive *right now. Doc said I should be dead.*

If I hadn't survived, where would I be? he wondered. *Just a sack of rotting meat buried in the ground? Like a candle snuffed out and gone? Or would I actually be in hell?*

The gruesome fever hallucinations flooded into his mind and he shuddered. He wondered if that's what hell was really like, if there really was such a place. He tried to remember what his ma had told him about it. There was supposedly fire, of course, and he seemed to remember something about worms that wouldn't die but he couldn't recall her saying anything about spiders.

Of course God existed.

Of course every man would face His Judgment.

That moment of crystal clarity suddenly came back to him. He remembered looking down at his shirt and seeing the blood foaming around the hole in his chest. And he remembered how knifelike—how powerful—those words were.

Of course God existed.

Of course every man would face His Judgment.

In that moment, he had known he was going to hell.

True, the words didn't seem to carry as much weight as they had before. What had seemed so sharp then, was now a little dim, a little far away. Even so, he could still remember the force it had carried in that moment.

Had his mind conjured it all up out of fear? That must be it. After all, his mother had been telling him for years that he was on his way to hell. That would be enough to scare anyone! Surely, that was the answer.

But something niggled at the back of his mind.

He brushed it off.

It returned.

He swept it aside.

It did not leave.

He denied it.

Yet it remained.

He could barely bring himself to admit it.

He *knew* it was true.

There it was.

Something in him *knew* it. And as he sat thinking about it he realized that if he kept pushing, he *could* push that knowledge down so far that he wouldn't have to deal with it anymore. He *could* push it down to the point that he would eventually be able to forget it was there. After all, that's what he had done for the majority of his life.

But there it was.

Of course God existed.

Of course every man would face His Judgment.

The more he pondered it, the more power those words seemed to have.

What if it were true?

Then the fact he was alive right now was a second chance. He had asked God for a second chance. Was there actually a God up there who heard him and granted his request?

He looked around the room. There it was, the family Bible, sitting on a chair beside the bed. He scooted to the side and began to lean over.

He stopped.

He realized if he went forward now there would be no turning back.

He would be admitting he'd been wrong, and his mother right, all these years.

His pride bucked.

He sat back and listened to the argument in his own head.

Don't give her the satisfaction! You'll never hear the end of it! She's been trying to use this religion garbage to control you for years. Are you finally caving in? Are you like a horse that's finally been broken? Has she finally beaten you into obedience? You milksop! You're letting her lead you around by the nose, you weakling! You don't really believe any of this, do you?

"Shut up," he said aloud to the empty room.

I'm turning into a lunatic. I'm talking out loud to myself.

He looked across at the Bible and felt his own determination growing. No one, *including himself*, was going to tell him he couldn't look at that Bible if he wanted to! He scooted the rest of the way and leaned over to grab it.

It felt a little awkward, since he only had use of his left hand. But as he brought it to his lap, it fell open to the newspaper clipping.

As he took it out he remembered that night, out on the porch, so long ago—at least it seemed like a long time ago. Ma had put it in his hand with so much hope in her face and he had stubbornly refused to even look at it.

As he was about to read it, he noticed that some words on the open Bible pages had been carefully underlined in pencil: "...the LORD revengeth; the LORD revengeth, and is furious; the LORD will take vengeance on his adversaries, and he reserveth wrath for his enemies."

Revenge.

That's what his own heart had been set on for so long.

He looked down to the next place that was underlined. "The mountains quake at him, and the hills melt, and the earth is burned at his presence, yea, the world, and all that dwell therein. Who can stand before his indignation? and who can abide in the fierceness of his anger? his fury is poured out like fire, and the rocks are thrown down by him."

It sounded like God was even *more* angry than he was.

He re-read, and his eyes stopped on, "he reserveth wrath for his enemies."

Immediately he thought of Garret.

God is reserving "wrath" for Garret.

That felt great to know.

God is reserving "wrath" for me.

Now that did not conjure the same feelings at *all*.

He looked over to the newspaper clipping. He remembered his ma had held it like a treasure. It looked so unimpressive—just a little piece of yellow paper.

"Everything changed that night," her words came back to him. "Your father became a new person."

He began to read.

My, hearer, does not the Law of God convince you of sin this morning? Under the hand of God's Spirit does it not make you feel that you have been guilty, that you deserve to be lost, that you have incurred the fierce anger of God?

Yes, I know I'm guilty. And I know God is angry. But what am I supposed to do about it? I can't go back in time.

Have you not broken these Ten Commandments; even in the letter have you not broken them? Who is there among you who has always honored his father and mother?

He cringed. *Just the opposite. Ma is ashamed of me. I've shamed her in front of the whole town.*

Who is there among us who has always spoken the truth? Have we not sometimes borne false witness against our neighbor?

Jake was a natural born liar. He could lie as easily as tell the truth and he secretly prided himself on the fact that no one could tell the difference. The hundreds of lies he'd told his mother over the years came back to haunt him. Even the Bible he held in his hands, with its charred edge, shouted his guilt. He winced.

Though you have never killed, yet we are told, he that is angry with his brother is a murderer ...

Jake suddenly remembered reading almost this exact same thing that day in the barn. It hadn't made any sense to him at the time but now he could fully see the truth of it.

Out-of-control rage drove him to get the pistol out of the wardrobe ride into town like some gun waving vigilantly and almost *murder* his dearest childhood friend.

He could see the truth of it—the man who squeezes the trigger is not that far removed from the man who *wishes he had the guts* to squeeze the trigger. Anger was the seed from which murders grew.

God counts me as a murderer.

He was starting to feel a little panicked. What did God want out of him? How could he ever make up for all this?

This Law does not only mean what it says in words, but it has deep things hidden in its bowels. It says, "Thou shalt not commit adultery," but it means, as Jesus has it, "He that looks on a woman to lust after her has committed adultery with her already in his heart."

Images of women he had slept with flashed across his mind. He knew that was wrong. However, the thought that God judged even his lust-filled *thoughts* to be a form of adultery astonished him.

"That's impossible!" he said aloud.

He thought to himself that he might be able to get control of his temper and he would surely never again visit a prostitute once he and Catrina were married. But the concept that *every* lustful thought he would *ever* have—for the rest of his *life*—would be counted against him by God as *adultery*? It was too much.

"That's impossible," he muttered hopelessly.

It says, "Thou shalt not take the name of the Lord thy God in vain," it means that we should reverence God in every place, and have his fear before our eyes, and should always pay respect unto his ordinances and evermore walk in his fear and love.

Jake thought about how casually, and continually, he had used "God" to "damn" this or that. Every guy he knew did it except around the ladies. He even remembered a dirty joke where God's name, taken in vain, was the punch line. Until this moment, he never cared but now he saw that he was guilty of a serious crime against an angry God.

Blasphemy. That's what Ma called it. I'm a blasphemer.

He turned away from the clipping. He didn't know if he could go on reading any more of this. It was too much to take. His eyes flitted back to the open Bible and unintentionally landed on the underlined verse, "who can abide in the fierceness of his anger? his fury is poured out like fire."

He took in his breath. He was actually afraid.

Ay, my brethren, surely there is not one here so foolhardy in self-righteousness as to say, "I am innocent." The spirit of the Law condemns us. Oh, are you this morning, my hearer, sad, because of sin? Do you feel that you have been guilty? Do you acknowledge your transgression? Do you confess your wandering?

I'm guilty. I'm guilty and doomed.

Oh! you that are self-righteous, let me speak to you this morning with just a word or two of terrible and burning earnestness. Remember, sirs, the day is coming when a crowd more vast than this shall be assembled on the plains of Earth; when on a great white throne the Savior, Judge of men, shall sit.

Judgment day.

Now, He is come; the book is opened; the glory of heaven is displayed, rich with triumphant love, and burning with unquenchable vengeance; ten thousand angels are on either hand; and *you* are standing to be tried.

I'm the one on trial and God's going to have vengeance on me—"unquenchable vengeance."

Now, self-righteous man, tell me now that you went to church three times a day! Come, man, tell me now that you kept all the Commandments! Tell me now that you are not guilty!

Jake had no such delusions.

Murderer. Blasphemer. Adulterer. Liar.

How am I ever going to make up for all this?

If you would know how we must be saved, hear this —you must come with nothing of your own to Christ. Christ has kept the Law. You are to have His righteousness to be your righteousness. Christ has suffered in the stead of all who repent. His punishment is to stand instead of your being punished.

It couldn't really be that simple. Could it?

It sounded too easy.

"Come with nothing of your own." "Christ has kept the Law." "Christ has suffered…in the stead of all who repent." All who "repent." So I have to repent. But what does that mean?

And through faith in the sanctification and atonement of Christ, you are to be saved. Come, then, you weary and heavy laden, bruised and mangled by the Fall, come then, you sinners, come, then, you moralists, come, then, all you that have broken God's Law and feel it, leave your own trusts and come to Jesus, He will take you in, give you a spotless robe of righteousness, and make you His forever.

"God," he closed his eyes and said aloud. "I really don't understand all this, but I know I need forgiveness. I'm guilty.

"I know you see me as no different as a murderer." Tears

were starting to pool in his eyes at the thought that he really was no different than Garret. The only thing separating the two of them was that his bullet had been knocked off course in mid-flight.

"And I'm a liar too. I'm probably one of the worst liars that's ever lived." He thought again of knocking this very Bible into the fire. He realized he was going to have to tell his ma the truth about it.

What else did he need to own up to?

"I'm also a blasphemer. I've used your name in vain more times than I can count. And I'm an adulterer—many times. And even in my mind, I guess I'm guilty of adultery there, too,however that works."

There were so many sins, he didn't know if he could even think of them all.

"Look, I know you have every right to hate me..." he swallowed and then forced the words out, "because I've hated you.

"I admit it. I've hated you because you let Pa get shot. And you let him die. You could have protected him, but you didn't," he looked up at the ceiling, "I still don't understand why. I don't know if I ever will."

He took a breath and wiped the tears off his face. "But even if I never understand, I still need forgiveness."

He paused. He listened. He wondered if he'd said everything he should.

"Please...I don't know what else to say.

"God, if Jesus dying on the Cross can somehow stand in my place, for all that I've done, please do it!" He squeezed his eyes shut and balled his one good hand into a fist, as if his effort could somehow make it happen. "Please..."

chapter

Catrina did not understand this joyful celebration she was witnessing. Just a few hours ago, they had all heard an indistinct shouting match between Julia and Jake, followed by a slammed door. Julia had come out of the room with lightning bolts crackling off her and everyone had given her a wide berth. Catrina knew about Jake's temper but had never seen Julia that way.

But she hardly had time to worry about it because now both Julia and Summer were crying with joy and embracing Jake in his bed. And Jake, for his part, was crying and laughing at the same time. Catrina really didn't understand what was going on but she was very glad that whatever the argument had been about, it seemed to now be beautifully resolved.

"Catrina," Jake called out to her. She was standing in the doorway, feeling almost shy at the display of emotion. He held out his good arm in her direction. "Come here."

He wiped off some of his tears, and then took her hand firmly. "I have not been the man I've pretended to be. But now I think I am, or at least I will be." Jake laughed aloud at how silly that sentence sounded.

She laughed along with him although she hardly knew why. "I don't understand," she said, shaking her head.

He realized he needed to take his time and do this right. "Ma? Summer? I need to talk to Catrina alone."

———

Julia was flying higher than she had ever been in her life! She could hardly believe that just a few hours ago she had taken her focus *so far* off the Lord.

She had given herself license to explode in a bitter, angry rant—well knowing that what she was doing was wrong. Yes, she could have controlled herself. Yes, she had felt the pull of the Holy Spirit. But like so many other times in her life, she had just ignored the Lord. She had willfully sinned, in rage. Now she felt ashamed. She ran back to the Cross with all her might.

There I was acting like an idiot, God, while you were working so mightily! You were answering the prayer of my heart! Oh God, I'm so sorry. I'm so sorry, Lord. Thank you for the precious blood of your Son poured out for me. Thank you for the forgiveness you provide. Thank you, Father.

She and Summer had never taken the clothes down off the line with such elation. They were both nearly euphoric, having waited and prayed for this for so long.

Summer began to sing energetically: "Praise Him! Praise Him! Jesus, our blessed Redeemer! Sing, O Earth, His wonderful love proclaim!"

Julia joined in: "Hail Him! Hail Him! Highest archangels in glory; Strength and honor give to His holy Name!"

The two of them had never sung so robustly and if the O'Neill's home hadn't been in such a public place, they might have even danced around the yard.

Julia couldn't stop closing her eyes and thanking God for this miracle, over and over again. Because that's what it really was. There had been so many days of praying and so many nights of crying. Now it had finally happened.

My son is saved! Nothing else matters. If we lose the house, the land, everything, I will praise you, Father! You saved my boy! Thank you, Lord Jesus!

father

As her father helped her climb up into the buggy, Catrina thought back over what a puzzling day it had been. What a whirlwind of emotions! Now here she was heading back to San Francisco with her father.

Jake had just had some kind of religious experience. He had spent about a half an hour explaining to her what an awful person he had been and how God was forgiving him. She didn't really understand why he thought he was so bad since most of the things he was confessing to her sounded like any normal human being.

She had heard of people seeing their lives "pass before their eyes" when they were close to death, so guessed that this whole thing must have had something to do with the injury and the fevers. However, whatever the significance, his mother and sister were certainly ecstatic about it. Moreover, she was glad for him too—whatever it was, because it obviously made him very happy.

She smoothed her skirts down as her father climbed in next to her. Actually, the timing of this trip couldn't have been better if Catrina had set it up herself. Up to this point, she had successfully cloistered herself inside the O'Neill's house. However, since Jake was now on the mend, it would become impossible for her to continue to turn down her father's requests to take walks together in town. Now it was more important than ever that she not be seen in town, especially by Garret.

Because of Jake's injury, Edwin had already stayed away from the jewelry store much longer than originally planned. Now he *had* to get back to San Francisco and since he and Catrina had been able to spend precious little time together, it only made sense to everyone that she would take this trip with him.

She was relieved as her father took the reins and directed the horses out of town. But suddenly two young men stepped out from between buildings across the street. She turned her head quickly away—but not quickly enough. She recognized them both as former customers.

"Miss Catrina!" they both exclaimed, as they jogged up, taking off their hats.

Her father stopped the horses out of courtesy.

"We had no idea you were back!" one said.

"It's so good to see your arm's all healed up," the other said genuinely.

"This is my father!" she blurted out to them in a panic.

A moment of silence passed.

"Oh," said one.

The other one awkwardly rubbed the back of his neck and then reached his hand out to shake. "Nice to meet you, Mr...."

"Edwin Salterson," he replied, shaking the young man's hand. The other young man shook his hand as well.

"Uh...well," the first one put his hat back on as he began to back away. "So nice to see you again, Miss Catrina."

She nodded toward him willing them with all her might to leave quickly.

"Good day," the other youth said as he replaced his hat and joined his friend.

The two went down the street together, taking turns at backwards glances.

"What did they mean about your arm?" her father asked her, clearly puzzled. "And how is it that you know those two young men and yet they don't know your last name?" He clucked at the horses in the hired buggy and they started on the road to San Jose.

How am I supposed to answer him?

She closed her eyes slowly. She had dreaded this moment for so long. Her only consolation was that it would only be the two of them until they arrived in San Jose to catch the San Francisco stagecoach.

"Papa, there are some things I need to tell you."

misfiled

"You realize that I can't actually destroy the Land Commission's copy." the pudgy, balding man leaned in closer to Garret across the table. "The best I could do was misfile it."

Garret narrowed his eyes. He'd already paid this fumbling idiot twice what he was worth. He would have had this free and clear if Matthews hadn't up and died of a heart attack. Now those carefully orchestrated portraits of him were worthless. This whole plan had taken entirely too long to execute.

Sensing Garret's extreme displeasure, the man almost whined. "There are just too many workers and the stacks are only open at the start of business each day. I would be seen. There's no way to take files out of there. It's done that way on purpose."

The man nervously babbled on as he wiped his perspiring forehead. "But don't worry, he won't be back. It just so happens that the *time* it was filed exactly coincides with the fire of '52. Can you believe it? What luck, huh?"

Garret took a drink. He wondered if this dunce had already outlived his usefulness. He stared at him without speaking and purposefully drew out the awkward silence.

Then he folded his hands slowly and leaned slightly forward. "If *that* is the best you can do, then you will check *frequently* to *make sure* it hasn't been located and re-filed." His voice was like polished marble—heavy and cold.

"Oh, yes sir...I..."

"And you will contact me by telegraph if there are any other issues that require my presence," he commanded with force.

"Yes, Mr. Garret."

somewhere

She still had her face turned slightly away from her father. "...and staying with Rebekah was probably one of the greatest turning points in my life. She was such a good person. Her death was very hard to take. I've often wondered why God didn't kill me instead."

She sniffed and dabbed at her puffy eyes. "She taught me a lot about religion. And then Jake and his family have taught me even more."

"But," she said in a warning tone, "Jake's family knows *nothing* about my former life. Jake never once stepped foot into the Dragón. He's a good man, Papa and he can *never* know what I once was," she went on as she wiped a lone tear from her cheek. "Their whole family can *never* know."

Her father pulled up the horses.

She waited for him to speak.

"I am so *sorry* for what you've been through." She could hear the pain in his voice and she turned to look at him for the first time since they had left town. He looked like he'd aged ten years.

He wrapped the reins and put his face in his hands. His voice sounded anguished. "My darling Treasure," he used the pet name she had not heard since she was a little girl. "Oh, how I wish that I could have protected you from all of it."

She couldn't believe he was blaming himself. This was not the reaction she had imagined.

"Papa, it's my fault. They were my choices, not yours."

"But you were too young to be allowed to make such choices. It was my duty to protect you." He was softly crying now. "So many times I've gone over it in my mind. I knew you were angry about your mother's death. I knew you thought it was my fault for bringing her home from the hospital. But the doctors told me there was *nothing more they could do.* I wanted your mother to be able to die at home, in her own bed. However, I knew you were angry. I should have guessed you would run away. I should have done something to keep you from leaving."

"It was *my* fault, Papa." She was crying with him now. "I had my mind made up and I honestly don't think you could have stopped me."

They put their arms around each other and cried together.

He pulled back and looked deeply into her eyes. "I'm so glad you're alive and safe. I'm so thankful to God for His providence."

"I love you, Catrina." He put one of his hands over hers. "And I will *never* break your confidence."

"But," he continued, "how can you expect to keep a secret like this when your future husband and his family live in this very town?"

"They won't for much longer." She sat up a little and wiped her eyes almost cheerfully. "It's only a couple more weeks till the judge comes through. Since they can't find the title, they're going to lose the land. Then Jake and I, and Julia and Summer, we can all go live somewhere else, somewhere far away, and have a new start on life."

"That seems an awfully glib attitude to have about someone losing everything they ever had," he replied.

Catrina's conscience smote her.

"Besides, supposing they find the title," he continued, "or the man relinquishes his claim on the land?"

"That's not going to happen, Papa," she said firmly. "Jake told us they don't even have a copy of the title in San Francisco. A clerk told him it was destroyed in The Great Fire. And the family turned the whole farm upside-down looking for it. Surely, if it was going to be found, it would have been when Dan moved all their things into the old meeting hall."

"And as for the man making the claim on the land," she said, almost shuddering at the thought of Garret, "he won't give it up. Believe me."

"No, we'll be going somewhere else to start a new life," she said dreamily. Just thinking about Jake made her heart swell. "He's a good man, Papa, a truly *good* man—and so humble. You should have heard the ridiculous things he was confessing to me earlier today. Like he was so grieved over having knocked the family Bible off the fireplace mantle right after his father died."

She shook her head, "Of course, that's nothing compared to what *I* did when Momma died."

They were almost to San Jose. Her father took up the reigns and they started off again. She smiled and adjusted her hat. "But I am determined to become a better person. Just being around Jake makes me a better person—I can feel it. I'm going to do everything I can to balance the scale.

With Jake's help, I'll become a good wife—and someday maybe even a good mother. I know it."

reading

It was mid-morning when Ma brought him a hot cup of tea. It had been two days since Catrina had gone to San Francisco with her father and it was a mere three weeks until the judge would come to town and take their land away for good.

Jake was still hoping for a solution. However, he did have a new take on the whole situation. His mother had shared a verse with him that was somehow comforting and disquieting in the same instant. *How did it go? Oh yes, "Our God is in Heaven and He does whatever pleases Him."*

So the truth of the situation was that God would be the ultimate decision maker about whether or not they lost the farm. Not Jake, not Sam Garret, and not even Judge Spence. Ma said he needed to "rest" in that knowledge.

In a sense, it was hard concept to stomach because it meant that God was allowing tragedy that he had the power to prevent. But on the other hand, knowing that God was big enough to take a tragedy and somehow turn it so that His own purposes would be fulfilled—and perhaps even bring something good out of it—well, it felt comforting to know that God was just that big.

It was drizzling outside but not too cool. Freshness rolled into the room when Ma opened the window. Jake breathed it in. He felt so grateful to God for every moment, every experience—the warmth of the cup in his hand, the cooling air that rustled the curtains, the softness of the pillows behind his back. He was grateful to God for life!

He had been devouring the Bible. He drank the words like water! He had already finished Matthew and Mark, and was halfway through Luke.

Both times he read about the Crucifixion it brought tears to his eyes. He couldn't believe the lengths God went to. Why should a perfect God send His perfect Son to die for people who would just as soon spit in His face?

Jake had been a hater of God—a fist shaker, shouting at the heavens, and yet Christ died in his place. He was overwhelmed with gratitude and found that tears came more easily now than they ever had in his life.

As he read, he had so many questions. He would have preferred to write them down so he could ask Ma all of them at once but he just couldn't write legibly with his left hand. So all day long he was calling out for her, over and over again, to come in and answer a question. He thought she would tire of that pretty quickly but he couldn't have been more wrong. She seemed delighted to answer whatever she could.

Just after getting his tea and opening the window, Ma brought in the stack of his father's papers that he had found on the printing press. Jake felt like he'd been handed a fortune in knowledge.

"Have you read all these?" he asked excitedly.

"I think so," she replied. "But it's been years. Probably since your pa was alive."

"Well, let's read them again together." He made an effort to sit up a little more. "Go get Summer and I'll read one to us all. Then we can talk about it!"

"I'll get her right now!" she said happily as she opened the door. "You pick which one you'd like to read."

Just like Luke, he really is a new man. Julia was smiling so much lately that her jaw hurt. Her face felt like it was perpetually glowing.

Lord, she prayed silently as she peeked out of the room looking for Summer, *if all of this happened just so that Jake could be saved, it was worth it a thousand times over! Thank you, Lord. Thank you!*

There she was, sitting on the front porch. "Summer, come in here. Jake wants to read something to us." She bounded out of the chair, all smiles, and came in the front door.

Julia sat in a chair and Summer sat on the side of the bed as Jake began, "Okay, I found this one." He took a breath to start reading, but stopped short. "Are you sure *you* don't want to read it to us, Ma?"

"No, you go right ahead." She and Summer were all grins waiting for him.

He began: "It is not the overt act, merely, that will damn a man; it is the thought, the imagination, the conception of sin, that is sufficient to ruin a soul. If you had never committed one single act of sin, yet the thought of sin, the imagination of it would be enough to sweep your soul to hell for ever. Oh! there is no man here that can hope to escape. We must every one of us bow our heads before God, and cry, 'Guilty, Lord, guilty—every one of us guilty…'"

Outside the window, a figure sat on a chunk of firewood. The drizzle had soaked him through to the skin but an oppressive hopelessness kept him from moving.

Dan felt like a man already dead. His guilt was overwhelming and his shame was even greater. He felt his soul had been hollowed out leaving nothing but skin. If he hadn't had such a sense of responsibility to care for his mother, he would have hung himself.

He could hear Jake speaking inside. Actually it sounded like he was reading something. He couldn't make out the words, but as he listened, he noticed the tone of Jake's voice and it took him aback.

He sounded sort of happy or excited. Actually almost joyful.

Dan furrowed his brow. *What does he have to be happy about? He's losing his farm, he's got no prospects on how he was going to support his mother and sister, he can't get out of bed or even move his right arm, and on top of that—his so-called "best friend" stabbed him in the back.*

At the thought of the last one, Dan closed his eyes and clenched his teeth. Oh, how he wished he could go back in time.

He turned and looked up at the window. The drizzle that had pooled on top of his hat now ran down his back causing him to shiver involuntarily.

He strained to catch the words but he couldn't hear. *What is he reading?*

He needed to get a little closer. Quietly, he stooped over and moved the big chunk of wood back closer to the wall of the house. Then he sat down almost directly under the window being careful not to make any noise and he listened.

sunday

Catrina awoke on Sunday morning in the room she remembered from her childhood. It was so *good* to be home. She stood up beside the bed, feeling the soft carpet beneath her feet and walked to the window. Father had left her room just as she remembered it and all the *good* memories from her childhood came flooding back to her. The tree in front of her bedroom window was taller now but other than that, it was like being transported back in time.

She looked out as the thin morning sunshine was breaking through the cooling ocean mist. She opened the window and breathed in the fresh air. The birds were singing and she could make out the distant sounds of the city waking up.

She felt alive, grateful, happy.

She felt new.

She closed her eyes and breathed deeply. All the bad choices she'd ever made seemed to fall away. She wondered if this is what it meant to be "born again."

She was looking forward to going to church with her father. They had only sporadically attended services when she'd been a child, and then only because father said it was good for business. But in the years they'd been apart, she was learning that her father had become quite a sincere and devout churchgoer.

He was eager for her to attend church with him but she had requested that they visit the little church Rebekah had been a part of instead. So after they dressed and had a delicious breakfast which Father's housekeeper had made for them, they boarded their buggy and headed just a few blocks down from where the laundry had once stood.

There was no sign announcing that this unassuming, little white building was Grace Mission. Only a beautiful window of stained glass shining in the morning sun above the dark wooden, double doors attested to the fact that this was a church.

Catrina thought the window was the prettiest feature of the church and she was relieved to see that it wasn't broken. Amazingly, the entire building appeared to have come through the earthquake unscathed.

She and her father entered and sat near the back on the worn wooden pews. As she looked out across the heads in front of her, she noticed there were fewer people than she remembered. She wondered how many, besides Rebekah, had been lost in the earthquake.

On the one hand, she was glad to be here but on the other, she was realizing how difficult it was to be here without Rebekah. As the congregation stood and began to sing "O Sacred Head, Now Wounded," Catrina felt a little stab of pain in her heart. This had been one of her friend's favorite hymns, so all Catrina could hear was the *absence* of Rebekah's voice.

O sacred Head, now wounded,
with grief and shame weighed down,
Now scornfully surrounded with thorns,
Thine only crown;
How pale Thou art with anguish,
with sore abuse and scorn!
How does that visage languish,
which once was bright as morn!
What Thou, my Lord, hast suffered,
was all for sinners' gain;
Mine, mine was the transgression,
but Thine the deadly pain.
Lo, here I fall, my Savior!
'Tis I deserve Thy place;
Look on me with Thy favor,
vouchsafe to me Thy grace.
What language shall I borrow
to thank Thee, dearest friend,
For this Thy dying sorrow,
Thy pity without end?
O make me Thine forever,
and should I fainting be,
Lord, let me never, never
outlive my love to Thee.

The congregation remained standing as Reverend Haddon took up his place behind the ornately carved wooden pulpit. He was so slightly built that a gust of wind could have blown him away. The massive pulpit he stood behind only intensified his small stature. If they had been sitting closer to the front where Rebekah had liked to sit, then all they could have seen was his shock of meticulously combed white hair bobbing up and down above the pulpit edge.

He opened the Bible and began to read with a voice so mild that one had to strain to understand him. "Our passage today is from the Apostle Paul's letter to the church in Galatia, chapter three."

He cleared his throat and began: "For as many as are of the works of the law are under the curse: for it is written, Cursed is every one that *continueth* not in *all* things which are written in the book of the law to do them."

He straightened the thick spectacles perched on the end of his nose. "May the Lord add His blessing to the reading of His Word."

"Amen," the congregants responded, and then took their seats.

As Reverend Haddon preached for the next hour, Catrina's mind wandered back through the times she'd been here with Rebekah...the earthquake...watching her die...meeting Jake.

She really was a new person now. Her life had been so changed and all because of Rebekah.

No, wait, she corrected herself. *I never would have known Rebekah if it hadn't been for Rob. Rob's really the one that got me out of there. I wonder how he's doing. I really wish I could have checked in on him more often, but I can't risk running into Garret again.* She shuddered at the thought.

The last time she had seen Garret in the alley beside the store, he had sworn to her that if he ever saw her face again, he would tell the Foresters all about her and, he reminded her, he had the pictures to prove it. Just remembering that encounter gave her the sensation of falling off a cliff. Even as she sat here, safe in this pew, the pit of her stomach dropped out as her mind concocted images of how Jake's face would distort as he found of the truth about what she really was.

Was.

Was, was, was. That's in the past. I'm not that way anymore. She tried to conjure up the feeling of newness and joy she had felt this morning while looking out the window, but she couldn't quite do it.

Catrina and Edwin sat side-by-side in comfortable silence as the church members filed out the back, shaking hands with the minister. Catrina was still lost in thought until her father spoke as he stood.

"Wonderful sermon," he said. "Powerful. It gives me a lot to think about. I've read that verse many times, but I'd really never felt the weight of *'continueth'* 'in *all* things which are written in the book of the law.' The Reverend made a wonderful point."

Catrina said, "Oh yes," as she stood up. But in truth she hadn't really listened so she wasn't following at all.

"It really does make salvation by works impossible," Edwin went on as he sidestepped his way out of the aisle. "If you have to *'continue'* 'in *all* things' from the first dawn of reason till the day you die—well, we are all under the curse; none of us righteous, but every one of us a wretched sinner."

She followed him and faintly smiled.

"So, thanks be to God for sending Jesus, right?" he said as she reached the end of the aisle.

"Yes," she nodded. "Yes, of course."

They were the last ones out of the church. Reverend Haddon stood outside the door, letting them take their time to leave.

Edwin clasped his hand. "Wonderful sermon."

"God bless you," the Reverend replied as he shook his hand. "And, don't I know you, Miss?" He extended his hand to Catrina.

"Yes, Reverend," she replied. "I was living with Rebekah Campbell at her laundry just before the earthquake. Catrina Salterson. And this is my father, Edwin."

"Oh yes." He nodded his head. "I remember now. What a precious saint Rebekah was. Did you know that ever since my wife passed away a few years ago she would bring me meals almost every week?"

Catrina nodded.

"Precious, precious, saint. She is greatly missed."

Catrina reached for her hanky. "Yes, I miss her too. It's greatly due to her that I am who I am today."

"And who are you today, Miss Salterson?" he asked with a twinkle in his eye, as if this was a bit of a joke. "A wretched sinner or a righteous woman?"

"Oh, a righteous woman, Reverend," she responded automatically. But immediately she could tell that must have been the wrong answer.

He cocked his head ever so slightly and his bushy gray eyebrows did a little perplexed dance. "Miss Salterson, as long as a person believes himself to be righteous, he is like the Pharisees of old. As long as a heart is saturated with an opinion of its own goodness, there also abides incomprehensible pride. Christ cannot enter into the heart of such a one."

Catrina felt embarrassed and even a little angry. "Oh, you misunderstand. I'm not proud."

Her father, sensing that this was evolving into a private conversation, tipped his hat politely and walked out of earshot several yards away next to the buggy.

Reverend Haddon reached out and took her hand in his. She looked down at it. It was thin and shook ever so slightly. An almost translucent skin, flecked with age spots, was wrapped like a sheet over the spidering ropes of blue veins.

She looked up into his milky-blue eyes and saw gentleness and genuine concern for her. It made her lower her defenses a little.

Rebekah always spoke so highly of Reverend Haddon, she thought. *She trusted him and I probably should too.*

"Miss Salterson, do you see yourself as condemned under God's judgment? Do you say, 'Oh God, I confess Thou wouldst be just and right to send me to the utter blackness of Hell? Do you feel you could *never* be saved by your own good works, but that you are utterly condemned by your sin?"

Catrina tried to think through that with an open mind before replying, "I think I *used* to see myself like that but I've become a much better person since then."

"Then, my dear lady, you were once much closer to heaven than you are today," he said sympathetically.

"This will not be comfortable but let me help you get back there. Hear these words of God's Law: 'Thou shalt have no other gods before me.' Have you *ever* loved anything better than God? Surely you dare not say you are guiltless here."

"Well, I..."

He went on, "'Thou shalt not make unto thee any graven image.' Have you ever, in your life, set up anything in the place of God? If your conscience speaks truly it will tell you that, just like me, you have been guilty of bowing before gold and silver, or honor, or pleasure or self-will."

"I suppose…"

"Can you say that you have *never* taken the name of the Lord thy God in vain? And what about, 'Remember the Sabbath day to keep it holy,'—have you gone your whole life, never breaking this command? Surely not. These four commandments alone are enough to condemn anyone."

He finally paused long enough for her to speak but now she didn't know what to say. She felt the uncomfortable weight of guilt coming down on her again. This morning's feeling of being light and free and new was gone.

"Reverend," she said, "I know I've broken God's Laws but surely I'm no worse than anyone else."

You were a prostitute for years! her conscience screamed at her.

Yes, she answered. *But he doesn't know that.*

"To be damned in a crowd is no more comfortable than to be damned alone," he said calmly. "When the wicked are cast into hell, it will be very little comfort to you if thousands are cast there with you."

The things he was saying seemed completely incongruous to the caring look in his eyes. She took her hand out of his with polite firmness.

"Sir, you do not know me. But *God* knows how hard I have tried to become a good person." Her mind quickly flitted to Garret for some reason. "And believe me, there are many people who are *much* worse than I am!"

"Miss Salterson, what do you have to do with other men's sins?" he asked softly. "You are not responsible for them. According to *your own deeds,* you will be judged. The murderer's guilt may far exceed your transgressions, but you will not be damned for the murderer. The harlot's sin may be grosser than yours, but you will not be condemned for *her* iniquities."

Catrina's heart jumped sickly. Maybe he *did* know who she was.

He continued, "Do not look upon your neighbor's, but upon your own heart."

Catrina was ready to get out of there. She saw her father out of the corner of her eye. He was still standing next to the buggy waiting patiently for her. She was suddenly aware of how long this was taking.

"Um…thank you for talking to me, Reverend," she said as she turned to go.

He gently grasped her forearm with one of his shaking hands. "I don't enjoy talking this way." She could see in his eyes that what he was about to say was not pleasant for him. "But I cannot let you leave before I sorrowfully tell you that you are under God's wrath as long as you refuse to humble yourself."

She became angry. How could he be so judgmental? But when she looked back at him she could tears forming in his eyes.

"You are young and I am old," he went on. "But one day, each of us shall lie upon our bed—the last bed upon which we shall ever sleep—we shall wake from our last slumber to hear the physician solemnly assure our relatives that it is all over. And we shall lie in that room where all is hushed except the ticking of the clock and the weeping of our loved ones, and we must die. What an awful thing it is to die without a Savior—and 'after death *the judgment.*'"

As he spoke, it was almost as if the picture came alive in her mind. She could feel her heart beating. She tried to swallow. Her mouth was dry. She was truly frightened.

God was still holding all her sins against her?

Nothing she'd done had made up for any of them?

She pulled her arm away from him with wide eyes. "You are condemning me!"

"Yes, but not I—God has done it," he said. "This place—this place of *conviction* of sin, and understanding of the *condemnation* of a Holy God—this is the place you *need* to be, Miss Salterson." A rosy light came into his cheeks, as if the sun was suddenly rising on his face, and he smiled widely. "And because you are here, I now have a sweet word for you..."

cat

Jake held the stack of papers in his hand. He had just finished reading a second one to the three of them. They were taking a break right now because Ma and Summer needed to prepare dinner.

He was amazed that he saw himself repeatedly in these writings. He could see why it had been his pa's dream to print these and get them into people's hands.

The wind seemed to be whipping up outside and the room was getting chilly, but he didn't want to have to call Ma back in here so soon. He wondered if he was well enough to get out of bed to shut the window.

Well, he decided, *there's only one way to find out.*

First, he worked to sit up all the way in bed, then he turned to the side so his feet were on the floor. Leaning heavily on his left arm, he pushed to stand. He was glad to find he could do it easily. He did feel a little weak, but it wasn't as bad as he had feared.

The window was only about two steps away. He could close it and be back in bed in a few seconds if he felt woozy. He took the steps and put his good hand up on the frame to close it, but stopped short. Almost directly underneath the window, he saw Dan's brown hat.

He took his hand away from the frame. *That must be what I heard out here a little while ago.* At the time he'd thought it was the O'Neill's cat prowling around.

As he watched, he saw Dan reach up to his face. Although he could only see the top of his hat and his shoulders—and it wasn't at a good angle to make a determination—it rather appeared that he might be wiping tears out of his eyes.

Was he out here listening the entire time?

Only now did he realize how much he really loved his friend. He felt a stab of terrible regret for everything that had happened on that day and silently thanked God that he hadn't pulled the trigger. It was unthinkable. He couldn't believe what he'd almost done, over, as his ma had called it, a "stupid rock."

Dan cut a mournful figure, soaking wet out there in the cold wind.

He probably still thinks I hate him, Jake thought. *But I don't.*

Jake shook his head realizing how truly amazing it was. There were honestly no feelings of hatred left for Dan at all, not anywhere. It was shocking, really.

He wondered if God had taken away *all* his anger and hatred forever? Maybe his *entire temper* had been taken away by God! To test it, he thought of Sam Garret, but immediately his stomach knotted up and he could feel his blood pressure rising.

So much for that idea.

Apparently God didn't take it *all* away.

Nevertheless, he could tell there had been a change. He realized he didn't exactly "hate" Garret anymore although he didn't feel any "love" for the man either. But, as he continued to search his mind and heart, he was astounded to find a teeny, tiny, almost infinitesimal glimmer of pity when he thought about Garret dying and going to hell.

Wow, he thought. *That's new.*

He couldn't believe how much he had changed.

He really was a "new creation"—a new man.

He felt a surge of energy! He wanted to tell Dan all about this! But not just Dan, he wanted to tell everyone! The desire to share this "good news" was beginning to dominate him and it felt great!

If we lose the farm maybe I'll become a preacher! he thought excitedly.

The idea would have been so ludicrous just a few days ago that he spontaneously laughed out loud.

That startled Dan below, who looked up with an expression on his face almost as if he'd been caught doing something wrong.

Jake smiled down at him. "Hey, you're awfully big to be a cat."

The warmth of the greeting seemed to melt a little of the gray out of Dan's cheeks. He allowed a tentative gladness to creep into his face and tried an experimental half-smile back.

"Get yourself dried off and come on in here," Jake said down to him. "Everything's changed and I've got a *lot* to tell you!"

meetings

Catrina had been so excited to come back to Pureza, especially to see Jake, of course. But what she returned to wasn't what she left.

The entire previous evening the two of them had spent together, he had rambled on for hours about this-and-that article, or this-and-that Bible passage. Everything was about God. It was fine at first, but he just kept going on and on. He'd never been this way before. She felt confused and frustrated at the change in him. It was a grumpy, almost resentful feeling.

She and Father were staying in the town's hotel. Coincidentally, from their window on the second floor, Catrina had a beautiful view of the O'Neill's home and storage building behind their storefront.

She was sitting in a chair beside the open window watching as Dan, Julia, and Summer gleefully carried things out of the storage building. She didn't see Kylie, but that was probably because she was working the store.

Jake was trying to help as well. His arm was no longer bound to his chest, but in a sling around his neck, still obviously useless. He was carrying whatever he could with his good left arm.

Even Catrina's father was out there. Edwin had happily joined in to help. He had his shirt sleeves rolled up and he was carrying things back and forth, occasionally mopping his brow with his handkerchief. She wondered how many years it had been since he'd done any real physical work like that? Still, he seemed in high spirits.

A little peal of laughter floated up through the window. They were down there telling jokes and having fun while they worked. She hated having to put on this charade of being too sick to go out, but she didn't know any other way to be *sure* she would not lay eyes on Garret again. She just couldn't take the chance that he would make good on his threat.

The previous night Jake had explained to her that what the O'Neill's had been using for years as a storage building had originally been a church meeting hall. In fact, the O'Neill's rather modest home was built to be the accompanying parsonage.

In the few days she'd been gone, apparently Jake and Dan had gotten it into their heads that they were going to clean the building out, put the pews back in place, and start inviting people to come hear Jake read these articles he'd been so up-in-arms about.

It sounded like a *ridiculous* idea to her. Who would come to hear someone read an article out of an old newspaper? But Jake was absolutely ecstatic about it.

She really couldn't understand the point. There were only two weeks left before the judge came through to make the final decision and then they would *have* to leave. They couldn't move in with the O'Neill's permanently. What was the use of trying to start up a church?

She heard footsteps on the stairs, leapt up, and ran on tiptoes to get back into the bed. But the steps passed by her door and continued down the hall to another room. She bit the inside of her lip. It wasn't going to be easy to keep up this "sickness" farce for two *entire* weeks. And what if Father became worried and called in the doctor?

She would have to think of something else, but right now nothing was coming to mind.

————•————

Sunday had finally arrived and all the work they'd done had paid off. Sunlight streamed in through clean windows and gleamed off freshly oiled pews. It seemed that almost every person they invited showed up. Still more were streaming in through the door. Word had spread and people were curious.

Everyone was dressed in their finest, and there was an air of excitement. There had not been Sunday Meetings in Pureza for more years than anyone could count. In fact, only the oldest members of the community could even remember when this building had been a church.

Jake had started off somewhat nervously. There was no elevated pulpit so he simply stood at the front next to a table. He was not accustomed to wearing a tie and he fought the urge to loosen it.

He cleared his throat. "So glad you could all make it out here on this Lord's Day morning."

He looked around at the smiling faces. There were people he only casually knew, people he knew well, and people he really didn't know at all. He even saw Rob, the barkeep from the Dragón, sneak into the back, take his hat off, and sit in the last pew. The poor man looked like he'd cried his soul out since his sister's death. Jake was suddenly struck with guilt that their family really hadn't reached out to him during his time of grief. He'd been so preoccupied with his own problems, he hadn't even thought about him since the day they lay his sister's body to rest. He was determined to approach him afterwards and ask what they could do for him.

Of course, he was disappointed that Catrina couldn't be there. She was still in her hotel room, too ill to venture out. He said a silent prayer asking the Lord to heal her.

"Most of you know I'm Jake Forester," he continued. "Many of you remember my father, Luke. Some of you know he had a life-changing experience not too long after moving out here to Pureza and he truly became a different man."

He saw various heads around the room begin to nod. "Well, just a few days ago, I had that *same* experience. And now, with the O'Neills generously letting us resurrect this old Meeting Hall, I'm excited to share this amazing message with you."

"Now, I'm not a preacher," he apologized somewhat self-consciously. "But I am going to do my best to read this sermon with the passion the original preacher must have felt when he first delivered this message. It's by a fellow named Charles Spurgeon, from England."

He took a breath and launched in, reading with all his heart. From time to time, he wondered if he was emphasizing too many words or pausing too long as he tried to give extra weight to different points. But each time he looked up he was grateful to see that most of the people appeared spellbound.

He was nearing the end of this article: "'On Mount

Sinai, when God's Law was given in *peace*, even Moses said, "I do exceedingly fear and quake." What will *you* do when the Law comes in *terror*, when the trumpet of the archangel shall tear you from your grave, when the eyes of God shall burn their way into your guilty soul, when the great books shall be opened, and all your sin and shame shall be published? Can you stand against an angry Law in that day?

"'Off with all your masks, and away with all excuses! Let every one of us turn our idle pretences to the wind,'" the pitch of his voice went up. "'Unless we have the blood and righteousness of Jesus Christ to cover us, we must every one of us acknowledge that this sentence shuts the gates of heaven against us, and only prepares us for the flames of perdition.

"'Now, poor sinner,'" he softened his voice again. "'With all your sin about thee, take this promise in your hands, go home *tonight*, down by the bedside, and pour out your heart saying, "O Lord, it is all *true* that that man said; I am *condemned*, and Lord, I deserve it. I have nothing to plead. Lord, I am a sinner; he came to save me; I trust in it—sink or swim—Lord, this is my only hope: I cast away every other, and hate myself to think I ever should have had any other. Lord, I rely on Jesus only."'"

Jake looked up from the article. That was the end.

There was a palpable silence. No one moved. People seemed to be staring at him with mouths gaping open as if they'd never heard anything like that before. He wondered if this was the kind of response he should have expected. Perhaps he had been *too* passionate in his reading?

He concluded, "May God bless these words and bring each of us to the foot of that blood-stained Cross where we can alone find mercy and forgiveness of sins."

A thought occurred to him. "Some of you may know that it was my pa's last living dream to print these up and get them into people's hands. And today, seeing your faces, and your reactions, so much like mine—my pa's dream has become mine as well.

"I'll try to make enough so that each of you can have two—one for yourself and one for you to give to a friend or neighbor."

There was a murmur of happy appreciation.

"I hope to have them for you next Sunday." Jake smiled. "Thank you for coming."

The last person had left and Jake went back up the steps to close the double doors. As he stepped inside the threshold, he was surprised to see Rob standing with his hat in his hands just out of sight in the corner as if he'd been waiting for him.

Jake quickly realized he'd forgotten to talk to him as he'd intended. "Rob, I'm so glad you're still here. I wanted to talk to you…"

"I need to get forgiveness for my sins," Rob interrupted almost desperately. "Now!"

"Okay!" Jake smiled broadly. "Let's sit down."

Jake went back over what he'd read this morning and twenty minutes later, Rob was on his knees, praying and sobbing, his massive head and shoulders heaving as he leaned over on the pew.

Jake was amazed at what God was doing. He couldn't even make out the words Rob was saying. That was just as well. Rob didn't need to confess his sins to Jake, but to God. Jake just sat beside the man and patted him on the shoulder now and then.

Finally Rob stopped weeping and spent a few moments wiping the tears off his face. His head came up and for a moment Jake was reminded of how he had looked the day they buried his sister. But this time the hopelessness was no longer there behind the tears.

"Thank you," Rob said sincerely, still on his knees but extending his hand to shake. Jake's hand was dwarfed in Rob's big one.

Rob pushed himself up to stand. He again took his hat in hand as he wiped his tears some more.

Jake also stood but he felt he had to say one more thing. "Rob, I'm so sorry we weren't there for you the way we should have been after Rebekah's death." He put his hand up on Rob's shoulder. "I confess to you that I was so self-centered. I hope you can forgive me. And please, our family wants to be here for you *now*. Just let us know what we can do."

Rob looked down at Jake for a moment, taking it in. For a moment, he looked as if he was going to begin to cry again. Then the look changed, as if the giant of a man was on the brink of some monumental decision—weighing how much he should say—how much he could trust.

"What is it?" Jake couldn't put his finger on it but something about that look made him feel a little alarmed.

"I need to tell you something." Rob furrowed his eyebrows. He peeked out the double doors and then stepped purposefully to the side so that he couldn't be seen by anyone outside.

Even though it was only the two of them, he lowered his voice to a whisper. "I was one of the men who rode along with Garret that day he shot your pa."

Rob searched Jake's eyes for a reaction. Jake felt numb.

A tear pooled up and slipped down his enormous cheek. "I'm so sorry I was ever a part of that. And I'm so sorry your pa died. I had always liked Luke. He was a good, decent man. He didn't deserve that...and neither did you, and your ma, and your sister..."

Jake remembered the tall man in the black hat, the one he'd immediately assumed was the gang's leader. He was back in the dugout, paralyzed with fear as he looked at those boots through the cracks overhead. *That was Rob?*

"I've done many things in my life that I'm ashamed of, but I think that's the worst of 'em all." He wiped the tear off his cheek just before it went into his beard.

"What does he want me to do?" Jake could hear the voice: *"Look under every stinkin' chicken?"*

Rob looked up from his hat, apparently trying to gauge whether or not he should go on. "I don't have any evidence—it would just be my word against his. But I can tell you this. He wasn't after the gold, he was after the land's title. And he's been years now putting some kind of plan into place to get a hold on your land. I don't know all the details, but I know some pretty highfalutin' people from San Francisco are in on it."

He turned and leaned so that he could just barely see out the door. "My life's worth nothing now that I've told you this. If Garret knew, I'd be dead by mornin'. I'm getting' out of town tonight. But I wanted to get clean."

Jake still hadn't completely processed this.

He hadn't even responded. He didn't know how.

"And one more thing." Rob said as he slid quickly out of the door. "I'm really sorry for shooting you in the back."

down

Business was down and Garret knew why.

The whole town was talking about it.

Apparently even Rob, his rock-solid employee for *years*, had gone to that revolting church meeting, gotten religion, and disappeared! Just like most all his other customers. The bar was nearly deserted. On a Friday night! It was unheard of!

Garret was galled at having to stand behind the bar like a common employee but he hadn't found anyone to take Rob's place yet. So he stood there wiping the counter and trying to look pleasant. Internally he was seething. Dark thoughts rolled like thunder heads through his brain.

He had heard of these kinds of "revival meetings" sweeping through other cities and completely shutting down businesses like his. Sometimes entire business *districts*!

But what would be even worse than the meetings was that he had heard that Jake had promised to start *printing* the sermons and distributing them. That meant that even people who *didn't go* were going to start being influenced!

He held the dishrag down below the edge of the bar so that no one could see and took out his growing rage by wringing it like a chicken's neck. All the while, he prided himself that nothing showed above the bar. Nothing. He appeared in complete control.

Releasing the stranglehold on the rag, he took a breath. Perhaps he should just be *patient* and wait until after the hearing? Surely the Foresters would move on to somewhere else once they *knew* they weren't getting back on their land.

But then again, Dan O'Neill seemed to be getting as religious as Jake.

What would keep *him* from continuing to have these meetings even after Jake's family moved away?

No. Something else had to be done.

It needed to be strong, and swift. And it needed to happen before Sunday.

Sunday morning, Jake stood at the front of the meeting hall looking out over what seemed like almost twice as many people as the previous week. Many of them must have been from neighboring towns because he'd never seen them before.

Best of all, Catrina, having finally gotten over her illness, was sitting on the front row smiling at him with her father on one side and Summer and Ma on her other side. She looked proud of him. It made him smile.

"So glad you could all make it out here on this Lord's Day morning," he began. He introduced himself and explained again that he was not a preacher but just a person reading a sermon.

He began to read with as much passion as he could muster, "Oh! how solemn will be that hour when we must struggle with that enemy, Death! The death-rattle is in our throat—we can scarce articulate—we try to speak, the death-gaze is on the eye: Death has put his fingers on those windows of the body, and shut out the light for ever; the hands well-nigh refuse to lift themselves, and there we are, close on the borders of the grave! Ah! that moment, when the Spirit sees its destiny; that moment, of all moments the most solemn, when the soul looks through the bars of its cage, upon the world to come! No, I cannot tell you how the spirit feels, if it be an ungodly spirit, when it sees a fiery throne of judgment, and hears the thunders of Almighty wrath, while there is but a moment between it and hell."

After he finished the sermon, he briefly prayed and then went to the back of the church to try to say personal farewells to each person as they left. Everyone was so appreciative. They were shaking his hand and telling him how much they were looking forward to hearing another one next Sunday.

As the crowd dispersed, he saw a well-dressed stranger waiting on the other side of the church apparently waiting to talk to him privately. Catrina, Summer, and Ma were the last ones out and were heading over to the O'Neill's home to make Sunday supper.

"Thanks for coming today," Jake said and extended his hand to the stranger.

The man smiled and reached out as his hand well. In it, he held a pistol. Before Jake realized what was happening, the man had shot him directly through the heart. As he fell to the floor, the man dashed out the door.

Everything moved in slow motion. The pain was incredible.

"Help..." His voice was barely above a whisper. "Help me..."

All of a sudden, he could hear Ma screaming. Then Catrina and Summer were screaming too. Dan was there kneeling over him shouting for the doctor. Then, as if by magic, Doc Thomas was at his side. Doc loosened Jake's tie and ripped his shirt open. Buttons flew everywhere in slow motion, landing on the wood floor like little spinning plates.

"Hurry!" the doctor shouted to Dan, "go get my…"

But as soon as the doctor looked back down at Jake's chest, his face turned ashen. He didn't finish his sentence. The gaping cavity was boiling blood. He covered his mouth with his hand. Then with great sadness, Doc took the sides of Jake's shirt and quietly pulled them back over his chest.

Doc Thomas looked up at Julia.

"It was right through the heart," he said by way of explanation. "He's losing blood too fast."

Julia gasped as if she'd been shot herself. She seemed to know what the doctor was going to say next.

"No!" she wailed. "No, God, please!"

She fell to her knees and tried to put her arms around Jake. She was trying to lift him into her arms like she'd done when he was a little boy. She seemed to be trying to hold him tightly enough to keep him in this world.

"I'm sorry, there's nothing I can do," the doctor sat back with tears in his own eyes. "He'll be dead in a few seconds."

Jake felt disconnected, almost as if he were floating. He wasn't in control of his body anymore, although he could still dimly feel his mother's arms around him.

He was sorry he'd gotten so much blood on her best dress.

He could see Summer, face down on the ground next to Ma, crying her heart out although it was getting harder to hear her. Sounds were becoming farther away as if he was going down a long tunnel.

On the other side, he could see that Catrina had fainted. Dan had apparently only partially caught her and he seemed to be checking to make sure she hadn't hurt her head.

Jake watched Dan take one more look at his chest. Then his friend turned away, squeezing his eyes shut and began to sob.

I'm dying.

This is it.

God, please receive me, because of the blood of Your Son, Jesus.

And please take care of Ma and Summer…and Catrina.

Jake's jaws began to hurt and the pain radiated through his face. He struggled to open his eyes but he saw only blackness. His thoughts were frighteningly confused. Suddenly his arms obeyed him and he pushed to sit up.

Where did everybody go? Where am I?

It was so dark.

What's happening?

His heart was hammering and he grabbed for the wound in his chest. It wasn't there. It wasn't there?

He felt all over. His chest was whole. He wasn't injured at all.

As the cobwebs began to clear realized he was in bed.

It was a nightmare!

He reached up and felt the sides of his jaws. They still hurt a little. He must have been grinding his teeth like he was trying to bite through a board. He stretched his mouth open widely and his jaw actually popped.

He could only remember a few times in his life that he'd had a dream *that* real. It seemed more real than this moment—sitting quietly in the dark. He wiped cold sweat out of his hair with both hands and shook his head again. It was Sunday morning but it was still black outside. It had to be before 5 a.m. He sat up on the edge of the bed and took several deep breaths.

Did God speak to people in their dreams? Was God showing him what was going to happen today? Or had that threatening note had more of an effect on him than he realized?

It had said simply, "If you get up and speak on Sunday, you are a dead man."

He and Dan found it on the press when they'd gone back to the farm to print the sermons. And whoever had broken in to leave it had also stolen both the printer's main counterbalance lever and the ornate cast-iron eagle counterweight. Of course, without those pieces, the four hundred pound platen couldn't be lifted to print anything.

They had reported the theft to the sheriff but the two of them had elected not to tell anyone about the note. Word traveled fast and they didn't want the growing crowds to be scared away from the meetings for nothing.

When the two of them had been standing out in that barn in the light of day, the idea that someone would actually try to kill him over a sermon seemed like nonsense. But now, Jake was alone in the dark confronted by the reality of his own fears.

Am I going to die today? he wondered, and then realized that the more important question was, "Am I *ready* to die today?"

Is anyone ever really *ready?*

He climbed out of the bed and got on his knees before God.

Lord, I am scared. I am really scared. I'm afraid of being shot. I don't want to leave my family or Catrina. The very thought of dying terrifies me. But I'm not afraid of what comes after. I know where I'm going. Help me today to share your Word without fear. Amen.

respectable

"Come on in, Rob," Catrina said in a weak voice as she leaned heavily on the hotel room door, still in her nightgown.

He almost had to duck as he came into the room, seemingly one shoulder at a time. He closed the door behind himself as she manufactured an exhausted cough and climbed fraily back into the bed.

Rob entered with a concerned look and hat in his hands. But after taking one look around the room, he relaxed and chuckled, "Your puttin' on. Admit it."

Catrina's eyes opened a little wider. She was caught.

"Okay," she smirked at him sitting straight up and folding her arms across her chest. "What gave me away?"

"Well, for one thing, you left your cards out." He indicated the table by the window where she'd been trying to pass the time.

He laughed and that laugh was contagious. She had to stifle her own.

"Shhh! Shhh! You're visiting a very sick woman, you know!"

"Your hidin' out here from Garret. Ain't ya?" he asked

in a more serious tone as he sat down on the edge of the bed.

She looked down at her hands. "He said that if he saw me again, he would..." Tears came to her eyes. She quickly wiped them away. "He would tell the Forester's all about me."

Rob looked puzzled.

"Don't you see?" She shook her head and wiped another tear away. "Jake doesn't know. His *family* doesn't know. He met me in San Francisco. He thinks I was *always* a laundry girl with Rebekah."

Rob looked like he was going to speak, but Catrina interrupted. "I love him, Rob. I'm going to be his wife. See?" She held out her hand right under his nose—her mother's ring sparkled.

"But, darlin', don't you think..."

"Haven't you ever done anything you were ashamed of?" she demanded of him.

His face darkened and he tipped his head down.

"Well," she continued in earnest, "I'm *ashamed* of what I used to be."

He continued to look down at his lap. "Me too," he said softly.

Catrina sucked in her breath as if she'd been wounded.

Rob quickly realized how that must have sounded. "No, no, no!" He grasped her hand. "I'm ashamed of what *I* used to be. *Me*, darlin', not you."

Now Catrina was the one puzzled. The way he spoke made it sound very serious. She didn't know what to say.

He slowly looked up at her and sighed. "I only come back to town to grab a few more of my things and I thought I'd sneak in and say a quick goodbye. But..." He tilted his head and grimaced. "But now I'm thinkin' that the Lord wants me to get clean of all this to you, too. Before I leave for good."

"'*Back* to town'? 'Get clean of all this'?" She questioned. "What are you talking about?"

"Miss Catrina, I'm so glad you're gonna marry that Jake. He really is a good, decent man and God-fearing." He took his hat back into his hands. "And this is hard for me to tell you, 'cause I'm afraid your gonna hate me for it, but..."

She was growing more concerned by the moment. "But what?" she asked.

He sighed. There just wasn't any other way to say it. "Well, I'm the one who shot him, that's what."

She couldn't believe what she'd just heard.

"What?" She blinked at him, confused.

"I'm the one who shot Jake that day, behind the saloon. It was me."

She looked up at him, utterly perplexed.

No. Not Rob, the "gentle giant!" Thoughts swirled through her head.

"No," she slowly shook her head. "That's impossible. My Jake almost died. I just can't believe it. You...you *couldn't...*"

He realized from the tone of her voice that she could never have imagined him doing *anything* to harm *anyone.* He raised his eyebrows at her naivety and then looked off to the side.

"It's not the even the *worst* thing I ever did for him." he said absently, almost to himself. "For Garret, I mean."

"But why? Why?" she cried out, plaintively.

He thought a moment and then answered as honestly as

he could, "Truth be told, I'm a wicked man."

Catrina just stared at him. *What kind of answer was that?*

He shrugged. "After Rebekah died, I just let my heart go black. I started hating everything and everybody. I gave up believin' in God. Or maybe I just hated God, too. My insides were like tar."

He sighed, and then admitted, "I know this may not seem reasonable, but I think I hated the whole Forester family more than just about anything else."

"But why?" she cried out. It seemed ludicrous for anyone to hate this family that had been nothing but love and kindness to her from the day she met them.

He shrugged his shoulders. "Well, I suppose I felt like they should have tried to comfort me during my grief."

He looked down, "I remembered how when I was a boy people came and comforted my family when our Granny died. They brought food, they sat with us even prayed with us. I guess I was expecting something like that…" he trailed off.

"But nobody ever came. Not a one of 'em. Ever. They just forgot about me." He didn't look up. "And then, since you didn't come either, I felt they must be keeping you away somehow." His voice betrayed a little bit of lingering pain.

Catrina felt like she'd received a blow in the chest. She had to admit that she had, indeed, deserted him. Right after Rebekah's death, she had thought of him now and again, but then she'd gotten wrapped up in her own selfish, self-centered, little world and had simply forgotten about him. How could she have done that?

It was just despicable.

"Oh Rob!" Tears began pooling in her eyes. "I am *so* sorry. I am so, *so*, sorry. Please forgive me."

"*Of course,* I forgive you." He quickly wiped his own eyes and his smile returned. "How could I not forgive, when *I've* been forgiven *so* much more? I mean, here I am. *I'm* the one who *shot* somebody. I'm a 'murderer at heart.' And yet, God has *forgiven* me."

He looked at her with wonderment. "I mean, think about it. God. God *himself* has forgiven me of *all* my sins. Can you believe it?"

She couldn't help being charmed by the childlike astonishment in his voice.

"That's great, Rob. I'm glad for you."

"It happened just last Sunday." He went on excitedly. "I went to hear Jake read, at the O'Neill's meeting house. Lord only knows why I even went in the first place. But while he was speakin', all the things Rebekah ever said to me seemed to come floatin' back up in my head. And I saw all my sins just like they were written on my tombstone. Then I realized as sure as the world, if I died, I was goin' straight to the devil's hell! I ain't never been so scared in all my life!"

She couldn't help listening with rapt attention.

"And then Jake explained how we can get clean of all our sin, just because of what sweet Jesus did dyin' on that cross." Tears were beginning to run down his cheeks. "He died for *me*—a *murderer*, or as good as."

In the midst of crying, he began to smile so widely his eyes all but disappeared. He looked just like his sister only bigger. It made Catrina want to giggle. She couldn't help it.

"And then last Sunday, God did it." He slapped himself on the leg as if it were the most remarkable thing. "He *really* did it! I got borned again and I'm clean of all my sins."

"That's really great, Rob."

"So, yes, I forgive you." He patted her hand. "And no, I won't tell nobody your fakin' up here."

She smiled back at him gratefully.

"But I will tell you, I think that Jake's a bigger man than you might think. I don't think he'd ever turn on you, darlin'. I told him some really awful stuff I done."

He looked down again. "I mean *really* awful and he didn't even bat an eye. Not even when I told him I was the one who shot him."

That *was* pretty remarkable. Catrina thought about it for a moment.

"Maybe you're right." She paused thoughtfully. "But let me find that out in my own time, okay? I'm not ready yet."

He squeezed her hand and smiled in response as he got up to leave.

"So where are you going? You said you're leaving 'for good'?" she asked.

"I'm actually goin' up to San Francisco. I gotta get away from Garret too. I told Jake some..." He paused and rubbed his beard. "Some *things*. And if Garret finds out I'm a dead man."

"So I'm hightailin' it." He slapped his hat with his hand. "Gonna see if I can start up Rebekah's laundry again. Do somethin' respectable with my life."

"Well," she replied cheerily, "maybe we'll be coming out to San Francisco too. After the judge comes through, I mean."

"Maybe so," he replied. "I guess you never can tell what the Lord's gonna do."

He leaned over and gave her a kiss on top of the head and she reached up to give him a hug.

Good 'ole Rob, she thought. *If it hadn't been for you, I'd probably be dead now.*

job

Garret was angry. Despite his best efforts, he had heard no talk around town about the service being cancelled this morning. Now he had to make good on his promise and this could get messy.

The man stood in the musty storeroom with his palm out. His dark brown suit coat and carefully greased hair along with the large black Bible he carried should enable him to slip into the crowd seamlessly.

Garret grudgingly put one of the bills in his hand. "You get the rest when the job is done."

tremor

Jake walked through the crowd to the front. There seemed to be almost twice as many people as the previous week and many of them were strangers. Just like his dream.

Dan was watching every person who came in closely. He still didn't believe anything was actually going to happen, but in order to be safe, he was closely monitoring every person as they came in, making sure that there were no weapons.

After everyone had been seated, he nodded to Jake and stationed himself outside the building like a sentinel to watch for anything suspicious. As Dan walked out, Jake felt sweat forming on forehead, chin, and scalp.

God help me.

He forced himself to walk quickly to the front before he lost his nerve. "Thank you for coming out this Lord's Day morning."

He could hear the tremor in his own voice, and wondered if anyone else could. But he saw only expectant faces, smiling up at him, so he began to read anyway.

Twenty minutes into the reading a man in a dark brown suit coat, sitting in the second to last row, began to shift uncomfortably. Jake couldn't help seeing him in his peripheral vision. The man seemed nervous and agitated. An icy feeling started in the back of Jake's skull and ran down his back. Something was very wrong.

The dark-haired stranger stood and walked around the pew to the back of the meeting hall, right next to the door.

Jake stumbled on an easy sentence and had to read it again. But he was barely aware of what he was saying. His mouth had gone stone dry.

The man opened a hollowed out black Bible and pulled out a small pistol.

Jake stopped and stared. He felt paralyzed like this was inevitable.

Here it comes.

The man seemed to be in a battle with himself. His mouth flattened into a straight line and he forced his shaking hand to take aim. He pulled the trigger, but nothing happened. He looked in unbelief at the gun in his hand. He tried to pull the trigger again, and again nothing happened.

His eyes grew wide with fear and he started glancing around nervously in all directions. Without a word, he ran quickly out the door frantically crossing himself as if to ward off whatever had jammed his gun.

By this time, several people noticing Jake had stopped were following his gaze toward the back of the meeting hall. But now, there was nothing there.

"Who was that? What happened?" Dan came bounding in the door. "Are you okay?"

People began to excitedly murmur amongst themselves. They were looking about in all directions trying to determine what had happened.

Jake finally breathed. He breathed out a sigh of relief

that was like a prayer of thanksgiving. He almost laughed aloud. He felt lightheaded and almost giddy although he had begun to shake so hard he had to sit down on the edge of the table that was at the front of the room.

Jake took out his handkerchief and wiped his face and the back of his neck.

Thank You, Lord.

"I hope you don't mind," he began breathlessly, "but I think I'm going to leave off there and speak to you from my heart for just a minute."

There seemed to be a general air of confusion but the people quieted to listen.

"Have you thought very much about your own death?" he began. "I had a very vivid dream last night that made me think about mine."

"Spend some time today thinking about your impending death," Jake said as he shakily stood to his feet. "Think about it long and hard. Are you ready to die? Are you ready to face a Holy God? Have all your sins been forgiven through the blood of Christ Jesus? Be sure. You are only one breath away from eternity."

The morning had finally arrived. Judge Spence had come in the previous night and was staying in the hotel. In just a couple of hours, they would know the final word on whether or not they would ever see their farm again.

Julia and Kylie worked side-by-side in the kitchen cutting out biscuits while Summer was setting the table and putting the kettle on.

Jake was sitting with Dan at the table reading the Bible aloud. Ma had picked this passage for the day and it seemed to be just what they needed to hear.

Jake read, "...Not that I speak in respect of want: for I have learned, in whatsoever state I am, therewith to be content. I know both how to be abased, and I know how to abound: everywhere and in all things I am instructed both to be full and to be hungry, both to abound and to suffer need. I can do all things through Christ which strengtheneth me."

He tried to digest all that and mused thoughtfully, "It is so hard to be *content* when you're being treated unjustly."

"Now, we don't *know* that we're going to lose the farm," his mother put in quickly as she tested the heat of the oven with her hand and slid the pan of biscuits in.

"Ma," Jake replied lovingly but firmly, "we've already *lost* it." He lifted both hands and motioned around the room, indicating that they were sitting in the O'Neill's home, not their own.

"God can still do a miracle," Summer said as she spooned tea leaves into the warming kettle. "But he doesn't *have* to do one either. It's up to Him. All He promises us is that He'll enable us to endure all kinds of trials—full or hungry—abounding or suffering need—He'll enable us to us to endure whatever comes our way…through Christ who strengthens us."

"You're right, of course, Summer," Julia said as she wiped the flour from her hands, and quoted, "After all, 'Our God is in the heavens: he hath done whatsoever he hath pleased.'"

"Yes," Jake wryly responded, "now let's all pray that God will be pleased to give us our farm back."

They all smiled at each other.

There was a knock at the door and Dan rose up to answer it. There was Edwin, and leaning heavily on his arm, a very weak and frail looking Catrina.

Jake jumped up and took her weight on his good arm. "Catrina, you should have let me know you were coming. I could have come over and helped." He and Edwin guided her carefully into a chair.

"She couldn't be persuaded to stay in bed," Edwin said, shaking his head. Summer quickly brought a quilt and tucked it in well around her legs. Then she leaned over and gave her future sister-in-law a quick hug and kiss on the cheek.

"I just hate being separated from you all day long,"

she said weakly as she looked lovingly up at Jake. "And I especially didn't want to be apart on this day." She squeezed his hand.

Kylie came around with a cup of hot tea. "Hasn't Doc Thomas figured out what's wrong with you yet, you poor dear? It's not the consumption, is it?"

"Thank you." Catrina took the cup of tea in trembling hands. "No. The doctor says I'm not coughing enough for it to be the consumption."

Catrina had had to modify her "sickness" to include *less* coughing, since consumption is exactly what the doctor had begun to suspect.

"He said it must just be a weakness in my constitution." She smiled bravely. "I'm of the belief that it must pass soon."

Hopefully today, right after the hearing, she thought. *I'm starting to go completely stir-crazy sitting in that hotel room.*

three

El Dragón Rojo was closed today. The curtains were drawn and only a few random rays of sunlight, dotted with dust, dimly illuminated the room.

Garret was annoyed that he'd hired such an amateur. He would just have to hope that all this religion nonsense could be dealt with after the Foresters were gone. He smoothed his hair in the dim light and adjusted his cufflinks one more time before walking through kitchen and out the back door.

Three men were standing in the alley waiting for him: an older man with a bushy white moustache, a lean man in an expensive suit, and a distinguished looking, Hispanic gentleman. Garret's annoyance went up a notch when he saw that the fourth man was not there. He was just about to consult his pocket watch when an overstuffed, balding, peacock of a man huffed and puffed his way around the corner of the building and then stood nervously fumbling with his hat in his hands.

All three of the men looked at Garret with contained malevolence. It was clear that each one of them hated him. Garret smirked inwardly.

"Let's get this right, gentlemen," he told them plainly. "Get this right and all your concerns go away forever."

appetite

"Take a little breakfast with us," Julia implored Catrina. "Well, I don't know," Catrina replied tentatively. In actuality she was ravenous. She'd purposefully been eating barely nothing since beginning this charade.

"You should try to eat something," her father urged.

"Okay," she forced out, and Summer brought her a steaming flour-flecked biscuit on a small plate. It was cut in half and covered in a layer of creamy, melting butter. The smell was mouthwatering. She could have eaten it in one bite but she forced herself to pick and poke at it in an uninterested fashion.

Jake watched her with concerned eyes. He didn't seem able to properly enjoy his meal while she was "suffering" so. Catrina couldn't stand to see him so worried like that. She felt like a heel. Felt like? She *was* a heel!

This was ridiculous. She lifted her biscuit and took a decent-sized bite.

"I believe I *am* getting my appetite back a little," she said with a smile.

Jake brightened greatly. In fact, so did everyone else as well.

Catrina would be *so* glad when this day was over.

coffee

Sheriff Morrell was working with Dan to move the table out a little from its place near the wall when Judge Spence walked in. He had a thin circlet of white hair and a neatly-trimmed white beard. His cheeks were unusually rosy and he wore wire-rimmed spectacles pushed down to the end of his nose. He'd been riding this circuit for nearly twenty years and was known to be a fair-minded man with a sharp and sometimes rapid-fire intellect.

"Good morning, George…Dan," he said as he came into the O'Neill's meeting hall. He looked around and nodded his approval. "I think this is going to work out just fine." He usually had to work out of the hotel's lobby but since the meeting hall was so much larger, he was glad to set up there for today's business.

"Morning," Sheriff Morrell replied.

"Good morning, Your Honor," Dan said.

He waved it off. "You can dispense with all that till we're in session, Dan."

"Yes sir…uh…" Dan tried, "Mr. Spence?"

"You're a grown man, now, Danny, and I've known you since you were a mewing babe." The judge rolled his eyes.

"I think 'Paul' will do just fine."

"Yes sir…uh…Paul."

The judge chuckled as he put his bag on the table. "Is this where I'm going to be?" he asked the sheriff.

"Uh-huh."

"Dan, could you try to rustle me up a cup of coffee? Mary, over at the hotel, usually does it for me but since we're here today…"

"Yes sir, right away." He jogged toward the door, but stopped and turned, "Say, Mr. Spe…I mean 'Paul'…about the Foresters' farm…"

"Never discuss a case with me, Dan," the judge shot back without looking at him. He slid a chair around behind the table as he got ready. "I can't talk about it."

"Yes sir."

"Now, how about that coffee?"

"Yes sir."

As soon as Dan was out the door, the judge stopped what he was doing and watched him through the window jogging over to his house. Then he turned to his old friend and shook his head. "I'm afraid this is going to be a very bad day, George."

"Yeah, Paul. So am I."

hour

Jake took his hat off and walked into the O'Neill's meeting hall. He could see Garret and four other men already sitting on the right-hand side of the room. Sheriff Morrell, who was standing up front, nodded to him as he came in.

Summer and Ma along with Dan and Kylie came in after him and sat down on the pew directly behind Jake. Edwin came in a few moments later and joined them in the same pew.

Jake didn't want to stare but couldn't help wondering who the other men were. He guessed one was probably the San Francisco attorney Sheriff Morrell mentioned when he served the papers, but who were the *other* three? He leaned forward and tried a little non-committal look to his right but Garret was the one seated directly opposite him and he couldn't really see past him very well.

"All rise," the sheriff said as the judge entered from the back door. "Court is now in session. The Honorable Paul T. Spence presiding."

Judge Spence walked around the table and took his seat. "Thank you. Be seated."

Everyone sat. Judge Spence paged through a stack of papers in silence.

Suddenly the lean, dark-haired man, sitting directly next to Garret, stood again and started to speak, "Your Hon…"

"I assume you're the counsel for the plaintiff," the judge cut him off without even looking up. "What's your name?"

"McMurdow, your Honor."

"Well, McMurdow," the judge said, looking up at him through the glasses on the end of his nose, "I'm not sure where you're from, but in my courtroom, I call the shots. ¿Comprende?"

"Well…Yes sir, your Hon…"

"Sit down, Counsel." The man closed his mouth abruptly and sat.

Judge Spence sat for several more moments shuffling intently through the stack of papers before he spoke. "Gentlemen, I've cleared the docket of any other cases so that we can get the matter before us settled *today*. Since this is the continuation of an already open case, I'm just going to begin by directly asking Mr. Forester: Can you produce the title to the land? Yes or no?"

Jake stood, "No sir, your Honor. We've not been able to find the title, sir."

"I see." The judge folded his hands and sat back in his chair. "And you, Mr. McMurdow, do you have any *evidence* relative to this case to present to this court?"

Jake sat back down and the attorney stood. "Yes sir, your Honor."

"Well, let's get on with it."

The first of the three men was the owner of a nearby ranchos. His name was Javier Sergio Alvarado, a wealthy

Ranchero, and the cousin of the man who gave Luke the land. However, this man testified that his cousin often spoke of how annoyed he was that the Foresters were squatting on his land but that he had been just too kind-hearted to kick them off.

Jake had to bite the inside of his lip to keep from shaking his head in disbelief. That was a complete lie. Jake could remember as a boy meeting Señor Alvarado on many occasions. There was no way this man could be telling the truth.

"Your Honor," Jake interrupted, grasping at straws, "how am I supposed to prove Señor Alvarado would never say that? Something about this doesn't seem right. How can anyone be expected to prove what a dead man did or didn't say?"

"Mr. Forester's objection is sustained, Counsel." The judge turned to McMurdow. "His instinct is right, and I think you know very well that such unsupported testimony is inadmissible."

"We have evidence to accompany it, your Honor." McMurdow rose and carried a piece of paper to the judge. "Mr. Alvarado, please tell the court what this is."

"It's a letter from my cousin," the man replied in his thick Spanish accent. "In it, he mentions what a problem it was having the Foresters squatting on some of his best farmland."

Jake couldn't believe what he was hearing. It *had* to be a forgery. He watched as the judge peered at it through his spectacles.

"Your Honor, we also have one of Señor Alvarado's ledgers," McMurdow said and retrieved a black, leather bound ledger from his bag. "You can compare the handwriting yourself. It's identical."

"Hmmm," the judge said as he compared the two.

"Excuse me, your Honor," Jake said. "Can I see that, too?"

"Certainly." The judge motioned for Jake to approach. He turned the ledger around to face Jake and laid the letter on top.

The handwriting *did* look identical. Jake couldn't believe it. He shook his head.

This is a lie! It has to be! Jake thought.

He turned swiftly to Alvarado and said in a pleading voice, "Why are you lying? Why did you fake all this?"

The man's face turned instantly red. "How dare you!" he said much too loudly. "You would *dare* to bring my *honor* into question? Do you have any idea who I am?"

"Yeah, I know who you are." Jake's temper was on the rise. "You're a liar."

"Your Honor!" McMurdow stood, demanding the judge's attention.

"Oh, sit down, Counsel." The judge turned to Jake. "Mr. Forester, you need to sit back down as well. I'm giving you a great deal of latitude here because you're acting as your own counsel. But what you just did is called 'badgering the witness.' If you think the man is lying, you need to ask him *questions* that will reveal that. The court deals in facts. And that's what I need to see. *Not* emotions."

"Yes sir, your Honor." Jake pulled himself back. His mind scrambled for something—anything he could ask that would prove this man was a liar. Nothing was coming to mind.

"Did you know your cousin was once almost killed in a bar fight?"

"Yes," the man replied.

"Do you know who saved his life?"

"Yes."

"It was Luke Forester…my pa. Your cousin gave my pa this land as a way of *honoring* him for putting his own life in danger to save his life. You say you care about *honor*?"

The man seemed to shrink inside himself a little.

"If you care about *honor* so much, why are you doing this?"

"Your Honor!" The opposing attorney didn't stand this time.

"Do you have any *questions*, Mr. Forester?" The judge leaned forward.

"I'm sorry, your Honor." Jake shrugged, and stood there stupidly. After a long moment, he said dejectedly, "I'm sorry, I don't know what to ask him."

The judge turned to Mr. Alvarado. "You may be seated, but do not leave."

"Okay, who's next?" Judge Spence said as he sat back.

McMurdow introduced the pudgy, balding man as Frank Johnson, a lawyer from San Francisco. Jake couldn't even begin to guess what was coming next.

"Please tell the court what happened in early April, 1852," McMurdow prompted him.

"Well, I received a visit from Luke Forester to my office on Kearney Street," Frank said. "I dealt mostly with land rights, back then. You see, that was before I'd become an associate at McKinnley and Carter. Of course, their office has always been on Pacific Stre…"

McMurdow cut him off, "Mr. Johnson, please just tell the court about Luke Forester's visit."

Jake turned back to look at his ma. She shook her head

and shrugged. *Why would Pa have visited a lawyer on his trip to the Land Commission?*

"Yes. Well he seemed a little agitated when he came in." He looked up as if thinking. "He introduced himself and told me about his situation. He said that this man by the name of Alvarado had promised him some land, but had never actually given him a title. He told me his family had been living on that land now for more than ten years, that he'd put his blood and sweat into it and he was sure that must amount to some kind of legal claim."

Jake's irritation was growing. This sounded exactly like what Garret had told him that day he confronted him. In fact it sounded *too* similar.

"When I told him that I didn't think he had a claim, he went into a rage." Johnson's eyes widened in his pudgy face. "It was unbelievable! He picked up a chair and busted out the front window of my office."

Jake turned quickly around to look at his ma. Summer looked at her, too. Julia silently mouthed the word "No," and shook her head vigorously.

Unfortunately, the story sounded disturbingly credible. Jake had heard stories about his pa's temper before he'd gotten saved. Throwing a chair out a window would be directly in line with Luke's pre-Christian personality.

Garret was at the root of this, Jake was sure of it. He had coached this man and he must be paying him or something. *But how many of the little details did Garret think to coach into him?* Jake wondered.

"Can I ask something, your Honor?" Jake said.

"Counsel?"

"I'm finished for now, your Honor." McMurdow sat back down.

"Go ahead, Mr. Forester."

"What color was my pa's shirt?" Jake stood and walked closer.

"I'm sorry?" The little fat man nervously looked around.

"Since you remember the day so vividly," Jake said, "I'm sure you can tell me the color of my pa's shirt."

The man's mouth opened a little and he looked directly into Garret's eyes. Garret looked away nonchalantly, but Jake could see the muscle on the side of his neck pop.

"Why are you looking at him?" Jake asked as he stepped closer to the man.

"I'm not looking at anyone," the man denied. "I just can't remember the color."

"What about the color of his hair or his eyes?" Jake continued. "How tall was he?"

"I...I...I think it was about the same coloring as you and, uh, he was about your height, wasn't he?"

"This will tell us for sure," Jake said aside to the judge. He leaned in close to the man's face. "Was his scar on his right or his left cheek?"

His eyes darted for a split second to Garret.

"Why do you keep looking at him?" Jake asked with passion.

The man's eyes danced back and forth frantically. Then he looked up with raised eyebrows. "It was on his left, wasn't it?"

"My father had no scars on his face," Jake finished. "You are making this whole thing up."

"No, no!" The man pulled a paper out. "I have proof! Here's the receipt for fixing my front window."

"That only proves your window got broken," Jake shot

back. "Not *who* broke it."

Jake began to turn but stopped short. "And isn't it strange that you would save a receipt like that for close to twenty years? What possible reason could you have for saving a receipt that long?"

"Well, I just…"

"This is a complete lie, your Honor!" Jake burst out.

"Your Honor, may I reexamine?" McMurdow asked.

"Yes, Counsel."

"Now, Mr. Johnson, we are talking about an incident that occurred close to twenty years ago, are we not?"

"Yes."

"Can you tell me what color shirt you were wearing the day Luke Forester visited you."

"No." The man started to relax, as he saw where this was going. "I can't remember."

"Can you tell me what you ate for breakfast that day?"

"No, I don't remember."

"Quickly," McMurdow droned on, "close your eyes."

Frank did and McMurdow asked, "Can you tell me what color *my* eyes are?"

"Uhhh…" The man seemed to be trying to remember. "I don't think I really looked. I'm sorry, I don't know."

Jake was looking at the side of the lawyer's head and realized that he didn't know what color McMurdow's eyes were either. What had seemed so promising just a few moments ago, now seemed inconsequential.

"Mr. Johnson," McMurdow said in the most reasonable voice possible, "you may open your eyes. Do you think there is anything *strange* about the fact that you can't remember *every* small detail about an incident that occurred close to *twenty years ago*?"

"No." He was visibly relieved at this point. "No, not at all."

"Does Mr. Forester's cross-examination cast any doubt in your mind as to whether or not the incident occurred?"

"No. None whatsoever."

"Just one more question." He turned to sit again. "Do you have any records…any files…any paperwork of any kind…that goes back even *further* than twenty years?"

"Yes, I do."

"That's all I have, your Honor."

"Mr. Forester?" Judge Spence asked.

"Yes, your Honor?" Jake felt dejected.

"Do you have any other questions for Mr. Johnson?"

"No. No sir, your Honor."

"Then we are in recess for lunch, and will reconvene at 1:30 p.m. precisely." He looked at Garret's attorney. "And I want all these witnesses back here—none of them have been excused. Understand?"

"Yes sir, your Honor."

"Okay then." The judge stood to stretch. "Sheriff can you clear the room? And Dan, I hate to make you my 'step-and-fetch-it-boy,' but would you mind bringing me something to eat?"

"Of course," Dan replied.

"Mary, at the hotel—she knows what I usually have." The judge turned his back and stood staring out one of the windows. "Thank you," he ended in a clipped manner.

"Yes sir."

Garret, his attorney, and his witnesses were making a quiet line out the door, when Jake got his first real a look at the last man, the one who hadn't been called yet.

"You?" It was out of his mouth before he even realized

he'd said it.

The man spun on his heel to look at Jake but he was grabbed by the arm by McMurdow and walked out the door with the rest of them.

The judge had turned to see what was happening, "Sheriff, please clear this room."

"But that man…" Jake started to explain.

Sheriff Morrell walked up to Jake with his thumbs in his pockets. He eyed him strongly. Jake opened his mouth, he had so much he wanted to say—so much that *needed* to be said. But as he looked back and forth between the sheriff and the judge, he knew he *had* to reign in that temper of his. God seemed to help him do it. He closed his mouth, nodded politely to them both, and walked out ahead of his family and friends.

liar

Catrina had eaten two more biscuits and was feeling full for the first time in a long time. She was so ready to be done with this "sickness." She sat close to the window, watching the meeting hall. She could hardly wait for this to be over. She'd spent the entire morning fantasizing about what their lives would be like in San Francisco.

Finally she saw Garret coming out of the building. He didn't look happy. Filing out behind him were four other men. Catrina gasped and stood up in shock. She quickly hid her body behind the drape and stared. They weren't very far away and she could see every one of their faces clearly. Her stomach turned over. Her heart was palpitating.

She turned around and covered her mouth with her hand. She could hear Garret's voice in her mind: *"Catrina, I've got someone here I want you to meet."* Pictures flashed through her mind—the lavish room, the beautiful clock, the ornate hammered copper plates.

Sheep to the slaughter.

She looked out again.

There had been a few others as well, but all four of those men for sure.

I did it. I'm the cause of this. I'm helping Garret. The realization sickened her like nothing she could have imagined. She wished she could disappear. She wanted to just wink out of existence, then and there.

Everything that's happened...it is all my *fault.*

She saw the family coming out of the meeting hall and across to the O'Neill's front porch. All except Dan who was jogging across the street to the hotel.

She didn't know what to do. She ran to the bedroom, shut the door behind her, and sat on the bed like a trapped prisoner. She could hear them talking amongst themselves as they came in.

Jake's voice was angry, but controlled. "It's been a set-up from the start! Every one of them are lying. Who knows how long Garret's been putting this thing together?"

"Who was that last man?" Summer asked.

"I didn't tell you about this, but when I went to try to get the title in San Francisco, Garret must have known it wasn't there." Jake stopped and thought a moment. "He's got to have someone inside the title office too!"

He shook his head as he put more things together. "Anyway, after they couldn't find the title, I left the building, and I was kinda just standing there on the steps, thinking about how we were going to lose the farm, when *that* guy walked up to me and told me he could hook me up to get the title forged!"

"Oh no!" Ma cried out. "But you didn't—did you, Jake?"

"Well, no," he admitted. "But it wasn't for lack of trying. I was going to use the other gold nugget to pay for a forged title. But well, that's when I saw it was missing, and..."

He thought again. "I guess that explains how they

forged the letter. Either that man is a forger himself or he's got contacts. I guess they figured they'd be ready to trap me if I produced a forgery."

They sat in silence for a minute or two. There seemed little left to be said. Jake suddenly realized Catrina wasn't in the chair she'd been sitting in when they left. "Where's Catrina?"

"Maybe she had to lay down," Edwin suggested.

Catrina could hear someone walking down the hall toward the room she was in. She quickly laid down and turned her face away from the door. She heard the knob turn and the door creak softly on the hinges. A moment passed and then it closed again.

"She's asleep," she heard Julia say softly. She heard her steps going back up the hallway. "The poor girl. Maybe there's a specialist in San Francisco we could take her to?"

The fact that they loved her so much and were so concerned for her was like salt in an open wound. She was despicable. She hated herself.

She listened as they all sat down and ate lunch together. They talked back and forth about everything that had been said, and from their descriptions of the men, she was doubly sure of their identity.

She listened till she just couldn't take it anymore. Then she put her hands up over her ears and began to cry without making a sound.

There's no way anyone will ever know, a voice in her head told her. *No one ever has to know. Just forget about it, it's in the past. You can still have a beautiful life with Jake in San Francisco.*

But how could I look in his eyes for the rest of my life, knowing he trusted me and I betrayed him? I could never live with myself!

You're going to have to tell the truth, another voice said. *Go over there and tell the judge the truth.*

Garret would kill me!

Well do it before he comes back.

No! I can't!

Just kill yourself and get it over with, said yet another voice. *If Jake knew what you really are he'd wish you were dead—they'd all wish you were dead!*

Jake loves me.

No. He loves what you've pretended *to be, not who you really* are. *He doesn't even* know *who you really are. You're a fake. A phony. You're an actress. A liar.*

I'm not a liar.

You're lying right now! Laying in here acting like you're sick! You're the biggest liar in the world! You remember what that Reverend said: "All liars have their part in the Lake of Fire!" And nobody deserves it more than you!

"Oh God," she whispered, "it's true. I know I deserve to go to hell."

The conversation she'd had with Reverend Haddon came back to her mind sharply: *"And who are you today, Miss Salterson? A wretched sinner or a righteous woman?"* She could see the correct answer to that question so clearly now.

Wretched sinner. Wretched. Wretched!

She thought she had done such a good job of cleaning up her life. Now here it was again, haunting her. Slowly it dawned on her—she hadn't really "cleaned up" anything, she'd only pretended it wasn't there. As if pretending something long enough could somehow make it true.

Time cannot forgive sins.

"Oh God," she whispered, "please save me. Please! Please, Jesus, forgive my sins because of the Cross! Oh please, God, please!" She cried a little louder, "And please show me what I need to do."

———•·•———

Summer was collecting the dirty dishes when she heard a sound like crying, coming from Catrina's room. She dropped what she was doing and sped to the door.

"What's wrong?" she cried out, as she came through. "Should I get Doc Thomas?"

Catrina was sitting up on the side of the bed. Her eyes were streaming tears. She stood up and walked over to Summer. She took the younger girl's face in her hands for a moment and kissed her on the cheek. "I want you to know that despite what's getting ready to happen, I really do *love* you, and your *ma*, and *Jake* most of all."

"We love you too, Catrina," Summer said in a perplexed way.

Catrina put her arms around Summer and hugged her tightly. "Jake will probably never want to see me again after what I'm about to do. But someday, when you think he's ready to listen, please tell him that I did *love* him, very, *very* much."

"What's going on?" Summer turned and followed as Catrina strode purposefully toward the front door. "Should you be out of bed? Aren't you weak?"

"I'm perfectly fine, Summer," Catrina turned and wiped the tears out of her eyes just before going out the front door. "I've not been sick a single day. I've been completely pretending the whole sickness from start to finish. And I'm so *sorry* for lying to you that way. Goodbye sweetie."

"What?" Summer stood dumbfounded. "What? Where are you going?"

"I'm going," her face contorted as she began to cry afresh, "...I'm going to confess."

confession

Judge Spence was turned toward Jake as he spoke. He had taken his glasses off and was cleaning them with a small white cloth, "...your story is an interesting one, Mr. Forester, but this court ca..."

The back door creaked open and in walked Catrina. The judge stopped speaking and everyone turned to look at her. Instant understanding shot through the eyes of every man on Garret's side.

The man with the bushy white mustache looked shocked, the Ranchero was concerned but calm, and the overstuffed peacock looked nearly stupefied with fear. Only McMurdow appeared entirely unruffled. For his part, he narrowed his eyes at her, as if to say, "You have no idea who you're dealing with here."

Garret had by far the most visible reaction...but perhaps it only seemed that way because he usually had no reactions whatsoever. For a split-second his eyes grew to twice their normal size and then for a second longer they blazed such hatred that Catrina wouldn't have been at all surprised to see flames shooting out of them. But then, just as suddenly as it had begun, it was gone. Garret quickly whispered something to his attorney, got up, and walked straight back down the middle aisle without a sound.

The sight of him coming straight toward her took her breath. She braced herself but Garret walked right past her not even looking her in the eye.

"Do you have business with this court, young lady?" the judge asked.

Jake was looking at her with concern. Catrina could see he was worried about her being up and about in such a "weakened" state. Looking into those eyes, so full of love, she found she almost couldn't go through with it. She wanted so badly to have one sweet moment of goodbye with Jake before she did this—but it just wasn't possible.

She looked at the judge. "Yes sir, your Honor."

Suddenly the little fat lawyer awoke from his stupefaction popped up out of his seat and almost *jogged* down the aisle past her and out the back door as well.

"Where's he going, Counseler?"

"I'm sorry. I don't know, your Honor," the attorney said coolly.

"What about Mr. Garret? Where did he go?"

"That was, um, the call of nature, your Honor. He said he'll be right back."

"Well, no one else is to leave this courtroom, understand? Sheriff, enforce that." He replaced his glasses. "It's not as though I called a recess."

He turned back to Catrina, still standing at the back of the meeting hall next to the door. "Does your business have to do with the case open before us."

"Yes sir, your Honor."

"Well don't stand about in the doorway. Come up here." He leaned forward. "What is it?"

"Your Honor, I am…I mean I used to be…a…a…" She wasn't going to be able to do this dispassionately as she wanted to. She began to cry. "Your Honor, I used to be a p…prostitute." She had to say it through almost clenched teeth.

The judge sat back quickly, clearly a little repulsed. "Well, what does that have to do with this case?"

Catrina's tears were flowing. She couldn't bear to think of what Jake's face must look like right now. "I used to be a prostitute for…for Garret. He has a special room at the Dragón, on the top floor, where he can make pictures of…" She couldn't bring herself to describe anything more.

"I was personally in that room with each of these men and that other man who ran out. Garret must be blackmailing them with the pictures…"

flames

Garret was so furious he wanted to roar! He had to act quickly. He ran in through the back of the bar and up the stairs to the photography room. The chemicals were already highly flammable, so that part would be easy. What he needed now was a fuse but it would have to last a while so that he could be back in front of the judge before the fire actually started.

His brain was already spinning on the angle he could take with this. *"Your Honor, they obviously set fire to my saloon so I wouldn't be able to prove them wrong. This woman is clearly a practiced liar, while I'm known as an honest businessman."*

"Why would I set fire to my own saloon? The land in question is almost worthless...the saloon is my money maker..."

"How can you trust a filthy prostitute?"

Okay, maybe that last one was a little over the top.

A fuse, a fuse... what would make a good fuse???

He stepped back into the hallway, and almost stepped right on top of Frank Johnson. But Frank was no longer the laughable, nervous little fat man. He was standing stock still with a look of incredible hatred gleaming out of his little piggish eyes and had a pistol pointed straight at Garret's heart.

"Frank?" Garret tried to assess how serious he was. Would he *really* pull that trigger? Garret decided playing 'friends' was the best strategy. "Frank, get back to the courtroom as quickly as you can. I'm going to set this fire and we're all going to walk away from this…"

"No." Frank shifted his jaw back and forth. "*You're* not going to walk away from it. Not *you*." He lowered the pistol and shot Garret in the left thigh.

"Aaaaa!" Garret cried out, and fell to his hands and knees. The box of matches skidded out of his hand. Still he tried to reason with the man. "Look, you can walk away from this rich! Richer than you can imagine! The land I'm getting from the Foresters has *gold* on it! Do you hear me? *Gold!*"

"After that girl gets finished talking, my life will be over," the man said in a high pitched voice and tears ran down his puffy cheeks as he slowly shook his head. "You can't buy my life back with gold."

He aimed and shot. The slug passed through Garret's right forearm, breaking the bone, and imbedded in his right thigh.

Garret howled in pain and rage as he fell on his face. The agony had taken away all his self-control. He burst out, "You fat little idiot! I'll get you for this!"

"No," the man said calmly, "no, you won't be 'getting' anyone anymore." He shot him once more in the left hand and Garret screamed again. The man dropped the gun and kicked it down to the other end of the hall where it clattered down the stairs. He picked up the box of matches Garret had dropped and walked into the photography room. A great whoosh was followed by the crackling of a massive fire. The man stepped back out of the room with his hand over his mouth as if the reality of what he was doing was finally sinking in.

"You can't leave me here!" All Garret's pride was gone. He began to cry as he begged with abandon, "You can't leave me here! Please, please don't leave me here!"

Frank looked at Garret's bloodied form like a man waking up. His eyes became wide, as if he couldn't believe what he was looking at. He screamed a little high pitched scream through his fat fingers.

Ropes of flame were starting to lick out of the photography room along the ceiling like writhing snakes. Frank looked down at Garret and up at the flames. Thick black smoke was beginning fill the air.

"Please...*please* don't leave me here!" Garret begged him again, lifting his bloody left hand for help.

Frank almost reached for it then drew back his hand in horror. He looked quickly around himself, blinking. He took a few steps backward then he turned and ran for the stairs.

"No!" Garret screamed after him. He listened hopelessly as the footsteps went down the stairs and out of the building.

Garret frantically began trying to drag himself to the steps, but the fire was growing by the second and the flames were catching up to him.

cufflink

ourt was abruptly adjourned because of the fire. Everyone
in town—men, women and children—came out in force,
forming a bucket brigade to put it out. It was a miracle
that the Dragón was the only building to be completely
destroyed. The entire town could have gone with it had it
not been for some unknown man who had run through the
street screaming "Fire!" just minutes after it had started.

Judge Spence splashed water over his head from the
horse trough. He leaned over and coughed. Edwin, Dan,
Jake, and all the other men were coughing and spitting,
wheezing, and blowing. The smoke was the worst. It still
hung in the air everywhere. There was no breeze to blow
it away. Most had wet cloths tied around their faces against
it. The sounds of coughing could be heard from every
direction.

They passed around a bowl of soft soap and rubbed it
in well all over their blackened hair and faces, then rinsed
under the pump as a young boy worked the handle up and
down. Every one of them looked exhausted.

Kylie, was going by with a bucket and dipper. "Here
you go, Judge."

"Oh thank you, Mrs. O'Neill." He drank gratefully. His eyes were bloodshot from smoke and his throat felt red and raw. He had worked as hard as men half his age out there and now he was feeling it. He took another drink from the dipper before she moved on to the next man. "Thank you," he said again.

Sheriff Morrell, still covered with ash, walked up to him. "Paul, we just found a body in the debris. I'm fairly sure it's Garret."

Jake and Dan, standing nearby, walked over to join them.

"How do you know?" the judge asked as he wiped his face and the top of his head with the rag he had had tied around his face.

"Here." George opened a once white handkerchief to reveal a gold cufflink covered in black ash. It was embossed with an ornate carving of the letter G.

Dan picked it up to examine it. "Yeah, this is his, alright. He was showing them off all around town about two years ago, bragging about how he'd made a bundle on some land deal." He handed it to the judge.

Judge Spence peered at it. "I'm surprised it didn't melt."

"Looks like it got a little soft, but not hot enough to completely melt it," the sheriff replied as he turned it over in hand. "The body didn't burn up completely either although it did get pretty mangled when the top floor collapsed." He wound the link back up in the handkerchief and stuffed it down into his pocket, then turned to Jake. "And, unless I miss my guess, I've got something over here that belongs to you."

Jake followed him back toward the smoldering timbers

and around to the side of the building, roughly where Garret's office used to be. He pointed and Jake saw the last thing he expected.

"The counterweight!" he exclaimed. There was the cast-iron eagle and next to it he could see the counterbalance lever. Neither one of them looked damaged at all.

"So now we know," Sheriff Morrell said to Jake. "I'd suggest letting them cool off for a few more hours." He turned and walked over to the trough to wash.

Jake made his way back over to where Dan was still standing with the judge. He gave Dan a signal to step away and give him a moment alone with the judge. No one else was standing close by and Jake half turned his back toward Judge Spence before speaking quietly in earnest tones. "Judge, isn't it obvious Garret was trying to burn the evidence?"

The judge sighed and looked down and in the opposite direction, so that it wouldn't be evident to anyone that they were speaking to each other. "I admit, that's the way it *looks*, Jake, but without any hard evidence…"

"The sheriff just found the parts from my printing press in what's left of Garret's office," Jake said exasperated.

"That's evidence that Garrett broke into your barn. But as far as I can tell, it doesn't have anything to do with him making pictures of important people in compromising situations. Without something more, what that girl said amounts to slander."

"Judge, she's not 'that girl,' all right? Her name is Catrina, and she's going to be my wife." He turned slightly so that the judge could see the earnestness in his eyes.

The judge met his gaze briefly then dropped his head and turned swiftly away again. "You'd better hope McMurdow doesn't know that or it will only make the situation *worse*. It casts *doubt*—makes it looks like *you* put her up to it in a desperate attempt to get your land back."

Jake wiped his face all over with his own rag and sighed desperately.

McMurdow walked up. He was entirely un-mussed. His shirt's white collar still stood up in starched glory. He held a white handkerchief over his mouth and nose and looked like he was trying to avoid touching anything. Jake shook his head. He must have been the only man in the town who didn't try to help put the fire out.

"Judge Spencer."

The judge looked him up and down and must have had the same thoughts as Jake. "McMurdow," he said with evident distain. He turned to sit on the edge of the General Store porch.

The attorney pulled an expensive watch out of his waistcoat pocket. "I'm sorry to have to press this but it would be so much more convenient for me if we could reconvene today and get this case settled. Surely all that's left for you to do is render a verdict and I have pressing matters waiting for me back in San Francisco."

The judge looked around at the disarray of the entire town—men coughing and wheezing, smoke everywhere. Finally he faced McMurdow, nonplussed. "You do realize your client is *dead*?"

"I know they found a body and a cufflink," McMurdow said, in a flat matter-of-fact way. "But I'm sure they've not yet been able to conclusively *prove* it was Samuel Garret. As far as I know, my client is only missing and I must continue to advocate for him."

The judge said something disgustedly under his breath.

"I'm sorry, your Honor?"

"Nothing," he replied forcefully. "Of *course*, we can reconvene today. Here, help me up." The judge wiped both his clean hands on his grimy, soot-covered trousers and reached up to grab the pristine white shirt sleeves of McMurdow.

"Thank you, thank you!" He smiled as he pulled himself up and then slapped the attorney on the back. "I'm getting up in years, you know. Hard to get up and down anymore."

McMurdow stood staring at the coal-black hand prints on his sleeves.

"You're *right*! We can't let a little thing like a *fire* and a *dead* man stand in the way of justice!" The judge grabbed the expensive pocket watch out of McMurdow's hand. "We'll reconvene at six o'clock sharp. How does that sound?"

The judge dropped the watch and it swung on its chain coming dangerously close to hitting the porch post.

"Oh, *sorry* about that," the judge said, as McMurdow scrambled to get control of his watch. Jake got the distinct impression that the judge was more sorry that the watch didn't bust into a thousand pieces than he was sorry for dropping it.

"Six o'clock, okay?" The judge smiled at McMurdow, a little too widely. "That will give everyone a chance to eat first." The judge slapped him on the back again in a seemingly friendly—if possibly too firm—manner.

McMurdow grimaced and seemed to grit his teeth. "Yes sir, your Honor." As he turned and headed back down the street, Jake almost smiled at the two soot-black hand slaps on the cream-colored silk backing of his waistcoat.

As soon as the attorney was out of earshot, the judge

tipped his head down and spoke softly. "I'm sorry, son, but you might as well try to get through this today. I'm afraid the outcome is inevitable."

The judge coughed once more and went down the steps, crossed the street, and headed toward the hotel.

Jake sighed as he watched him go. He guessed it *was* inevitable. He looked around at the town—not the buildings, but the people—standing together in small groups, coughing and consoling each other. He knew them all by name. He sighed again. He didn't want to leave.

Lord, he prayed silently, *please don't let this happen. Please don't let us lose the farm. I know you can prevent it from happening. But...but even if you don't...I will still praise you. Please help me to not become bitter—my emotions can be a mess, and I'm prone to it. You'll have to help me, Lord. Please.*

The stagecoach from San Francisco rounded the corner of the lane and even from here where he stood, could hear the driver exclaim, "Jumpin' Jehoshaphat! What happened here? You folks need help?" The driver bounded down off his rig and even several of the men riding in the coach filed out quickly to help. He could see the sheriff walk over and start talking to them. He could hear them muttering that they'd gone slow the last several miles when they'd seen the smoke, fearing it was a forest fire.

Jake was hungry and his throat hurt. He needed to eat something. The women of the town had been putting together a community meal of sorts. Apparently they were all bringing whatever they'd been making for their own family's supper to the O'Neill's meeting house. He'd seen women going back and forth with pots and dishes. He'd seen his ma and Summer among them but only now did he realize he hadn't seen Catrina. In fact, he realized he hadn't seen her since they'd heard the call of "Fire!" and had all run out of the meeting house.

He scanned around looking for her. He needed to talk with her. He caught Edwin's eye as the man took a drink from the bucket and dipper that Kylie was still carrying around.

"Have you seen Catrina?"

Edwin swallowed and looked around too. "No. Not since we were in the meeting hall."

Jake needed to find her.

cleansed

Julia was making her third trip back and forth from the meeting hall when she almost walked full force into Catrina who was coming out of the O'Neill's home. Catrina's arms were full of plates and cups and Julia's were empty.

"Oh!" they both exclaimed.

"I'm sorry," Catrina said and looked down quickly. She tried to walk on but Julia put her arm out to stop her. This was the first time they'd been alone.

"Wait," Julia said in a loving tone. "I want to talk to you."

Catrina kept looking down. "I'm so sorry, Julia. I know you have every reason…"

"Now stop a minute," Julia went on. "I need to tell you something. Here, let me take those dishes first." Julia took the dishes out of her hands and put them on the table. Then she gently closed the front door.

"Please come and sit with me." Julia pulled a chair out at the table for her.

Catrina reluctantly came back in and sat. She stared resolutely at her hands folded in her lap.

"We love you, Catrina," Julia said quietly.

The vision before Catrina's eyes was wavering as two tears dropped onto her folded hands.

"You remind me so much of myself," mused Julia as she looked at her.

Oh sure! Catrina thought to herself. The idea was so ludicrous that she actually looked up and laughed a little. She thought Julia might be trying to cheer her up with a little humor.

"It's how I met Jake's father." Julia raised her eyebrows to Catrina. "Luke was one of my customers at 'The Citro' in San Francisco. But I've never had to tell that fact to a whole courtroom."

"What?" Catrina was astonished and Julia could hardly keep from chuckling at her open-mouthed reaction.

"I'm a different woman today because of Jesus," Julia went on. "He cleansed me of that sinful old life and gave me a new heart."

Julia was about to launch into a gospel message when Catrina exclaimed, "He did me too! It happened right there in the bedroom. I had seen the men come out and I knew at once that what I'd done was causing all this. I felt so awful and the words of this Reverend I met at Rebekah's old church came back to me. I just felt this horrible weight of my sin. I knew I deserved to go to hell..." She knew she was rambling. "Well, I asked the Lord to save me and I think He did because the first thing I knew I *had* to do, was go over there and tell the truth."

Julia could feel the infectious joy in her voice as she listened. "Well, I'd say that certainly sounds like fruit to me." This time she did chuckle.

Jake burst in the door. "Ma, have you seen...Catrina."

"Well, as a matter of fact, I have," she said with good humor as she stood up to go.

Thank you, Lord, she silently prayed. She had been worrying about Jake being unequally yoked but it seemed the Lord had taken care of that as well.

Thank you, Lord. Thank you.

Julia grabbed up the pile of dishes and headed out the door. "They need these over there."

"Catrina!" He stepped forward and picked her up off the ground in a bear hug. "I'm so thankful to God you're not sick!"

She felt completed by his embrace. She could have hung there in the air with his arms around her, forever. Suddenly she exclaimed, "Your arm!"

"It's fine," he replied as he swung her gently back and forth. "It's healed up completely."

"Jake…Jake, I'm so sorry," she started, "please forgive me for all the lies, the deception…"

He put her back down on the ground so he could look at her face. "I forgive you, freely, and without reserve because I've been forgiven so much!"

He grabbed her up in a second embrace. He could feel his heart beginning to race at the closeness of her. He sat her back down again more slowly this time.

"Here we are," he said almost nervously, "without our chaperone…"

Catrina's golden eyes sparkled with love for him. Her lips were slightly parted and her face was tilting up toward him. An involuntary shudder ran through his body and he realized *he had to get out of there right now!*

It was like a wrestling match just to take the first step backwards. The second was a little easier. The fog started clearing out of his head as he took the third and fourth.

"The judge is going to reconvene the court at six and this will all be settled," he said as he stepped backwards out the front door of the house.

"I'll hope..." Catrina corrected herself, "no, I'll *pray* for the best. I love you, Jake."

"I love you too," he said as he turned and went down the steps.

lost

"Very well, Counsel," the judge said to McMurdow, who was sitting on his side all alone seemingly deserted by the other so-called "witnesses."

"You're *sure* you have nothing else, Mr. Forester?" Judge Spence eyed him with sympathy.

"No, your Honor," Jake sat back down. Everything seemed hopeless.

The judge looked down at the table as if he was dreading what he was about to say. "Seeing as Jacob Forester has been unable to produce a title *and* seeing as there appears to be no copy filed with the Land Commission *and* seeing as the plaintiff has produced witnesses that bring the claim of the land into question it is the judgment of this court that the land in question will revert to the ownership of the State of California. Court is adjourned."

Jake felt his heart take a sickening tumble. *That's it. The end.*

McMurdow stood. "Your Honor." he acknowledged the judge with a slight tip of his head. Gathering his things, he made his way to the door. He was no fool. He knew there must be something valuable about that land. There was no other reason Garret would have gone to such lengths to get it. He was heading straight back to San Francisco to make his own claim on it.

"George, can you spread the word that I'll be staying another day for anyone else that has business?"

"Sure Paul." The sheriff put his hand briefly on Jake's shoulder as he passed by. "I'm sorry this happened, Jake."

Jake nodded up to him as he left.

The judge remained seated for a few moments longer. He rose and opened his mouth as if he were going to say something, but then shut it again. He walked almost past him, then without looking down, reached over and gave Jake's shoulder a firm squeeze.

His footsteps continued down the aisle and out the door.

Jake sighed and looked down at his hands.

Okay Lord, now what? How am I supposed to take care of Ma and Summer and Catrina? Where are we going to live? What's going to happen to us?

The room remained silent.

He heard soft footsteps and turned to see his ma walking up the aisle with the Bible in her hands.

He turned to her. "I'm sorry, Ma. We lost it. I don't know what we're…"

She put her finger up to shush him, opened the Bible and pointed to an underlined passage. She smiled at him, then kissed his forehead and walked back out.

He looked down to the passage which looked like it had been underlined several times over. And as he began to read it, he recognized it as the one ma had read aloud so often after supper.

Therefore I say unto you, Take no thought for your life,

what ye shall eat, or what ye shall drink; nor yet for your body, what ye shall put on. Is not the life more than meat, and the body than raiment? Behold the fowls of the air: for they sow not, neither do they reap, nor gather into barns; yet your heavenly Father feedeth them. Are ye not much better than they? Which of you by taking thought can add one cubit unto his stature? And why take ye thought for raiment? Consider the lilies of the field, how they grow; they toil not, neither do they spin: And yet I say unto you, That even Solomon in all his glory was not arrayed like one of these. Wherefore, if God so clothe the grass of the field, which today is, and tomorrow is cast into the oven, shall he not much more clothe you, O ye of little faith? Therefore take no thought, saying, What shall we eat? or, What shall we drink? or, Wherewithal shall we be clothed? (For after all these things do the Gentiles seek:) for your heavenly Father knoweth that ye have need of all these things. But seek ye first the kingdom of God, and his righteousness; and all these things shall be added unto you.

He thought for the first time about what a frightening prospect his mother had faced at having to raise two children on her own. Now that he was the one with the responsibilities, he felt that fear too.

But God's Word was telling him that he shouldn't be focused on those fears—the Lord could effortlessly provide for their every need. The job God had given him was "seek ye first the kingdom of God" and that's where his focus needed to be.

That's what I'm going to do, he prayed. *I don't feel very strong to do this, Lord, but I'm going to try my best to keep focused on you. And somehow if you'll give me the faith, I'm going to trust you to provide the rest.*

He took up the Bible and walked back to the town center where the air was still filled with smoke and ash and men were still crowding around in groups.

As he gazed at the smoldering remains of the Dragón, he began to feel a deep pity for Garret. Yes, Jake had lost his land, but Garret had lost his *life*.

Jake couldn't even imagine how horrific Garret's last moments must have been.

Last moments? Jake's newly-found faith continued to inform his thinking. *Those weren't Garret's last moments at all, were they?*

He slowly put his hand over his mouth. Regret washed over him. He had never even *tried* to tell Garret about the Lord. He had never even *tried*. It hadn't even occurred to him.

He looked around at the groups of men standing in the street. Any number of them could have been killed today when the building had finally collapsed. It was a mercy of God that it had crumbled back onto itself instead of outwards into the street.

How many of them are just like I was, lost and lying to themselves?

"I've *got* to print those sermons," he said with determination.

counterweight

an took the chain off the barn door while Jake got the eagle counterweight and the counterbalance lever out of the back of the wagon. Both pieces were covered with soot and still a little warm to the touch but they didn't appear to have been damaged at all.

"I guess we're going to have to move the press now anyway," Dan said as they went in. "And all these cabinets."

Jake replied "Yeah, but not before we print out enough of these to go around town."

"I think the press will fit in the back of the meeting house," Dan continued. "Maybe you can even make a living as a printer?"

Jake was looking around for the pin that held the lever at its pivot point. "Who knows, maybe I'll become a circuit preacher!"

The two of them chuckled together at just how crazy that would have sounded a year ago.

Jake found it. "Here it is."

Dan held the lever in place and Jake carefully tapped the pin back in.

"Wow! It seems like forever since I saw this thing completely put together," he hefted the eagle up and slid it onto the end of the lever.

The platen and the print bed creaked apart for the first time in more than ten years.

Jake smiled. "Still works!"

Dan returned the smiled and slapped him on the back.

"What's this?" Jake spied the corner of something hanging down from the platen. Jake realized his pa must have been in the process of printing up one of the sermons.

"I guess we won't have to set type after all," Jake said cheerfully as he went to pull it off. "We'll just print whichever one Pa was doing."

The paper was stuck to the platen and a corner of it was coated in black ink. As he began to peel it back something didn't seem right. The paper was thicker than his pa would have used to print and the color was strange. It was a soft yellow. Jake's heart began to beat faster.

Along the ink-soaked corner, he could just make out what might be the wing of a bird. It took his breath away for a second and almost made him feel faint as the blood rushed to his head. Carefully he peeled and tugged until it came off into his hands. And there it was—the wing of a stately eagle.

Jake's hands began to tremble. He drew it close to his face and read and re-read the lines. He could barely believe what he was holding.

"What?" Dan was startled by the look on his face. "What is it?"

"The title," he whispered, and tears sprang to his eyes. "The title! Praise God, it's the title! It was here all the time." He wiped his eyes.

Dan grabbed it from his hands and read it himself. "Well, I'll be! Thank God!" He grinned from ear to ear. "Let's get this back to the judge before McMurdow leaves town! I can't wait to see the look on his face!"

They bounded into the wagon and took off in high spirits. As they bounced along the road Jake thought through it all. He had always assumed when his pa took the counterweight off, that it had something to do with storing the press—but that wasn't it at all. Now he could see that his pa had purposefully sealed the title in the press for safekeeping.

The day of the shooting, Garret's men had torn the place apart looking for the title. If his pa hadn't put it in there, they probably would have found it. The press was an ingenious hiding place. Who would think to put it back together unless they were getting ready to print something? It seemed that printing those sermons was the only way to find the title.

He closed his eyes chuckled to himself. "'Seek ye first the Kingdom of God and all these things will be added to you!'"

"What's that?" Dan asked cheerfully as he clucked to the horses.

"It's a *wonderful* passage. Praise God, I think I'm going to preach on it this Sunday!" Jake gripped the title even tighter. "Let's get it back to the judge. He's probably just sitting down to eat."

rocks

It had only taken a few moments with the judge in the morning session of court to have the entire monstrous nightmare behind them. Judge Spence had hardly been able to contain his own delight at being able to so quickly reverse his previous decision. Even the sheriff was smiling from ear to ear.

McMurdow simply looked annoyed. Annoyed at this hick town. Annoyed he'd been forced to stay another night. Annoyed that he'd been roped into this whole situation in the first place. He stomped out past them, doubtless on his way to take the first stage back to San Francisco.

Julia was crying with relief and gratitude as they emerged from the meeting house. Summer was embracing her mother from the side and Catrina was beaming with her arm around Julia's other shoulder.

Jake was filled with a restless, excited energy. As soon as they were past the door he threw his hat into the air and shouted, "Thank you, Lord!"

Then he turned and scooped all three women up into an embrace.

Dan laughed and the girls did, too, because Jake couldn't

properly lift them all together like that. He put them back down and retrieved his hat.

"I'm so thankful to God!" Catrina exclaimed.

"It will be so good to be back home," Summer said happily. "Maybe we can take some of our things back to the house today?"

"Wonderful idea," Julia joined in. "You three go and see what you can load up and take back to the house. Jake and I are going to take a little walk together."

The others raised questioning eyebrows.

"A mother's prerogative," she responded with a smile as she grasped his arm and began to walk.

Jake looked back briefly to the others and shrugged, then said with a laugh, "Hey, if it keeps me from having to load the wagon, I've got no objections."

Dan had a good laugh at that.

Jake put his hand over his mother's in the crook of his arm as the two of them walked along together. Hardly a word passed between them all the way back to the farm but the silence was warm and beautiful.

When they arrived back home, she led him through the east field toward the creek and the straggly bush land.

He felt an anticipation building in his chest.

"Jake," she said casually, "haven't you ever wondered why your pa abandoned the northwest field?"

He raised a suspicious eyebrow at her. He felt sure he knew where this was going. "Well, the other two fields are on much better land. I've always assumed Pa abandoned it because it's just got too much slope."

"That sounds like a good reason." She let go of his arm, took a few steps and turned. "But your pa told me it was because that field is full of *rocks*."

She couldn't keep from smiling broadly at him.

Suspicions confirmed, he took his hat off again and threw it as high as it would go as he shouted, "Praise God! We can get three presses! Or...three *hundred*! Thank you, Jesus!"

appendix

Historically, Charles Haddon Spurgeon's sermons began to be published in 1854, and continued to be published, worldwide, until he delivered his last message in 1891.

Several of his most famous sermons have been woven throughout *Jake's Fortune*. For example, every article Jake reads is taken from Spurgeon's writings. Additionally, Reverend Haddon is not only named after Spurgeon, but virtually everything he says to Catrina comes from his writings.

Spurgeon is recognized as one of the foremost preachers of the nineteenth century. Even in his day, he was known as "The Prince of Preachers." His works are, quite literally, filled with "gold nuggets" of God's truth. You can glean even more from the book *Spurgeon Gold*, also published by Bridge Logos.

On the following pages we are providing two of Spurgeon's most powerful sermons in their unaltered, original form. The first is titled, "A Call to the Unconverted,"[1] and the second one is "The Uses of the Law."[2] We hope you enjoy reading through them fully and noting the places that connect to the story in *Jake's Fortune*.

A Call to the Unconverted

A Sermon (No. 174)
Delivered on Sabbath Evening, November 8, 1857
by the Rev. C. H. Spurgeon
at New Park Street Chapel, Southwark

*"For as many as are of the works of the law are under
the curse: for it is written, Cursed is every one that
continueth not in all things which are written in the
book of the law to do them."*— Galatians 3:10

MY HEARER, ART THOU a believer, or no? for, according
to thine answer to that question, must be the style in which I
shall address thee to-night. I would ask thee as a great favor
to thine own soul, this evening to divest thyself of the thought
that thou art sitting in a chapel, and hearing a minister who
is preaching to a large congregation. Think thou art sitting
in thine own house, in thine own chair, and think that I am
standing by thee, with thy hand in mine, and am speaking
personally to thee, and to thee alone; for that is how I desire
to preach this night to each of my hearers—one by one. I
want thee, then, in the sight of God, to answer me this all
important and solemn question before I begin—Art thou
in Christ, or art thou not? Hast thou fled for refuge to him

who is the only hope for sinners? or art thou yet a stranger to the commonwealth of Israel, ignorant of God, and of his holy Gospel? Come—be honest with thine own heart, and let thy conscience say yes, or no, for one of these two things thou art to-night—thou art either under the wrath of God, or thou art delivered from it. Thou art to-night either an heir of wrath, or an inheritor of the kingdom of grace. Which of these two? Make no "ifs" or "ahs" in your answer. Answer straight forward to thine own soul; and if there be any doubt whatever about it, I beseech thee rest not till that doubt be resolved. Do not take advantage of that doubt to thyself, but rather take a disadvantage from it. Depend upon it, thou art more likely to be wrong than thou art to be right; and now put thyself in the scale, and if thou dost not kick the beam entirely, but if thou hangest between the two, and thou sayest, "I know not which," better that thou shouldst decide for the worst, though it should grieve thyself, than that thou shouldst decide for the better, and be deceived, and so go on presumptuously until the pit of Hell shall wake thee from thy self-deception. Canst thou, then, with one hand upon God's holy word, and the other upon thine own heart, lift thine eye to heaven, and say, "One thing I know, that whereas I was blind, now I see; I know that I have passed from death unto life, I am not now what I once was; 'I the chief of sinners am, but Jesus died for me.' And if I be not awfully deceived, I am this night "a sinner saved by blood, a monument of grace?'" My brother, God speed you; the blessing of the Most High be with you. My text has no thunders in it for you. Instead of this verse, turn to the 13th, and there read your inheritance: "Christ hath redeemed *us* from the curse of the law, being made a curse for us: for it is written, Cursed is every one that hangeth on a tree." So Christ was cursed in the stead of you, and you are secure, if you are truly converted, and really a regenerated child of God.

But my hearer, I am solemnly convinced that a large proportion of this assembly dare not say so; and thou to-night (for I am speaking personally to thee), remember that thou art one of those who dare not say this, for thou art a stranger to the grace of God. Thou durst not lie before God, and thine own conscience, therefore thou dost honestly say, "I know I was never regenerated; I am now what I always was, and that is the most I can say." Now, with you I have to deal, and I charge you by him who shall judge the quick and the dead, before whom you and I must soon appear, listen to the words I speak, for they may be the last warning you shall ever hear, and I charge my own soul also, be thou faithful to these dying men, lest haply on thy skirts at last should be found the blood of souls, and thou thyself shouldst be a castaway. O God, make us faithful this night and give the hearing ear, and the retentive memory, and the conscience touched by the Spirit, for Jesus' sake.

First, to-night we shall *try the prisoner;* secondly, we shall *declare his sentence;* and thirdly, if we find him confessing and penitent, we shall *proclaim his deliverance;* but not unless we find him so.

I. First, then, we are about to TRY THE PRISONER.

The text says: "Cursed is every one that continueth not in all things which are written in the book of the law to do them." Unconverted man, are you guilty, or not guilty? Have you continued "in all things that are written in the book of the law to do them?" Methinks you will not dare to plead, "Not guilty." But I will suppose for one moment that you are bold enough to do so. So, then, sir, you mean to assert that you have continued "in all things which are written in the book of the law." Surely the very reading of the law would be enough to convince thee that thou art in error. Dost thou know what the law is? Why, I will give thee what I may call the outside of it, but remember that within it there is a broader spirit than the mere words. Hear thou these words of the law—*"Thou shalt have no other gods before me."* What! hast thou never loved anything better than God? Hast thou never made a God of thy belly, or of thy business, or of thy family, or of thine own person? Oh! surely thou durst not say thou art guiltless here. *"Thou shalt not make unto thee any graven image, or any likeness of anything that is in heaven above, or that is in the earth beneath, or that is in the water under the earth."* What! hast thou never in thy life set up anything in the place of God? If thou hast not, I have, full many a time. And I wot, if conscience would speak truly, it would say, "Man, thou hast been a mammon worshiper, thou hast been a belly worshiper, thou hast bowed down before gold and silver; thou hast cast thyself down before honor, thou hast bowed before pleasure, thou hast made a God of thy drunkenness, a God of thy lust, a God of thy uncleanness, a God of thy pleasures!" Wilt thou dare to say that thou hast never taken *the name of the Lord thy of God in vain?* If thou hast never sworn profanely, yet surely in common conversation thou hast sometimes made use of God's name when thou oughtest not to have done so. Say, hast thou always hallowed that most holy name? Hast thou never called upon God without necessity? Hast thou never read his book with a trifling spirit? Hast thou never heard his gospel without paying reverence to it? Surely thou art guilty here. And as for that fourth commandment, which relates to the keeping of the Sabbath—*"Remember the Sabbath day to keep it holy,"*—hast thou never broken it? Oh, shut thy mouth and plead guilty, for these four commandments were enough to condemn thee! *"Honor thy father and thy mother."* What! wilt thou say thou has kept that? Hast thou never been disobedient in thy youth? Hast thou never kicked against a mother's love, and striven against a father's rebuke? Turn over a page of your history till you come to your childhood; see if you cannot find it written there; ay, and your manhood too may confess that you have not always spoken to your parents as you should, or always treated them with that honor they deserved, and which God commanded you to give unto them. *"Thou shalt not kill;"* you may never have killed any, but have you never been angry? He that is angry with his brother is a murderer; thou art guilty here. *"Thou shalt not commit adultery."* Mayhap thou hast committed unclean things, and art here this very day stained with lust; but if thou hast been never so chaste, I am sure thou hast not been quite guiltless, when the Master says, "He that looketh on a woman to lust after her, hath committed adultery already with her in his heart." Has no lascivious thought crossed thy mind? Has no impurity ever stirred thy imagination? Surely if thou shouldest dare to say so, thou wouldest be brazen-faced with impudence. And hast thou never stolen? *"Thou shalt not steal;"* you are here in the crowd to-night with the product of your theft mayhap, you have done the deed, you have committed robbery; but if you have been never so honest, yet surely there have been times in which you have felt an inclination to defraud your neighbor, and there may have been some petty, or mayhap some gross frauds which you have secretly and silently committed, on which the law of the land could not lay its hand, but which nevertheless, was a breach of this law. And who dare say he has not borne *false witness against his neighbor?* Have we never repeated a story to our neighbor's disadvantage, which was untrue? Have we never misconstrued his motives? Have we never misinterpreted his designs? And who among us can dare to say that he is guiltless of the last—*"Thou shalt not covet?"* for we have all desired to have more than God has given us; and at times our wandering heart has lusted after things which God has not bestowed upon us. Why, to plead not guilty, is to plead your own folly; for verily, my brethren, the very reading of the law is enough, when blessed by the Spirit, to make us cry, "Guilty, O Lord, guilty."

But one cries, "I shall not plead guilty, for though I am well aware that I have not continued 'in all things which are written in the book of the law,' yet I have done the best I could." That is a lie—before God a falsehood. You have not! You have not

done the best you could. There have been many occasions
upon which you might have done better. Will that young man
dare to tell me that he is doing the best he can *now?* that he
cannot refrain from laughter in the house of God? It may be
possible that it is hard for him to do so, but it is just possible
he could, if he pleased, refrain from insulting his Maker to his
face. Surely we have none of us done the best we could. At
every period, at every time, there have been opportunities of
escape from temptation. If we had had no freedom to escape
from the sin, there might have been some excuse for it; but
there have been turning points in our history when we might
have decided for right or for wrong, but when we have chosen
the evil and have eschewed the good, and have turned into that
path which leadeth unto Hell.

"Ah, but," saith another, "I declare, sir, that while I have
broken that law, without a doubt, I have been no worse than
my fellow-creatures." And a sorry argument is that, for
what availeth it thee? To be damned in a crowd is no more
comfortable than to be damned alone. It is true, thou hast been
no worse than thy fellow-creatures, but this will be of very
poor service to thee. When the wicked are cast into Hell, it
will be very little comfort to thee that God shall say, "Depart
ye cursed" to a thousand with thee. Remember, God's curse,
when it shall sweep a nation into Hell, shall be as much felt
by every individual of the crowd, as if there were but that one
man to be punished. God is not like our earthly judges. If their
courts were glutted with prisoners, they might be inclined to
pass over many a case lightly; but not so with Jehovah. He is
so infinite in his mind, that the abundance of criminals will
not seem to be any difficulty with him. He will deal with thee
as severely and as justly as it there were never another sinner
in all the world. And pray, what hast thou to do with other
men's sins? Thou art not responsible for them. God made thee
to stand or fall by thyself. According to thine own deeds thou
shalt be judged. The harlot's sin may be grosser than thine, but

thou wilt not be condemned for her iniquities. The murderers guilt may far exceed thy transgressions, but thou wilt not be damned for the murderer. Religion is a thing between God and thine own soul, O man; and therefore, I do beseech thee, do not look upon thy neighbor's, but upon thine own heart.

"Ay, but," cries another, "I have very many times striven to keep the law, and I think I have done so for a little." Hear ye the sentence read again—"Cursed is every one that *continueth* not in all things which are written in the book of the law to do them." Oh! sirs; it is not some hectic flush upon the cheek of consumptive irresolution that God counts to be the health of obedience. It is not some slight obedience for an hour that God will accept at the day of judgment. He saith "continueth;" and unless from my early childhood to the day when my gray hairs descend into the tomb, I shall have continued to be obedient to God, I must be condemned. Unless I have from the first dawn of reason, when I first began to be responsible, obediently served God, until, like a shock of corn, I am gathered into my Master's garner, salvation by works must be impossible to me, and I must (standing on my own footing), be condemned. It is not I say, some slight obedience that will save the soul. Thou hast not continued "in all things which are written in the book of the law," and therefore thou art condemned.

"But," says another, "there are many things I have not done, but still I have been very virtuous." Poor excuse that, also. Suppose thou hast been virtuous; suppose thou hast avoided many vices: turn to my text. It is not my word, but God's—turn to it—*all things.* It does not say *"some things."* "Cursed is every one that continueth not in *all things* which are written in the book of the law to do them." Now, hast thou performed all virtues? Hast thou shunned all vices? Dost thou stand up and plead, "I never was a drunkard?"—Yet shalt thou be damned, if thou hast been a fornicator. Dost thou reply, "I never was unclean?" Yet thou hast broken the Sabbath. Dost thou plead guiltless of that charge? Dost thou declare thou hast never broken the Sabbath? Thou hast taken God's name in vain, hast thou not? Somewhere or other God's law can smite thee. It is certain (let thy conscience now speak and affirm what I assert)—it is certain thou hast not continued "in *all things* which are written in the book of the law." Nay, more, I do not believe thou hast even continued in any one commandment of God to the full, for the commandment is exceeding broad. It is not the overt act, merely, that will damn a man; it is the thought, the imagination, the conception of sin, that is sufficient to ruin a soul. Remember, my dear hearers, I am speaking now God's own word, not a harsh doctrine of my own. If you had never committed one single act of sin, yet the thought of sin, the imagination of it would be enough to sweep your soul to Hell for ever. If you had been born in a cell, and had never been able to come out into the world, either to commit acts of lasciviousness, murder, or robbery, yet the thought of evil in that lone cell might be enough to cast your soul for ever from the face of God. Oh! there is no man here that can hope to escape. We must every one of us bow our heads before God, and cry, "Guilty, Lord, guilty—every one of us guilty—'Cursed is *every one* that continueth not in *all things* which are written in the book of the law to do them.'" When I look into thy face, O law, my spirit shudders. When I hear thy thunders, my heart is melted like wax in the midst of my bowels. How can I endure thee? If I am to be tried at last for my life, surely I shall need no judge, for I shall be mine own swift accuser, and my conscience shall be a witness to condemn.

I think I need not enlarge further on this point. O thou that art out of Christ, and without God, dost thou not stand condemned before him? Off with all thy masks, and away with all excuses; let every one of us turn our idle pretences to the wind. Unless we have the blood and righteousness of Jesus Christ to cover us, we must every one of us acknowledge that this sentence shuts the gates of heaven against us, and only prepares us for the flames of perdition.

II. Thus have I singled out the character, and he is found guilty; now I have TO DECLARE THE SENTENCE.

God's ministers love not such work as this. I would rather stand in this pulpit and preach twenty sermons on the love of Jesus, than one like this. It is very seldom that I meddle with the theme, because I do not know that it is often necessary; but I feel that if these things were kept altogether in the background, and the law were not preached, the Master would not own the gospel; for he will have both preached in their measure, and each must have its proper prominence. Now, therefore, hear me whilst I sorrowfully tell you what is the sentence passed upon all of you who this night are out of Christ. Sinner, thou art cursed to-night. *Thou art cursed,* not by some wizard whose fancied spell can only frighten the ignorant. Thou art cursed— not cursed by some earthly monarch who could turn his troops against thee, and swallow up thy house and thy patrimony quick. Cursed! Oh! what a thing a curse is anyhow! What an awful thing is the curse of a father. We have heard of fathers, driven to madness by the undutiful and ungracious conduct of their children, who have lifted their hands to heaven, and have implored a curse, a withering curse upon their children. We can not excuse the parent's mad and rash act. God forbid we should exempt him from sin; but oh, a father's curse must be awful. I can not think what it must be to be cursed by him that did beget me. Sure, it would put out the sunlight of my history for ever, if it were deserved. But to be cursed of God—I have no words with which to tell what that must be. "Oh, no," you say, "that is a thing of the future; we do not care about the curse of God; it does not fall upon us now." Nay, soul, but it does. The wrath of God *abideth* on you even now. You have not yet come to know the fullness of that curse, but you are cursed this very hour. You are not yet in Hell; not yet has God been pleased to shut up the bowels of his compassion, and cast you for ever from his presence; but notwithstanding all that, you are cursed. Turn to the passage in the book of Deuteronomy, and see how the curse is a present thing upon the sinner. In the 28th chapter of Deuteronomy, at the 15th verse, we read all this as the sentence of the sinner: "Cursed shalt thou be in the city"—where you carry on your business God will curse you. "Cursed shalt thou be in the fields"—where you take your recreation; where you walk abroad, there shall the curse reach you. "Cursed shall be thy basket and thy store. Cursed shall be the fruit of thy body and the fruit of thy land, the increase of thy kine, and the flocks of thy sheep. Cursed shalt thou be when thou comest in, and cursed shalt thou be when thou goest out." There are some men upon whom this curse is very visible. Whatever they do is cursed. They get riches, but there is God's curse with the riches. I would not have some men's gold for all the stars, though they were gold: and if I might have all the wealth of the world, if I must have the miser's greed with it, I would rather be poor than have it. There art some men who are visibly cursed. Don't you see the drunkard? He is cursed, let him go where he may. When he goes into his house, his little children run up stairs to bed, for they are afraid to see their own father; and when they grow a little older, they begin to drink just as he did, and they will stand and imitate him; and they too will begin to swear, so that he is cursed in the fruit of his body. He thought it was not so bad for him to be drunk and to swear; but O what a pang shoots through the fathers conscience, if he has a conscience at all, when he sees his child following his footsteps. Drunkenness brings such a curse upon a man, that he can not enjoy what he eats. He is cursed in his basket, cursed in his store. And truly, though one vice may seem to develop the curse more than others, all sin brings the curse, though we can not always see it. O! thou that art out of God, and out of Christ, and a stranger to Jesus, thou art cursed where thou sittest, cursed where thou standest; cursed is the bed thou liest on; cursed is the bread thou eatest; cursed is the air thou breathest. All is cursed to thee. Go where thou mayest, thou art a cursed man. Ah! that is a fearful thought. O! there are some of you that are cursed to-night. O, that a man should say that of his brethren! but we must say it, or be unfaithful to your poor dying souls. O! would to God that some poor soul in this place would say, "Then I am cursed to-night; I am cursed of God, and cursed of his holy angels—cursed! cursed! cursed!—for I am under the law." I do think, God the Spirit blessing it, it wants nothing more to slay our carelessness than that one word—"cursed!" "Cursed is every one that continueth not in all things which are written in the book of the law to do them."

But now, my hearer, thou that art in this state, impenitent and unbelieving, I have more work to do before I close. Remember, the curse that men have in this life is as nothing compared with the curse that is to come upon them hereafter. In a few short years, you and I must die. Come, friend, I will talk to you personally again—young man, we shall soon grow old, or, perhaps, we shall die before that time, and we shall lie upon our bed—the last bed upon which we shall ever sleep— we shall wake from our last slumber to hear the doleful tidings that there is no hope; the physician will feel our pulse, and solemnly assure our relatives that it is all over! And we shall lie in that still room, where all is hushed except the ticking of the clock, and the weeping of our wife and children; and we must die. O! how solemn will it be that hour when we must struggle with that enemy, Death! The death-rattle is in our throat—we can scarce articulate—we try to speak; the death-glaze is on the eye: Death hath put his fingers on those windows of the body, and shut out the light for ever; the hands well-nigh refuse to lift themselves, and there we are, close on the borders of the grave! Ah! that moment, when the Spirit sees its destiny; that moment, of all moments the most solemn, when the soul looks through the bars of its cage, upon the world to come! No, I can not tell you how the spirit feels, if it be an ungodly spirit, when it sees a fiery throne of judgment, and hears the thunders of Almighty wrath, while there is but a moment between it and Hell. I can not picture to you what must be the fright which men will feel, when they realize what they often heard of! Ah! it is a fine thing for you to laugh at me to-night. When you go away, it will be a very fine thing to crack a joke concerning what the preacher said; to talk to one another, and make merry with all this. But when you are lying on your death-bed, you will not laugh. Now, the curtain is drawn, you can not see the things of the future, it is a very fine thing to be merry. When God has removed that curtain, and you learn the solemn reality, you will not find it in your hearts to trifle. Ahab, on his throne laughed at Micaiah. You never read that Ahab laughed at Micaiah when the arrow was sticking between the joints of his harness. In Noah's time, they laughed at the old man; they called him a gray-headed fool, I doubt not, because he told them that God was about to destroy the earth with a flood. But ah! ye scorners, ye did not laugh in that day when the cataracts were falling from heaven, and when God had unloosed the doors of the great deep, and bidden all the hidden waters leap upon the surface; then ye knew that Noah was right. And when ye come to die, mayhap ye will not laugh at me. You will say, when you lie there, "I remember such-and-such a night I strolled into Park street; I heard a man talk very solemnly; I thought at the time I did not like it, but I knew he was in earnest, I am quite certain that he meant good for me; oh, that I had hearkened to his advice; oh, that I had regarded his words! What would I give to hear him again!" Ah! it was not long ago that a man who had laughed and mocked at me full many a time, went down one Sabbath day to Brighton, to spend his day in the excursion—he came back that night to die! On Monday morning, when he was dying, who do you suppose he wanted? He wanted Mr. Spurgeon! the man he had laughed at always; he wanted him to come and tell him the way to heaven, and point him to the

Saviour. And although I was glad enough to go, it was doleful work to talk to a man who had just been Sabbath breaking, spending his time in the service of Satan, and had come home to die. And die he did, without a Bible in his house, without having one prayer offered for him except that prayer which I alone did offer at his bedside. Ah! it is strange how the sight of a death-bed may be blessed to the stimulating of our zeal. I stood some year or so ago, by the bedside of a poor boy, about sixteen years of age, who had been drinking himself to death, in a drinking bout, about a week before, and when I talked to him about sin and righteousness, and judgment to come, I knew he trembled, and I thought that he had laid hold on Jesus. When I came down from those stairs, after praying for him many a time, and trying to point him to Jesus, and having but a faint hope of his ultimate salvation, I thought to myself, O God! I would that I might preach every hour, and every moment of the day, the unsearchable riches of Christ; for what an awful thing it is to die without a Saviour. And then, I thought how many a time I had stood in the pulpit, and had not preached in earnest as I ought to have done; how I have coldly told out the tale of the Saviour, when I ought to have wept very showers of tears, in overwhelming emotion. I have gone to my bed full many a season, and have wept myself to sleep, because I have not preached as I have desired, and it will be even so to-night. But, oh, the wrath to come! the wrath to come! the wrath to come!

My hearers, the matters I now talk of are no dreams, no frauds, no whims, no old wives' stories. These are realities, and you will soon know them. O sinner, thou that hast not continued in all things written in the book of the law; thou that hast no Christ; the day is coming when these things will stand before thee, as dread, solemn, real things. And then; ah! then; ah! then; ah! then what wilt thou do?—"And after death *the judgment.*"— O, can ye picture—"The pomp of that tremendous day, When Christ with clouds shall come."

I think I see that terrible day. The bell of time has tolled the last day. Now comes the funeral of damned souls. Your body has just started up from the grave, and you unwind your cerements, and you look up. What is that I see? O! what is that I hear? I hear one dread, tremendous blast, that shakes the pillars of heaven, and makes the firmament reel with affright; the trump, the trump, the trump of the arch-angel shakes creation's utmost bound. You look and wonder. Suddenly a voice is heard, and shrieks from some, and songs from others—he comes—he comes—he comes; and every eye must see him. There he is; the throne is set upon a cloud, which is white as alabaster. There he sits. 'Tis He, the Man that died on Calvary—I see his pierced hands—but ah, how changed! No thorn-crown now. He stood at Pilate's bar, but now the whole earth must stand at his bar. But hark! the trumpet sounds again: the Judge opens the book, there is silence in heaven, a solemn silence: the universe is still. "Gather mine elect together, and my redeemed from the four winds of heaven." Swiftly they are gathered. As with a lightning flash, the angel's wing divides the crowd. Here are the righteous all in-gathered; and sinner, there art thou on the left hand, left out, left to abide the burning sentence of eternal wrath. Hark! the harps of heaven play sweet melodies; but to you they bring no joy, though the angels are repeating the Saviour's welcome to his saints. "Come ye blessed, inherit the kingdom prepared for you from the foundations of the world." You have had that moments respite, and now his face is gathering clouds of wrath, the thunder is on his brow; he looks on you that have despised him, you that scoffed his grace, that scorned his mercy, you that broke his Sabbath, you that mocked his cross, you that would not have him to reign over you; and with a voice louder than ten thousand thunders, he cries, "Depart, ye cursed. And then—No, I will not follow you. I will not tell of quenchless flames: I will not talk of miseries of the body, and tortures for the spirit. But Hell is terrible; damnation is doleful. Oh, escape! escape! Escape, lest haply, being where you are, you should have to learn what the horrors of eternity must mean, in the gulf of everlasting perdition. "Cursed is the man that hath not continued in *all things* that are written in the book of the law to do them."

III. DELIVERANCE PROCLAIMED.

"You have condemned us all," cries one. Yes, but not I—God has done it. Are you condemned? Do you feel you are tonight? Come, again, let me take thee by the hand, my brother: yes, I can look round upon the whole of this assembly, and I can say, there is not one now in this place whom I do not love as a brother. If I speak severely unto any of you, it is that you may know the right. My heart, and my whole spirit are stirred for you. My harshest words are far more full of love than the smooth words of soft-speaking ministers, who say, "Peace, peace," where there is no peace. Do you think it is any pleasure to me to preach like this? Oh? I had far rather be preaching of Jesus; his sweet, his glorious person, and his all-sufficient righteousness. Now, come, we will have a sweet word before we have done. Do you feel you are condemned? Do you say, "O God, I confess thou wouldest be just, if thou shouldest do all this to me?" Dost thou feel thou canst never be saved by thine own works, but that thou art utterly condemned through sin? Dost thou hate sin? Dost thou sincerely repent? Then, let me tell thee how thou mayest escape.

Men and brethren, Jesus Christ, of the seed of David, was crucified, dead, and buried; he is now risen, and he sitteth on the right hand of God, where he also maketh intercession for us. He came into this world to save sinners, by his death. He saw that poor sinners were cursed: he took the curse on his own shoulders, and he delivered us from it. Now, if God has cursed Christ for any man, he will not curse that man again. You ask me, then, "Was Christ cursed for me?" Answer me this question, and I will tell you—Has God the Spirit taught you that you are accursed? Has he made you feel the bitterness of sin? Has he made you cry, "Lord, have mercy upon me, a sinner?" Then, my dear friend, Christ was cursed for you; and you are not cursed. You are not cursed now. Christ was cursed for you. Be of good cheer; if Christ was cursed for you, you can not be cursed again. "Oh!" says one, "if I could but think he was cursed for me." Do you see him bleeding on the tree? Do you see his hands and feet all dripping gore? Look unto him, poor sinner. Look no longer at thyself, nor at thy sin; look unto him, and be saved. All he asks thee to do is to look, and even that he will help thee to do. Come to him, trust him, believe on him. God the Holy Spirit has taught you that you are a condemned sinner. Now, I beseech you, hear this word and believe it: "This is a faithful saying, and worthy of all acceptation, that Jesus Christ came into the world to save sinners." Oh, can you say, "I believe this Word—it is true— blessed be his dear name; it is true to me, for whatever I may not be, I know that I am a sinner; the sermon of this night convinces me of that, if there were nothing else; and, good Lord, thou knowest when I say I am a sinner, I do not mean what I used to mean by that word. I mean that I am a real sinner. I mean that if thou shouldest damn me, I deserve it; if thou shouldest cast me from thy presence forever, it is only what I have merited richly. O my Lord I am a sinner; I am a hopeless sinner, unless thou savest me; I am a helpless sinner, unless thou dost deliver me. I have no hope in my self-righteousness; and Lord, I bless thy name, there is one thing else, I am a sorrowful sinner, for sin grieves me; I can not rest, I am troubled. Oh, if I could get rid of sin, I would be holy, even as God is holy. Lord, I believe. But I hear an objector cry out, "What, sir, believe that Christ died for me simply because I am a sinner!" Yes; even so. "No, sir; but if I had a little righteousness; if I could pray well, I should then think Christ died for me." No, that would not be faith at all, that would be self-confidence. Faith believes in Christ when it sees sin to be black, and trusts in him to remove it all. Now, poor sinner, with all thy sin about thee, take this promise in thy hands, go home to-night, or if thou canst, do it before thou gettest home—go home, I say, up stairs, alone, down by the bed-side, and pour out thine heart, "O Lord, it is all true that that man said; I am condemned, and Lord, I deserve it. O Lord, I have tried to be better, and have done nothing with it all, but have only grown worse. O Lord, I have slighted thy grace, I have despised thy gospel: I wonder thou hast not damned me years ago; Lord, I marvel at myself; that thou sufferest such a base wretch as I am to live at all. I have despised a mother's teaching, I have forgotten a father's prayers. Lord, I have forgotten thee; I have broken thy Sabbath, taken thy name in vain. I have done everything that is wrong; and if thou dost condemn me, what can I say? Lord, I am dumb before thy presence. I have nothing to plead. But Lord; I come to tell thee to-night, thou hast said in the Word of God, "Him that cometh unto me, I will in no wise cast out." Lord, I come: my only plea is that thou hast said, 'This is a faithful saying, and worthy of all acceptation, that Jesus Christ came into the world to save sinners.' Lord, I am a sinner; he came to save *me;* I trust in it—sink or swim—Lord, this is my only hope: I cast away every other, and hate myself to think I ever should have had any other. Lord, I rely on Jesus only. Do but save me, and though I can not hope by my future life to blot out my past sin, O Lord, I will ask of thee to give me a new heart and a right spirit, that from this time forth even for ever I may run in the way of thy commandments: for, Lord, I desire nothing so much as to be thy child. Thou knowest, O Lord, I would give all, if thou wouldest but love me; and I am encouraged to think that thou dost love me; for my heart feels so. I am guilty, but I should never have known that I was guilty if thou hadst not taught it to me. I am vile, but I never should have known my vileness, unless thou hadst revealed it. Surely, thou wilt not destroy me, O God, after having taught me this. If thou dost, thou art just, but:

Save a trembling sinner, Lord,
Whose hopes still hovering round thy Word,
Would light on some sweet promise there;
Some sure support against despair.

If you can not pray such a long prayer as that, I tell you what to go home and say. Say this, "Lord Jesus, I know I am nothing at all; be thou my precious all in all."

Oh, I trust in God there will be some to-night that will be able to pray like that, and if it be so, ring, the bells of heaven; sing, ye seraphim; shout, ye redeemed; for the Lord hath done it, and glory be unto his name, for ever and ever.

The Uses of the Law

A SERMON (NO. 128)
DELIVERED ON SABBATH MORNING, APRIL 19, 1857,
BY THE REV. C. H. SPURGEON
AT THE MUSIC HALL, ROYAL SURREY GARDENS.

"Wherefore then serveth the law?" — GALATIANS 3:19

THE APOSTLE, by a highly ingenious and powerful argument, had proved that the law was never intended by God for the justification and salvation of man. He declares that God made a covenant of grace with Abraham long before the law was given on Mount Sinai; that Abraham was not present at Mount Sinai, and that, therefore, there could have been no alteration of the covenant made there by his consent; that, moreover, Abraham's consent was never asked as to any alteration of the covenant, without which consent the covenant could not have been lawfully changed, and, besides that, that the covenant stands fast and firm, seeing it was made to Abraham's seed, as well as to Abraham himself. "This I say, that the covenant, that was confirmed before of God in Christ, the law, which was four hundred and thirty years after, cannot disannul, that it should make the promise of none effect. For if the inheritance be of the law, it is no more of promise: but God gave it to Abraham by promise." Therefore, no inheritance and no salvation ever can be obtained by the law. Now, extremes are the error of ignorance. Generally, when men believe one truth, they carry it so far as to deny another; and, very frequently, the assertion of a cardinal truth leads men to generalise on other particulars, and so to make falsehoods out of truth. The objection supposed may be worded thus: "You say, O Paul, that the law cannot justify; surely then the law is good for nothing at all; 'Wherefore then serveth the law?' If it will not save a man, what is the good of it? If of itself it will never take a man to heaven, why was it written? Is it not a useless thing?" The apostle might have replied to his opponent with a sneer—he must have said to him, "Oh, fool, and slow of heart to understand. Is it proved that a thing is utterly useless because it is not intended for every purpose in the world? Will you say that, because iron cannot be eaten, therefore, iron is not useful? And because gold cannot be the food of man, will you, therefore, cast gold away, and call it worthless dross? Yet on your foolish supposition you must do so. For, because I have said the law cannot save, you have foolishly asked me what is the use of it? and you foolishly suppose God's law is good for nothing, and can be of no value whatever." This objection is, generally, brought forward by two sorts of people. First, by mere cavillers who do not like the gospel, and wish to pick all sorts of holes in it. They can tell us what they do not believe; but they do not tell us what they do believe. They would fight with everybody's doctrines and sentiments, but they would be at a loss if they were asked to sit down and write their own opinions. They do not seem to have got much further than the genius of the monkey, which can pull everything to pieces, but can put nothing together. Then, on the other hand, there is the Antinomian, who says, "Yes, I know I am saved by grace alone;" and then breaks the law—says, it is not binding on him, even as a rule of life; and asks, "Wherefore then serveth the law?" throwing it out of his door as an old piece of furniture only fit for the fire, because, forsooth, it is not adapted to save his soul. Why, a thing may have many uses, if not a particular one. It is true that the law cannot save; and yet it is equally true that the law is one of the highest works of God, and is deserving of all reverence, and extremely useful when applied by God to the purposes for which it was intended.

Yet, pardon me my friends, if I just observe that this is a very natural question, too. If you read the doctrine of the apostle Paul you find him declaring that the law condemns all mankind. Now, just let us for one single moment take a bird's eye view of the works of the law in this world. Lo, I see, the law given upon Mount Sinai. The very hill doth quake with fear. Lightnings and thunders are the attendants of those dreadful syllables which make the hearts of Israel to melt Sinai seemeth altogether on the smoke. The Lord came from Paran, and the Holy One from Mount Sinai; "He came with ten thousand of his saints." Out of his mouth went a fiery law for them. It was a dread law even when it was given, and since then from that Mount of Sinai an awful lava of vengeance has run down, to deluge, to destroy, to burn, and to consume the whole human race, if it had not been that Jesus Christ had stemmed its awful torrent, and bidden its waves of fire be still. If you could see the world without Christ in it, simply under the law you would see a world in ruins, a world with God 8 black seal put upon it, stamped and sealed for condemnation; you would see men, who, if they knew their condition, would have their hands on their loins and be groaning all their days—you would see men and women condemned, lost, and ruined; and in the uttermost regions you would see the pit that is digged for the wicked, into which the whole earth must have been cast if the law had its way, apart from the gospel of Jesus Christ our Redeemer. Ay, beloved, the law is a great deluge which would have drowned the world with worse than the water of Noah's flood, it is a great fire which would have burned the earth with a destruction worse than that which fell on Sodom, it is a stern angel with a sword, athirst for blood, and winged to slay; it is a great destroyer sweeping down the nations; it is the great messenger of God's vengeance sent into the world. Apart from the gospel of Jesus Christ, the law is nothing but the condemning voice of God thundering against mankind. "Wherefore then serveth the law?" seems a very natural question. Can the law be of any benefit to man? Can that Judge who puts on a black cap and condemns us all this Lord Chief Justice Law, can he help in salvation? Yes, he did; and you shall see how he does it, if God shall help us while we preach. "Wherefore then serveth the law?"

I. The first use of the law is to manifest to man his guilt.

When God intends to save a man, the first thing he does with him is to send the law to him, to show him how guilty, how vile, how ruined he is, and in how dangerous a position. You see that man lying there on the edge of the precipice; he is sound asleep, and just on the perilous verge of the cliff. One single movement, and he will roll over and be broken in pieces on the jagged rocks beneath, and nothing more shall be heard of him. How is he to be saved? What shall be done for him—what shall be done! It is our position; we, too, are lying on the brink of ruin, but we are insensible of it. God, when he begins to save us from such an imminent danger, sendeth his law, which, with a stout kick, rouses us up, makes us open our eyes, we look down on our terrible danger, discover our miseries, and then it is we are in a right position to cry out for salvation, and our salvation comes to us. The law acts with man as the physician does when he takes the film from the eye of the blind. Self-righteous men are blind men, though they think themselves good and excellent. The law takes that film away, and lets them discover how vile they are, and how utterly ruined and condemned if they are to abide under the sentence of the law.

Instead, however, of treating this doctrinally, I shall treat it practically, and come home to each of your consciences. My, hearer, does not the law of God convince you of sin this morning? Under the hand of God's Spirit does it not make you feel that you have been guilty, that you deserve to be lost, that you have incurred the fierce anger of God? Look ye here, have ye not broken these ten commandments; even in the letter have ye not broken them? Who is there among you who hath always honored his father and mother? Who is there among us who hath always spoken the truth? Have we not sometimes borne false witness against our neighbor? Is there one person here who has not made unto himself another God, and loved himself, or his business, or his friends, more than he has Jehovah, the God of the whole earth? Which of you hath not coveted your neighbour's house, or his man-servant, or his ox, or his ass? We are all guilty with regard to every letter of the law; we have all of us transgressed the commandments. And if we really understood these commandments, and felt that they condemned us, they would have this useful influence on us of showing us our danger, and so of leading us to fly to Christ. But, my hearers, does not this law condemn you, because even if you should say you have not broken the letter of it, yet you have violated the spirit of it. What, though you have never killed, yet we are told, he that is angry with his brother is a murderer. As a negro said once, "Sir, I thought me no kill—me innocent there; but when I heard that he that hateth his brother is a murderer, then me cry guilty, for me have killed twenty men before breakfast very often, for I have been angry with many of them very often." This law does not only mean what it says in words, but it has deep things hidden in its bowels. It says, "Thou shalt not commit adultery," but it means, as Jesus has it, "He that looketh on a woman to lust after her hath committed adultery with her already in his heart." It says, "Thou shalt not take the name of the Lord thy God in vain," it meaneth that we should reverence God in every place, and have his fear before our eyes, and should always pay respect unto his ordinances and evermore walk in his fear and love. Ay, my brethren, surely there is not one here so fool-hardy in self-righteousness as to say, "I am innocent." The spirit of the law condemns us. And this is its useful property; it humbles us, makes us know we are guilty, and so are we led to receive the Saviour.

Mark this, moreover, my dear hearers, *one breach of this law is enough to condemn us for ever.* He that breaketh the law in one point is guilty of the whole. The law demands that we should obey every command, and one of them broken, the whole of them are injured. It is like a vase of surpassing workmanship, in order to destroy it you need not shiver it to atoms, make but the smallest fracture in it and you have destroyed its perfection. As it is a perfect law which we are commanded to obey, and to obey perfectly, make but one breach thereof and though we be ever so innocent we can hope for nothing from the lay; except the voice, "Ye are condemned, ye are condemned, ye are condemned." Under this aspect of the matter ought not the law to strip many of us of all our boasting? Who is there that shall rise in his place and say, "Lord, I thank thee I am not as other men are?" Surely there cannot be one among you who can go home and say, "I have tithed mint and cummin; I have kept all the commandments from my youth?" Nay, if this law be brought home to the conscience and the heart we shall stand with the publican, saying, "Lord, be merciful to me a sinner." The only reason why a man thinks he is righteous is because he does not know the law. You think you have never broken it because you do not understand it. There are some of you most respectable people; you think you have been so good that you can go to heaven by your own works. You would not exactly say so, but you secretly think so; you have devoutly taken the sacrament, you have been mightily pious in attending your church or chapel regularly, you are good to the poor, generous and upright, and you say, "I shall be saved by my works." Nay, sir, look to the flame that Moses saw, and shrink, and tremble, and despair. The law can do nothing for us except condemn us. The utmost it can do is to whip us out of our boasted self-righteousness and drive us to Christ. It puts a burden on our backs and makes us ask Christ to take it off. It is like a lancet, it probes the wound. It is, to use a parable as when some dark cellar has not been opened for years and is full of all kinds of loathsome creatures, we may walk through it not knowing they are there. But the law comes, takes the shutters down, lets light in, and then we discover what a vile heart we have, and how unholy our lives have been; and, then, instead of boasting, we are made to fall on our faces and cry, "Lord, save or I perish. Oh, save me for thy mercy's sake, or else I shall be cast away." Oh, ye self-righteous ones now present, who think yourselves so good that ye can mount to heaven by your works—blind horses, perpetually going round the mill and making not one inch of progress—do you think to take the law upon your shoulders as Sampson did the gates of Gaza? Do you imagine that you can perfectly keep this law of God? Will you dare to say, you have not broken it. Nay, surely, you will confess, though it be in but an under tone, "I have revolted." Then, this know: the law can do nothing for you in the matter of forgiveness. All it can do is just this: It can make you feel you are nothing at all; it can strip you; it can bruise you; it can kill you, but it can neither quicken, nor clothe, nor cleanse—it was never meant to do that. Oh, art thou this morning, my hearer, sad, because of sin? Dost thou feel that thou hast been guilty? Dost thou acknowledge thy transgression? Dost thou confess thy wandering? Hear me, then, as God's ambassador, God hath mercy upon sinners. Jesus Christ came into the world to save sinners. And though you have broken the law, he has kept it. Take his righteousness to be yours. Cast yourself upon him. Come to him now, stripped and naked and take his robe as your covering, Come to him, black and filthy, and wash yourself in the fountain opened for sin and uncleanness; and then you shall know "wherefore then serveth the law?" That is the first point.

II. Now, the second. The law serves to slay all hope of salvation of a reformed life.

Most men when they discover themselves to be guilty, avow that they will reform. They say, "I have been guilty and have deserved God's wrath, but for the future I will seek to win a stock of merits which shall counterbalance all my old sins." In steps the law, puts its hand on the sinner's mouth, and says, "Stop, you cannot do that, it is impossible." I will show you how the law does this. It does it partly thus, by reminding the man that *future obedience can be no atonement for past guilt.* To use a common metaphor that the poor may thoroughly understand me, you have run up a score at your chop. Well, you cannot pay it. You go off to Mrs. Brown, your shopkeeper, and you say to her, "Well, I am sorry, ma'am, that through my husband being out of work," and all that, "I know I shall never be able to pay you. It is a very great debt I owe you, but, if you please ma'am, if you forgive me this debt I will never get into your debt any more. I will always pay for all I have." "Yes," she would say, "but that will not square our accounts. If you do pay for all you have, it would be no more than you ought to do. But what about the old bills? How are they to be receipted? They won't be receipted by all your fresh payments." That is just what men do towards God. "True," they say, "I have gone far astray I know; but then I won't do so any more." Ah, it was time you threw away such child's talk. You do but manifest your rampant folly by such a hope. Can you wipe away your trangression by future obedience? Ah, no. The old debt must be paid somehow. God's justice is inflexible, and the law tells you all your requirements can make no atonement for the past. You must have an atonement through Christ Jesus the Lord. "But," says the man, "I will try and be better, and then I think I shall have mercy given to me." Then the law steps in and says, "You are going to try and keep me, are you? Why, man, you cannot do it." *Perfect obedience in the future is impossible.* And the ten commandments are held up, and if any awakened sinner will but look at them, he will turn away and say, "It is impossible for me to keep them." "Why, man, you say you will be obedient in the future. You have not been obedient in the past, and there is no likelihood that you will keep God's commandments in time to come. You say you will avoid the evils of the past. You cannot. 'Can the Ethiopian change his skin, or the leopard his spots? then may ye also do good that are accustomed to do evil.'" But you say, "I will take greater heed to my ways." "Sir, you will not; the temptation that overcame you yesterday will overcome you to-morrow. But, mark this, if you could, you could not win salvation by it." The law tells you that unless you perfectly obey you cannot be saved by your doings, it tells you that one sin will make a flaw in it all, that one transgression will spoil your whole obedience. It is a spotless garment that you must wear in heaven; it is only an unbroken law which God can accept. So, then, the law answers this purpose, to tell men that their acquirements, their amendings, and their doings, are of no use whatever in the matter of salvation. It is theirs to come to Christ, to get A new heart and a right spirit; to get the evangelical repentance which needeth not to be repented of, that so they may put their trust in Jesus and receive pardon through his blood. "Wherefore then serveth the law?" It serveth this purpose, as Luther hath it, the purpose of a hammer. Luther, you know, is very strong on the subject of the law. He says, "For if any be not a murderer, an adulterer, a thief, and outwardly refrain from sin, as the Pharisee did, which is mentioned in the gospel, he would swear that he is righteous, and therefore he conceiveth an opinion of righteousness, and presumeth of his good works and merits. Such a one God cannot otherwise mollify and humble, that he may acknowledge his misery and damnation, but by the law, for that is the hammer of death, the thundering of Hell, and the lightning of God's wrath, that beateth to powder the obstinate and senseless hypocrites. For as long as the opinion of righteousness abideth in man, so long there abideth also in him incomprehensible pride, presumption, security, hatred of God, contempt of his grace and mercy, ignorance of the promises and of Christ. The preaching of free remission of sins, through Christ, cannot enter into the heart of such a one, neither can he feel any taste or savor thereof; for that mighty rock and adamant wall, to wit, the opinion of righteousness, wherewith the heart is environed, doth resist it. Wherefore the law is that hammer, that fire, that mighty strong wind, and that terrible earthquake rending the mountains, and breaking the rocks, (1 Kings 19:11-13) that is to say, the proud and obstinate hypocrites. Elijah, not being able to abide these terrors of the law, which by these things are signified, covered his face with his mantle. Notwithstanding, when the tempest ceased, of which he was a beholder, there came a soft and a gracious wind, in the which the Lord was; but it behoved that the tempest of fire, of wind, and the earthquake should pass, before the Lord should reveal himself in that gracious wind."

III. And now, a step further. You that know the grace of God can follow me in this next step. *The law is intended to show man the misery which will, fall upon him through his sin.*

I speak from experience, though young I be, and many of you who hear me will hear this with ears of attention, because you have felt the same. There was a time with me, when but young in years, I felt with much sorrow the evil of sin. My bones waxed old with my roaring all day long. Day and night God's hand was heavy upon me. There was a time when he seared me with visions, and affrighted me by dreams; when by day I hungered for deliverance, for my soul fasted within me: I feared lest the very skies should fall upon me, and crush my guilty soul. God's law had got hold upon me, and was strewing me my misery. If I slept at night I dreamed of the bottomless pit, and when I awoke I seemed to feel the misery

I had dreamed. Up to God's house I went; my song was but a groan. To my chamber I retired, and there with tears and groans I offered up my prayer, without a hope and without a refuge. I could then say with David, "The owl is my partner and the bittern is my companion," for God's law was flogging me with its ten-thonged whip, and then rubbing me with brine afterwards, so that I did shake and quiver with pain and anguish, and my soul chose strangling rather than life, for I was exceeding sorrowful. Some of you have had the same. The law was sent on purpose to do that. But, you will ask, "Why that misery?" I answer, that misery was sent for this reason: that I might then be made to cry to Jesus. Our heavenly Father does not usually make us seek Jesus till he has whipped us clean out of all our confidence; he cannot make us in earnest after heaven till he has made us feel something of the intolerable tortures of an aching conscience, which has foretaste of Hell. Do you not remember, my hearer, when you used to awake in the morning, and the first thing you took up was *Alleine's Alarm,* or *Baxter's Call to the Unconverted?* Oh, those books, those books, in my childhood I read and devoured them when under a sense of guilt, but they were like sitting at the foot of Sinai. When I turned to Baxter, I found him saying some such things as these: "Sinner, bethink thee, within an hour thou mayest be in Hell. Bethink thee; thou mayest soon be dying—death is even now gnawing at thy cheek. What wilt thou do when thou standest before the bar of God without a Saviour? Wilt thou tell him thou hadst no time to spend on religion? Will not that empty excuse melt into thin air? Oh, sinner, wilt thou, then, dare to insult thy Maker? Wilt thou, then, dare to scoff at him? Bethink thee; the flames of Hell are hot and the wrath of God is heavy. Were thy bones of steel, and thy ribs of brass, thou mightest quiver with fear. Oh, hadst thou the strength of a giant, thou couldst not wrestle with the Most High. What wilt thou do when he shall tear thee in pieces, and there shall be none to deliver thee? What wilt thou do when he shall fire off his ten great guns at thee? The first commandment shall say, 'Crush him; he hath broken me!' The second shall say, 'Damn him; he hath broken me!' The third shall say, 'A curse upon him; he hath broken me!' And so shall they all let fly upon thee; and thou without a shelter, without a place to flee to, and without a hope." Ah! you have not forgotten the days when no hymn seemed suitable to you but the one that began:

> *Stoop down my soul that used to rise*
> *Converse awhile with death*
> *Think how a gasping mortal lies,*
> *And pants away his breath.*

Or else:

> *That awful day shall surely come,*
> *The 'pointed hour makes haste,*
> *When I must stand before my Judge,*
> *And pass the solemn test.*

Ay, that was why the law was sent—to convince us of sin, to make us shake and shiver before God. Oh! you that are self-righteous, let me speak to you this morning with just a word or two of terrible and burning earnestness. Remember, sirs, the day is coming when a crowd more vast than this shall be assembled on the plains of earth; when on a great white throne the Saviour, Judge of men, shall sit. Now, he is come; the book is opened; the glory of heaven is displayed, rich with triumphant love, and burning with unquenchable vengeance; ten thousand angels are on either hand; and you are standing to be tried. Now, self-righteous man, tell me now that you went to church three times a day! Come, man, tell me now that you kept all the commandments! Tell me now that you are not guilty! Come before him with a receipt of your mint, and your anise, and your cummin! Come along with you!

Where are you? Oh, you are fleeing. You are crying, "Rocks hide us; mountains on us fall." What are you after, man? Why, you were so fair on earth that none dare to speak to you; you were so good and so comely; why do you run away? Come, man, pluck up courage; come before thy Maker; tell him that thou wert honest, sober, excellent, and that thou deservest to be saved! Why dost thou delay to repeat thy boastings? Out with it—come, say it! No, you will not. I see you still flying, with shrieks, away from your Maker's presence. There will be none found to stand before him, then, in their own righteousness. But look! look! look! I see a man coming forward out of that motley throng; he marches forward with a steady step, and with a smiling eye. What! is there any man found who shall dare to approach the dread tribunal of God? What! is there one who dares to stand before his Maker? Yes, there is one; he comes forward, and he cries, "Who shall lay anything to the charge of God's elect?" Do you not shudder? Will not the mountains of wrath swallow him? Will not God launch that dreadful thunderbolt against him? No; listen while he confidently proceeds: "Who is he that condemneth? It is Christ that died; yea, rather, that hath risen again." And I see the right hand of God outstretched—"Come, ye blessed, enter the kingdom prepared for you." Now is fulfilled the verse which you once sweetly sang:

> Bold shall I stand in that great day,
> For who aught to my charge shall lay?
> While, through thy blood, absolv'd I am
> From sin's tremendous curse and shame.

IV. And now, my dear friends, I am afraid of wearying you; therefore, let me briefly hint at one other thought. "Wherefore then serveth the law." *It was sent into the world to shew the value of a Saviour.* Just as foils set off jewels, and as dark spots make bright tints more bright, so doth the law make Christ appear the fairer and more heavenly. I hear the law of God curse, but how harsh its voice. Jesus says, "come unto me;" oh, what music! all the more musical after the discord of the law. I see the law condemns; I behold Christ obeying it. Oh! how ponderous that price—when I know how weighty was the demand! I read the commandments, and I find them strict and awfully severe—oh! how holy must Christ have been to obey all these for me! Nothing makes me value my Saviour more than seeing the law condemn me. When I know this law stands in my way, and like a flaming cherubim will not let me enter paradise, then I can tell how sweetly precious must Jesus Christ's righteousness be, which is a passport to heaven, and gives me grace to enter there.

V. And, lastly, "Wherefore serveth the law." It was sent into the world *to keep Christian men from self-righteousness.*

Christian men—do they ever get self-righteous? Yes, that they do. The best Christian man in the world will find it hard work to keep himself from boasting, and from being self-righteous. John Knox on his death-bed was attacked with self-righteousness. The last night of his life on earth, he slept some hours together, during which he uttered many deep and heavy moans. Being asked why he moaned so deeply, he replied, "I have during my life sustained many assaults of Satan; but at present he has assaulted me most fearfully, and put forth all his strength to make an end of me at once. The cunning Serpent has labored to persuade me, that I have merited heaven and eternal blessedness by the faithful discharge of my ministry. But blessed be God, who has enabled me to quench this fiery dart, by suggesting to me such passages as these: 'What hast thou that thou hast not received?' and, 'By the grace of God I am what I am.'" Yes, and each of us have felt the same. I have often felt myself rather amused at some of my brethren, who have come to me, and said, "I trust the Lord will keep you humble," when they themselves were not only as proud as they were high, but a few inches over. They have been most sincere in prayer that I should be humble, unwittingly nursing their own pride by their own imaginary reputation for humility. I have long since given up entreating people to be humble, because it naturally tends to make them proud. A man is apt to say, "Dear me, these people are afraid I shall be proud; I must have something to be proud of." Then we say to ourselves, "I will not let them see it;" and we try to keep our pride down, but after all, are as proud as Lucifer within. I find that the proudest and most self-righteous people are those who do nothing at all, and have no shadow of presence for any opinion of their own goodness. The old truth in the book of Job is true now. You know in the beginning of the book of Job it is said, "The oxen were ploughing, and the asses were feeding beside them." That is generally the way in this world. The oxen are ploughing in the church—we have some who are laboring hard for Christ—and the asses are feeding beside them, on the finest livings and the fattest of the land. These are the people who have so much to say about self-righteousness. What do they do? They do not do enough to earn a living, and yet they think they are going to earn heaven. They sit down and fold their hands, and yet they are so reverently righteous, because forsooth they sometimes dole out a little in charity. They do nothing, and yet boast of self-righteousness. And with Christian people it is the came. If God makes you laborious, and keeps you constantly engaged in his service, you are less likely to be proud of our self-righteousness than you are if you do nothing. But at all times there is a natural tendency to it. Therefore, God has written the law, that when we read it we may see our faults; that when we look into it, as into a looking-glass, we may see the impurities in our flesh, and have reason to abhor ourselves in sackcloth and ashes, and still cry to Jesus for mercy. Use the law in this fashion, and in no other.

And now, says one, "Sir, are there any here that you have been preaching at?" Yes, I like to preach at people. I do not believe it is of any avail to preach to people; preach right into them and right at them. I find in every circle a class, who say, in plain English, "Well, I am as good a father as is to be found in the parish, I am a good tradesman; I pay twenty shillings in the pound; I am no Sir John Dean Paul; I go to church, or I go to chapel, and that is more than everybody does; I pay my subscriptions—I subscribe to the infirmary; I say my prayers; therefore, I believe I stand as good a chance of heaven as anybody in the world." I do believe that three out of four of the people of London think something of that sort. Now, if that be the ground of your trust, you have a rotten hope; you have a plank to stand upon that will not bear your weight in the day of God's account As the Lord my God liveth, before whom I stand, "Unless your righteousness exceed the righteousness of the Scribes and Pharisees, ye shall in no wise enter into the kingdom of heaven." And if ye think the best performance of your hands can save you, this know, that "Israel, which followed after the law of righteousness, hath not attained to the law of righteousness." Those who sought not after it have attained it. Wherefore? Because the one hath sought it by faith, the other hath sought it by the deeds of the law, where justification never was to be found. Hear, now, the gospel, men and women; down with that boasting form of your righteousness; away with your hopes, with all your trusts that spring from this:

> *Could your tears for ever flow,*
> *Could your zeal no respite know,*
> *All for sin could not atone;*
> *Christ must save, and save alone.*

If ye would know how we must be saved, hear this—ye must come with nothing of your own to Christ. Christ has kept the law. You are to have his righteousness to be your righteousness. Christ has suffered in the stead of all who repent. His punishment is to stand instead of your being punished. And through faith in the sanctification and atonement of Christ, you are to be saved. Come, then, ye weary and heavy laden, bruised and mangled by the Fall, come then, ye sinners, come, then, ye moralists, come, then, all ye that have broken God's law and feel it, leave your own trusts and come to Jesus, he will take you in, give you a spotless robe of righteousness, and make you his for ever. "But how can I come?" says one; "Must I go home and pray?" Nay, sir, nay. Where thou art standing now, thou mayest come to the cross. Oh, if thou knowest thyself to be a sinner, now—I beseech you, ere thy foot shall leave the floor on which thou standest—now, say this: "Myself into thy arms I cast: Lord, save my guilty soul at last."

Now, down with you, away with your self-righteousness. Look to me—look, now; say not, "Must I mount to heaven and bring Christ down?" "The word is nigh thee, on thy mouth and in thy heart; if thou shalt confess with thy mouth the Lord Jesus, and believe with thy heart, thou shalt be saved." Yes, thou—thou—thou. Oh! I bless God, we have heard of hundreds who have in this place believed on Christ. Some of the blackest of the human race have come to me but even lately, and told me what God has done for them. Oh, that you, too, would now come to Jesus. Remember, he that believeth shall be saved, be his sins never so many; and he that believeth not, must perish, be his sins never so few. Oh, that the Holy Spirit would lead you to believe; so should ye escape the wrath to come? and have a place in paradise among the redeemed!

ENDNOTES

1   http://www.spurgeon.org/sermons/0174.htm
2   http://www.spurgeon.org/sermons/0128.htm